THE BLOOMSBURY GROUP

EX LIBRIS

THE BLOOMSBURY GROUP

Henrietta's War by Joyce Dennys
Henrietta Sees It Through by Joyce Dennys
The Brontës Went to Woolworths by Rachel Ferguson
Miss Hargreaves by Frank Baker
Love's Shadow by Ada Leverson
A Kid for Two Farthings by Wolf Mankowitz
Mrs Tim of the Regiment by D.E. Stevenson
Mrs Ames by E.F. Benson
Mrs Harris Goes to Paris and Mrs Harris Goes to New York
by Paul Gallico

A NOTE ON THE AUTHOR

ROHAN O'GRADY is the pseudonym for June Margaret O'Grady, who was born in Vancouver in 1922. O'Grady began writing poetry and stories as a young child and ventured into full length fiction in her late thirties after her marriage to newspaper editor Frederick Skinner. By 1963, O'Grady had published three novels in three years, *O'Houlihan's Jest* in 1961, *Pippin's Journal* in 1962, and *Let's Kill Uncle* in 1963. The latter two books were illustrated by Edward Gorey. In 1966, William Castle directed the Hollywood horror movie *Let's Kill Uncle* starring Nigel Green and Mary Badham (the young star of *To Kill a Mockingbird*). Several unproduced screenplays and two novels followed: *Bleak November* in 1970 and *The Mayspoon* in 1981. June Skinner has resided in West Vancouver since 1959.

First published in Great Britain by Longmans, Green and Co., 1964
This paperback edition published 2010 by Bloomsbury Publishing Plc

Copyright © June Skinner 1963

The moral right of the author has been asserted

Ex libris illustration © Penelope Beech 2010
Illustration on p.v © Edward Gorey

Bloomsbury Publishing Plc, 36 Soho Square, London W1D 3QY

A CIP catalogue record for this book is available from
the British Library

ISBN 9 781 4088 0857 3
10 9 8 7 6 5 4 3 2 1

Typeset by
MPS Limited, A Macmillan Company
Printed in Great Britain by Clays Ltd, St Ives plc

www.bloomsbury.com/thebloomsburygroup

Let's kill Uncle

In an idyllic, peaceful island setting
two charming children on summer holiday
conspire to execute the perfect murder
—and get away with it.

by Rohan O'Grady

1

'LIAR! LIAR! LIAR!'

Even the pounding of the engines couldn't drown out the sound.

The first mate, leaning against the deck rail of the S.S. *Haida Prince*, winced. That shrill little voice had been bouncing on his eardrums for three hours.

'Cheer up, this is their stop.'

The purser joined him, and they stood watching a sea gull waddle along the deck rail.

'It's a beautiful place,' the first mate pointed to the Island. 'Well, it won't be for long. Not after they land. This is your first trip on this run, isn't it?'

The purser nodded.

'It isn't always this bad, you know.'

The seagull gave a hoarse shriek of delight, cocked a reptilian-bright eye past his feathered shoulder, then rose to the air, skimming over the choppy waters to the Island.

'I've shipped all over the world,' said the first mate, 'and this is my favorite. Someday I'm going to retire to one of these islands. I'll get myself a cottage on the beach, and a nice little sloop. Maybe on Benares - it has a beer parlour. The best salmon fishing on the coast is here.'

The deck steward, an ex-fighter with sloping, powerful shoulders, approached them.

'Excuse me, sir,' he said. 'Do you know anything that will dissolve chewing gum? Something that won't dissolve a dog?'

The first mate and the purser exchanged glances.

'*Them?*' asked the first mate.

'Yes, sir. One of the border collies in the hold. Its muzzle is glued together. They just thought he'd like a wad of gum, the little bastards.'

'Try rubbing alcohol,' suggested the purser.

'And keep them off the bridge!' said the first mate, his ears still burning from the captain's salty expletives.

He turned to the purser.

'When I've got my master's papers and run my own line, there'll be an iron-clad rule: no kids on board unless accompanied by their jailers, and even then they'll be confined to the hold.'

They stood gazing at the Island as the ship plowed nearer the dock.

'You can't beat these islands,' he continued. 'Get yourself a couple of acres, keep a small vegetable garden, with maybe a dozen fruit trees. A man can live well on next to nothing. Driftwood for fuel, fish in the water, crabs, clams, oysters on the beach, and venison when the Mountie's back is turned.'

'Are you really going to settle on one?'

'Yes, but not this one.'

'Why not?' The purser laughed. 'Oh, those kids.'

'No,' said the first mate, 'not because of them. This island is the most beautiful of the lot, but it's cursed.'

'Who are you kidding?'

'I mean it,' said the first mate. 'It's hexed. Any of the others, but not this one. And I'm not kidding. You can check the records if you want. In two world wars thirty-three men have left it to fight for their country. Only one has come back alive. See that Mountie on the dock? He's the fellow. All the rest killed, down to the last man. If there's such a thing as a dead island, this is it.'

They turned their eyes to the curly arbutus trees crowning the sloping, moss-covered rocks, down to the white sand, with the ocean wind fanning softly and smelling like perfume to an old sailor.

'I don't care how beautiful it is. I've been at sea too long not to be superstitious, and you couldn't pay me to live on this island. Well, I'd better check the cargo.'

As the first mate went down the companionway, he stopped to remove a fire axe which had been lifted from its wall bracket and left temptingly, blade up, on the stairs. He replaced it and continued, only to glance to the upper deck where a lifeboat was swinging crazily on its davit.

'Good God!' he said, and bumped into the dining steward.

'They left a piece of blueberry pie on a sofa in the lounge!' said the steward. 'Admiral Featherstonehaugh, Retired, Royal Navy, sat on it. He was wearing white flannels. He says he's going to sue the company.'

'I know, I know,' said the first mate. 'They have also spilled ink on the captain's charts.'

'Forty-two years at sea, I signed on as a boy of twelve,' said the steward, 'and never, never an afternoon like this. I wish you could see the dining saloon. Why, I've been through typhoons in the Orient with less damage. Then the girl threw a salt cellar at the boy and hit him on the head, so he threw a plate of salad at her and hit that lady missionary. You remember the one, she gave us tracts and said we were all going to die on the fields of Armageddon.'

'If we live through this afternoon,' said the first mate. 'Well, don't tell me your troubles. I've got enough of my own. I'm not a nursemaid. Kids shouldn't be allowed on board alone!'

Sergeant Coulter of the Royal Canadian Mounted Police watched the S.S. *Haida Prince* docking. Like a tourist's snapshot brought to life, he was a shining symbol of impassive and impartial justice. His shoulders bulged through his immaculate shirt, his Sam Browne belt hugged his narrow waist, the leather polished to the same gleaming russet as his riding boots. His steel spurs flashed in the sun, as hard and cold as his blue eyes, and his broad-brimmed hat was set squarely and stubbornly on his head.

Others might wilt in the summer heat, but not Sergeant Albert Edward George Coulter. He stood as though guarding the Khyber Pass, his back as solid as his royal names and his brick-red neck immovable in his tight collar.

Mr Brooks, the elderly keeper of the post office and general store, approached the police officer, the top of his silvery head barely reaching the august shoulders of Sergeant Coulter.

'Good afternoon, Sergeant.'

Mr Brooks was waving an open letter in his hand.

The Mountie's face relaxed and he nodded.

'I've just received some rather upsetting news, Sergeant.' Mr Brooks looked up at the policeman. 'Our cottage was leased for the summer by a Major Gaunt, no, let me see, Major Murchison-Gaunt. His lawyers wrote he would be here to open the place on July 2nd.'

He paused and gazed up at Sergeant Coulter again.

'It is now July 4th, Sergeant, and Major Murchison-Gaunt has not yet arrived,' he announced.

The officer stared down at him.

'Well?'

'Well,' said Mr Brooks, 'I've just received another letter from Major Murchison-Gaunt's lawyer saying he has been unavoidably detained and he may not be able to get here for several weeks.'

'Yes, Mr Brooks?'

'Oh, I forgot to tell you. Major Murchison-Gaunt's young nephew is being sent here from his private school, to join his uncle for the summer. The boy is an orphan. He's on the *Haida Prince* now.'

'I suppose he'll have to be sent back to Vancouver,' said the Mountie. 'If that's where he's from, of course.'

'But that's impossible! The school is closed and the child has no relatives except his uncle, who is in Europe now.'

Mr Brooks's nose twitched nervously, but Sergeant Coulter, who quelled riots single-handed, was not upset by the untimely arrival of a small boy.

'I imagine Major Murchison's lawyer will look after the situation.'

Mr Brooks nibbled the edge of the letter as though it were a piece of lettuce.

'But that's just it! Murchison-Gaunt, by the way. The lawyer writes that Major Murchison-Gaunt is the boy's legal guardian, and that he, the lawyer, wants no part of the boy whatsoever. As a matter of fact, he seems very explicit on that point.'

'I'll file a report with the child welfare department.'

Sergeant Coulter stared over Mr Brooks's head, to the *Haida Prince*, as the ship neared the dock.

Mr Brooks cleared his throat meekly.

'The lawyer suggests - he - he almost implores, that Mrs Brooks and I see to the lad until his uncle arrives.'

'Is that agreeable with you and Mrs Brooks?'

There was a pause.

'Mrs Brooks and I have talked it over, Albert. We hate to think of the little fellow being knocked about from pillar to post, and now that— ' a look of self-pity came to Mr Brooks's eyes, 'and now, of course, our own boy being gone, well, we'd be only too glad to do what we can for this little fellow. It may be lonely for him here, with no children left on the Island, but - but - Mrs Brooks and I would like to do what we can for him.'

As the expression on Mr Brooks's face softened, the expression on Sergeant Coulter's hardened.

'Very well, Mr Brooks. If you'll give me the address, I'll see that the lawyer is notified.'

Sergeant Coulter stared at the ship without seeing it. Was he to be always silently reproached for being the only one to return? He came back, the son of the poor addled old Sergeant-Major Coulter. The sons of admirals were coral in the briny deep, the sons of generals had little white crosses over them in all the graveyards of Europe, and the young eagles, like old Brooks's son, Dickie, hardly through school, they had flown back to the motherland. Like glorious phoenixes, they had plunged flaming to earth and burned, young and pure and untouched. Only the son of the old Sergeant-Major had returned.

He glanced up at the war monument in the center of the village square. A tall, plain granite shaft. 'To the Memory of our Island Boys' and then the long list of names, his own the only one absent.

CHAPTER ONE

No, there were no children left on the Island. The widows and their young broods had moved away, to the cities, and it was no wonder. There was no electricity on the Island, no doctor, no dentist. There was a church but services were held only a few times a year, when the minister came over from the neighbouring island of Benares.

Two world wars had bled the Island white. Now only a few farmers and the old people were left. The old people, remittance men, aged pensioners, ancient exiled aristocrats, living in sweet and poor gentility.

On rare occasions American tourists and summer visitors came. Sometimes commercial fishermen and Indians tied their seiners and gas boats at the wharf, but apart from them, the Island was as silent as a tomb.

'Ah, there's the goat-lady.'

A middle-aged woman came heavily down the wharf and scanned the decks of the *Haida Prince*.

'Good afternoon, Mrs Nielsen. Are you expecting someone on the *Prince* too?' Mr Brooks was at her side.

She nodded and craned her neck at the sightseers hanging over the rails of the boat.

'Yes, a little girl. Her mother worked in the ward of the hospital when I was in two years ago.'

Her eyes flitted over the passengers.

'She's coming for the summer. It's the first time I've had anyone to board with me, but I thought I'd try it. It's lonely now Per's away fishing.'

She turned to Mr Brooks.

'I don't see any little girl. I hope she isn't lost. She had to get on the boat by herself because her mother was working.'

'She's probably inside,' said Mr Brooks, and then his face brightened. 'A little girl? How nice! Mrs Brooks and I are

7

having a young lad with us for a few weeks. They'll be company for each other.'

He paused. 'It'll seem strange, children on the Island again.'

The goat-lady nodded, but said nothing.

Sweating deckhands heaved lines to the wharf and the ship, like a big horse backing into a stall, shuddered against the pilings. Finally the gangplank was shoved across and freight was hoisted to the dock, swinging dizzily. Winches groaned, commands were shouted, Mr Brooks and Mrs Nielsen strained their eyes and Sergeant Coulter stood lordly and impassive.

A bent old gentleman, carrying a knobby stick and followed by two border collies, came slowly down the gangplank.

'Oh, Mr Allen,' shouted Mr Brooks, 'how did you do in the sheep trials?'

The old man fumbled in his shabby overcoat and brought out a blue satin ribbon.

'Good! Very good indeed.' Mr Brooks gave him a friendly wave. 'Oh, Mr Allen, you didn't see a young boy on board, did you? Or a little girl?'

One of the border collies cringed. Mr Allen gave Mr Brooks a horrified look, and motioning to his two collies, he sprinted up the wharf, pausing only once to stop and shake a crotchety fist.

Mr Brooks and Mrs Nielsen approached the first mate.

'Did you see— '

'Yes! Yes!' he said irritably. 'Thank God somebody's claiming them.'

Sergeant Coulter moved to the foot of the gangplank. The first mate turned to him, shook his head and wiped his brow.

'Whew!' he said.

'What's the trouble?' asked the Mountie.

The mate gave a sigh of relief, realising his watch was over.

'Oh,' he said wearily, 'I guess the girl isn't *too* bad. But that boy!'

The burly steward in his wilted white jacket arrived panting at the top of the gangplank, a squirming child under each arm.

'Time, ladies and gentlemen!' he shouted with a harsh Cockney accent. 'The end of the line for you two!'

He set the two children on their feet and gave a comic salute to the Mountie.

'You'll wish you was back on the quiet beaches of Dunkirk!' he called as he beat a hasty retreat.

A smaller steward, carrying a leather suitcase and a paper shopping bag, dashed between the children, down to the wharf, dropped the bags, raced up the gangplank and fled into the bowels of the ship.

The children stood spitting at each other and refused to come down the gangplank.

'You did!'

'I didn't!'

'You did too!'

'I did not!'

'You're a liar!'

'I am not! So are you!'

'*I saw you!*'

Mr Brooks and Mrs Nielsen, with empty waiting arms, stood ignored, and the big Mountie watched with hard eyes.

'You went in the captain's cabin!'

'How do you know? I did not! You must of been up there too!'

'You dumped ink on his charts!'

'Liar! I bumped it with my elbow!'

'Liar! Liar! Liar!' The girl drew back and faced the boy triumphantly. Then, as a final insult she turned and hissed: 'And I don't care if you are going to get ten million dollars. You haven't got a mother!'

With this parting shot, she stalked down the gangplank.

Sergeant Coulter thought he had never seen such an unprepossessing child, not that he cared much for children in any form. They were miniature grown-ups, and as such bore careful watching.

The child, her lank, straw-colored hair hanging lifelessly about her pinched white face, looked straight ahead, and marched down like a small royal personage.

Sergeant Coulter noticed that, though her clothes were shabby, they were neat and clean, and somehow she already had the air of an indomitable Island spinster.

When she reached the waiting group she looked about, and her eye settled on Mrs Nielsen.

'Are you Mrs Nielsen, the goat-lady?'

Mrs Nielsen nodded, unsure of how to greet the child.

'And you are Christie,' she said finally.

'My mother told me you had a little house. She said you had a cow and a cat and a dog.' She paused while she looked the goat-lady up and down. 'Have you?'

Mrs Nielsen nodded.

The child became aware of the policeman.

'Who's he?' she gasped.

Mr Brooks, with his courtly, old-world manner, stepped forward.

'This is Sergeant Coulter of the Royal Canadian Mounted Police, and I'm Mr Brooks. I run the store here. Welcome to the Island.'

Sergeant Coulter did not look at all welcoming.

Christie gazed up at him and down again, from the top of his broad-brimmed hat to his polished boots. Then she smiled and her face was radiant.

'A real Mountie,' she said softly. She remembered her fellow traveller who still stood at the top of the gangplank, and she jerked her thumb at him.

'Can you put him in jail? He's a bad boy. He tells lies and he's not nice.'

Picking up the paper shopping bag, she turned to the goat-lady.

'Well, let's go.'

As she and Mrs Nielsen walked up the wharf she looked over her shoulder to Sergeant Coulter and smiled again.

'A real Mountie,' she repeated.

The boy suddenly hurtled down the gangplank, his face sullen and his bold eyes insolent.

'I am not a liar! I have so got ten million dollars! She threw the salt cellar at me!' He pointed to a purple bump on his forehead, 'and she said she'd push me overboard if I didn't shut up!'

When the Mountie stood expressionless and silent, the boy's outburst stopped and he looked about.

Mr Brooks stepped forward.

'You must be Barnaby,' he said and held out his hand.

Barnaby took no notice of the gesture.

'Where's my uncle? And I am not a liar! She's a liar!'

His voice was shrill, almost hysterical.

Mr Brooks put his arm about the boy's shoulder.

'Of course you aren't. Your uncle isn't here, Barnaby. At least, not yet, so you are going to stay with Mrs Brooks and me for a little while.'

He patted the boy's flaxen head, but the child drew away from him.

'Won't that be nice, Barnaby? We're so happy to have you, we've wanted a little boy like you for such a long time.'

Barnaby turned to Sergeant Coulter.

'Are you a real Mountie?'

'Of course he is,' said Mr Brooks. 'He always meets the boat when he's on the Island. This is Sergeant Coulter, Barnaby, and he was born here. Now then, shall we go up to the store and see Mrs Brooks? She's so anxious to meet you.'

The boy ignored Mr Brooks, his admiring eyes fixed on the policeman.

'When I grow up, I'm going to be a Mountie.'

'Why?' asked Sergeant Coulter, speaking for the first time.

'Because you can put people in jail if you don't like them.'

The policeman smiled and turned to Mr Brooks.

'It's not quite as simple as that, is it, Mr Brooks?'

'Shall we go and see Mrs Brooks, Barnaby?'

'Where's my uncle?'

Mr Brooks and Sergeant Coulter looked at each other.

'But I just told you, Barnaby, he couldn't get here in time.'

'You mean he's really not here? He's not playing a game?'

The child's manner changed, his face crumpled and he looked dependent and pathetic as he gazed in a confused way from Mr Brooks to Sergeant Coulter.

'No, of course he's not playing a game, Barnaby. He's been detained, but he'll be here soon. Everything will be all right, my boy, and in the meanwhile, I know you'll be happy with us. Now come along.'

He offered Barnaby his hand again, and this time, looking dazed, the child took it.

They walked together for several yards, then the boy pulled away from Mr Brooks and ran back to the policeman.

'But if he isn't here, where is he?'

His face was desperate.

The Mountie pointed to Mr Brooks.

'He's in Europe. Mr Brooks will explain everything to you. Go with him like a good boy. We'll get in touch with your uncle. Don't worry, we'll look after you.'

The boy stared up at him.

'You mean you'll really look after me?'

'Mr and Mrs Brooks will.'

'And nothing will happen to me?'

Puzzled, the Mountie stared down at the boy.

'No, of course not. You run along with Mr Brooks now. Mrs Brooks is waiting to meet you.'

Barnaby returned to Mr Brooks, and as they walked up the wharf he turned and shouted: 'I'm going to be a Mountie. Just like you.'

Sergeant Coulter sat in the police launch, pondering. One small boy unmet by uncle.

He was a precise, dedicated man who rarely made snap judgements, but he felt that there was something very much the matter with that boy.

He leaned back and lit a cigarette. When you stopped to think of it, there was something the matter with most children these days. They needed more discipline. Take that boy, rude, spoiled, private-school brat. 'I've got ten million dollars!' Imperious little devil. A good hiding was what he needed. But that sort of treatment was considered old fashioned today. It worked when he was a boy, though.

Well, the boy was, after all, only a child. Frightened when his uncle wasn't there to meet him. Left stranded on the dock like a lost puppy.

Sergeant Coulter, smiled as he remembered the admiration in the boy's eyes. They all wanted to be Mounties.

But the smile faded. There was something the matter with that boy. He was more than frightened. He looked almost insane, and that expression on his face when he asked about the uncle ...

What was it? Where had he seen that expression before? The policeman's mind couldn't let it go. Then things clicked into place and he remembered. The prisoner reprieved from the gallows.

Oh, no. He was imagining things.

Sergeant Coulter put his fountain pen away and brushed a speck of dust from his hat. The old people of the Island weren't used to boys. Especially bad boys. He'd be breaking windows and cheeking the old birds.

That boy needed a firm hand. Yes, he'd watch that boy.

CHRISTIE LOOKED AROUND the goat-lady's kitchen. A Big Ben alarm clock ticked noisily on the window sill, while under the window on an old black leather sofa, a cat and dog napped. The cat, a large tom, was curled in a tight circle at one end of the sofa, his tryst-scarred head half tucked under his paws. At the other end a tiny brown-and-white dog woke up and opened its mouth as if it were barking. Nothing came out but hoarse gasps.

The child turned a puzzled face to the goat-lady.

'It doesn't make any noise.'

'She never has,' said the goat-lady. 'Even when she was a puppy. Nobody knows why. Her name is Trixie.'

Christie put out her hand and then drew it back.

'Does she bite?'

The goat-lady smiled. 'No. Would you like some dinner?'

The child fondled Trixie's silken ears as she shook her head. 'No, thank you.'

'Then I'll make some cocoa for you.'

She changed her sensible black oxfords for a comfortable, sloppy pair of carpet slippers.

There were chickens on her little farm, she said, as she made the cocoa, and ducks and a few geese. There was an old dog called Shep who had once helped her tend her goats. She didn't keep goats any more because not enough people bought the milk. Instead she made bread now and sold it to the Islanders. Then there were Trixie and Tom who stayed in the house, and of course, Gudrun the cow, who lived in the barn.

Suspecting the child was homesick, she chatted on, but if Christie heard her, she gave no indication. Her little old-maid's face was preoccupied as she gazed around the kitchen, so different from the small, clinically neat apartment she and her mother shared.

The kitchen, though clean, was cheerfully untidy, and fragrant with the scent of cedar. On the window sill a clutter of soap coupons, knitting needles, wool and stray buttons was flanked by a handful of wild roses crammed in an empty jam jar. The wood in the huge, black iron stove crackled merrily and the soothing sound of the kettle in the background made Christie's eye droop with sudden weariness.

She blinked her eyes again to wake herself and stared at the embroidered cloth on the kitchen table. In the center were a blue-and-white-striped milk jug and sugar bowl. Behind them, looking out of place in the simple surroundings, stood a cut-glass cruèt set in a silver stand, the diamondlike surfaces glittering in the lamplight.

The floor was plain, unvarnished scrubbed boards, and in front of the stove, the sofa and an old rocking chair, were hand-hooked rag rugs in gay colours.

Inside the fluted glass of the lamp chimney a delicate flame burned, narrow, orange and tall. Almost hypnotised, Christie watched it flicker.

The goat-lady, receiving neither interest nor answers to her conversation, gave up. She put the steaming cup of cocoa on the table, pointed to it and nodded to Christie.

The child rose without enthusiasm, and sitting at the table, obediently sipped the drink. Her eyes were resting on the two little windows framed by frivolous sprigged curtains.

In the distance a giant jagged fir tree, one of the last of the old forest monarchs, stood proudly among the second-growth dwarfed timber, and as the moon rose behind it its feathery boughs were etched like black lace against the darkening summer sky.

'Do you like it?'

Reluctantly the child drew her eyes from the window.

'It's beautiful.'

The goat-lady looked puzzled, then she laughed.

'I meant the cocoa.'

Christie turned her tight little face to the goat-lady.

'I meant the tree.'

The goat-lady sighed. It appeared she and Christie were not destined to share many spirited conversations during the course of the summer.

'You must be tired. It's time for bed.' In a kindly fashion she put her hand on the child's lank, pale hair. 'Come, you'll sleep in Per's room. In his bed.'

She pointed to a ladder in the corner of the room which led to an attic above the kitchen.

'Up here. Per is my son. He's a fisherman and he's away until November.'

She pointed to a door beside the stove.

'My bedroom is there. If you're frightened or lonely, you have only to call; I'll hear you and come.'

But already Mrs Nielsen had a feeling that this self-contained, dour child was not likely to call for assistance.

Lighting a candle, she picked up the brown-paper shopping bag containing Christie's possessions and began climbing the ladder. Christie followed her.

The room in the attic was tiny, tinier even than the kitchen, and the child looked about her with interest.

A narrow, ornately carved wooden bed was beneath the lattice window, and Christie could still see the big fir tree, standing like a sentinel in the distance.

'You mean this will be my room while I'm here?'

She sat on the patchwork counterpane, her eyes those of a suspicious child listening to a fairy tale.

'Yes. Do you like it?'

Christie nodded.

'Well.' The goat-lady gave a sigh of relief. 'That's something, isn't it?'

Christie gazed up at the sloping roof beams, only a few inches above the goat-lady's head. Between the cedar shakes tiny glimpses of the evening sky flashed.

Christie pointed her index finger up.

'Rain come through there?'

'No. You get undressed and washed now.'

On a carved chest of drawers near the foot of the bed stood a big water jug and washbowl. Fat cabbage roses, pink and red, romped across the white china and the child suddenly stretched her hand out and patted them.

The goat-lady put the candle on the chest of drawers, took Christie's nightgown from the paper bag and handed Christie a white linen towel.

As Christie dried her face, she sniffed the towel.

'It smells nice,' she said, then, pointing to the water jug and washbowl, she added in her begrudging way, 'they're nice too.'

A breeze, laden with the warm scents of the forest, blew softly in the little window.

'Into your nightgown and say your prayers now. Remember, I'll be downstairs if you want me.'

Christie looked at her in surprise.

'I don't say prayers.'

'You don't? Don't you go to church?'

'No. My mother was brought up a Presbyterian, and MacNab, that's my father, he used to be a Catholic, so my mother says we'll just leave well enough alone with me.'

Her manner was polite, but irritatingly adult.

'Well, goodnight, Christie.' She leaned over to kiss the child's cheek, but Christie took a step back.

'Blow out the candle when you are through, Christie. I left matches next to it on the dresser if you want to light it again, but be careful.'

She backed heavily down the ladder, leaving the child standing in the middle of the room.

Looking small and forlorn now she was alone, Christie blew out the candle and crawled into the snug, bunk-like bed. By moonlight she could see strange little trolls carved on the headboard, laughing and hiding behind ferns. She touched them gently and then sank back, pulling the covers up to her neck.

She lay for a long time thinking of her mother. Though she knew her mother would not wish her to be unhappy on the first night of her holiday, her small, plain face became sadder by the minute. She sniffed as she thought of the acres of hospital floors her mother scrubbed, of the endless hospital beds she made, so that Christie could escape from that baking little apartment in the heart of the city.

Dwelling on her mother's sacrifices only made Christie sadder still, and so, burying her head on the crisp pillowcase, she decided to think about how much she hated the boy on the boat.

Soon she was asleep, and when the moon rose like a large golden coin and shone on her face she was smiling.

When she awoke, the sun had already been up for hours, and the fir tree, now a bright green, was motionless in the morning heat.

The sounds of the day came pouring in her little window, urging her to get out of bed. Ducks quacked, chickens clucked, Tom mewed, Trixie gasped, and from the barn Gudrun the cow lowed moodily.

A delightful morning on the farm, with all the animals calling welcome to a city-bred child.

But Miss MacNab was plainly not impressed with the rustic atmosphere, for as she climbed down to the kitchen her face wore its usual prim look of disapproval.

The goat-lady was cooking at the stove.

'Good morning, Christie. Did you sleep well?' She turned, and pointing her cooking fork to the table, motioned Christie to sit down.

'It's noisy here in the morning,' replied her guest courteously.

The goat-lady placed a bowl before Christie. It was filled with fresh-picked wild blackberries, winking like garnets and half covered with clotted cream.

Christie picked at the dish.

When the goat-lady put a steaming platter on the table, Christie looked up.

'What's this?'

'Your breakfast.'

With a royal wave Christie dismissed the plate of golden fried potatoes, pink ham curling prettily brown about the edges and scarlet tomatoes cut in thick slices.

'I only have cornflakes and tea for breakfast.'

She pointed to the homemade white bread, already buttered, and a jar of raspberry jam, which sat behind the platter. 'I don't eat things like that. Just cornflakes and a cup of tea.'

The goat-lady sat in her rocking chair and regarded Christie with astonishment.

'No wonder you've got a complexion like a chicken's foot.' As she rocked back and forth she took out her knitting.

'Listen,' she said finally, 'your mother is paying for your board. You know how hard she works, and you know she'd like you to eat properly.'

'Cornflakes and tea,' repeated Christie, and looking at the ceiling she added, 'when I was a year old, my mother took me to the very best baby doctor there was and I only weighed six pounds more than when I was born.'

'Well, if all she fed you was cornflakes and tea, it's no wonder.'

Christie gave her a level look.

'I was a very delicate baby. The doctor told my mother, he said it was love and love alone that kept that child alive.'

The goat-lady sniffed and counted stitches.

'Christie,' she said, when she reached sixty-two, 'what do you want more than anything in the world?'

'Curly hair,' said Christie without hesitation. 'But my mother won't let me have a permanent until I'm eighteen. She says they're vulgar on children.'

'Curly hair?'

'No,' Christie sighed patiently. 'Permanents on children.'

The goat-lady poured herself a cup of coffee.

'Well,' she said after a pause, 'let's have a bargain. I'll curl your hair for you every night, and you eat a good breakfast every morning.

Christie thought carefully.

'No, thank you.'

'Why not?'

'Because,' and she primped her whispy hair, 'because I want a permanent.'

The goat-lady took up her knitting again.

'Try and eat just a bit.'

The child took a token bite of tomato, one small potato slice and a morsel of ham; then she pushed her plate away.

'Cornflakes and tea,' she repeated with the persistence of a bill collector. 'Cornflakes and tea. That's all I ever eat for breakfast.'

A large humble-looking dog stood at the door, mouth watering, mournful eyes gleaming and tail wagging hopefully.

'You're going to be awfully hungry by September,' said the goat-lady. 'Well, give it to Shep. He'll eat it.'

The dog put a tentative foot in the doorway, testing his welcome.

'Does he bite?' asked Christie.

'Old Shep? No.' The goat-lady stroked his grizzled head affectionately.

The silent little Trixie, who had been napping on the sofa, suddenly flew like an angry wasp at the big dog and drove him out of the door.

'Trixie's jealous,' said the goat-lady, sweeping the little dog up in her arms. 'She won't let him in the house.'

Christie put the plate on the porch and stood watching the old dog as he gulped down her colourful breakfast.

'Hello.' Barnaby Gaunt sauntered to the door and looked the goat-lady up and down.

'They told me at the store, Mr and Mrs Brooks, to come over here and play with *her*.' He jerked his thumb at Christie.

'Good morning,' said the goat-lady. 'What did you say your name was?'

'Barnaby. Barnaby Gaunt.'

'I'm Mrs Nielsen, but you can call me Auntie.'

He didn't answer her. Licking his lips, he stared enviously at the dog, which was still wolfing down Christie's breakfast.

'Gee,' he said finally, 'that looks good.'

The goat-lady put some cookies in a paper bag and handed it to him.

'Why don't you two run along and play? Take Shep with you so you won't get lost.'

'I don't want to play with him,' whined Christie. 'He's not nice. My mother wouldn't like me to play with him. He swears and tells lies.'

'Oh, he doesn't.' The goat-lady patted Barnaby's bright yellow hair. 'You don't, do you? It's such a nice day, off you two go now and play. I've got a lot of work to do, the dough has risen and it's nearly time to get the bread in the oven.'

The old dog trotted along, and the goat-lady watched the little party disappear down the path.

What an odd child that Christie was. Polite and obedient enough, but with a very decided mind of her own. She needed to play with other children, boisterous, normal children. Like Barnaby.

The children walked slowly down the path until they came to a dusty lane. Timid Christie did not want to go too far away. The country looked all the same to her, with no landmarks. She looped her hand in the old dog's collar for confidence, but Barnaby Gaunt forged ahead as if he owned the Island.

They came to a large field, girdled with a cedar snake fence. Climbing the first two bars, and shielding their eyes from the bright morning sun, they peered in all directions.

A monstrous bull, tethered in the field, lowered his head and bellowed, rolling a fearsome, bloodshot eyeball at them.

Christie climbed hastily down, but the boy merely took a stone from his pocket and tossed it in the direction of the bull.

Past the bull an elderly man was painting a barn bright blue. He stopped his work and shook an angry fist at the boy. Barnaby climbed down from the fence and stuck out his tongue.

On the other side of the field, in the distance, the children could see a tall, red-haired woman plowing behind two giant Clydesdales.

'Everything's big here,' said Christie, staring first at the bull, then at the horses.

The woman stopped plowing and waved. The children waved back, watching the horses tugging lightly, like locomotives harnessed to a toy implement.

'They're pretty,' said Barnaby. The horses' coats gleamed like polished mahogany and their powerful rumps dimpled as they lifted ponderous fetlocked feet.

The children moved aimlessly on, down the leafy country lane.

Fifteen minutes later, dusty and whining again, Christie was back at the goat-lady's.

'He pushed me down, that Barnaby Gaunt! He's a bad boy.'

The goat-lady, relieved it was nothing more serious, brushed Christie's lank hair from her face.

'How did it start? Did you push him?'

'Well - yes,' said Christie.

'Did you push him first?'

'Yes,' said Christie.

'Why?'

'He wouldn't give me the cookies! They're mine! I came here to stay with you, not him! It's not fair he got the cookies.'

The goat-lady sighed.

'Never mind now, it's all right. Come along, we'll get the milk from the well, and you can have a nice cool glass with a cinnamon bun.'

From a covered stone well beside the house, she drew up a milk can. Carrying it under one arm, and with the other about Christie's thin shoulders, she led her into the house.

'You haven't any brothers or sisters, Christie, and you're not used to sharing things. You'll have to learn to. And you and the little boy must learn to be friends, or you'll be lonely here.'

Christie sat miserably on the leather sofa, munching the bun and drinking the milk. The little dog Trixie licked her face and begged for a snack.

It was comforting to be back in the goat-lady's snug kitchen. She watched as the goat-lady cleared off the table and began kneading dough. The yeasty scent and the heat from the roaring fire in the black stove made her drowsy again. She hugged the little dog and gave the goat-lady a wan smile.

'You're almost asleep. Lie down and have a nap.'

When Christie awoke, shiny loaves of bread with golden crusts were lined up on the kitchen table. The room was much cooler now, and the goat-lady sat in her rocking chair, shelling peas.

'Your little friend Barnaby was back. He wouldn't come in, but he said he was sorry. He'll be around tomorrow morning to play with you again.'

'Do I have to play with him?'

The goat-lady put down the bowl of peas and thought for a few minutes before answering.

'He's not a bad boy, Christie. You try and get along with him. You two could have lots of good times this summer, if you'll just learn to get along with each other. You'll try, won't you?

After a long pause, Christie nodded. She was an obedient child - in most things.

BARNABY GAUNT lost no time in fulfilling Sergeant Coulter's direst prophecies. Before the sun had set on his first full day on the Island, Sergeant Coulter had already received three complaints about the boy.

Mr Brooks, busy sorting the mail, looked up to find Sergeant Coulter standing at the counter of the store.

'I'm sorry, Sergeant, I hope you haven't been waiting long.'

'No. I just dropped by. Is there a parcel here from London for me?'

'Nothing yet, Albert.'

The quiet of the country store was suddenly rent with a childish treble that made the rafters ring.

'I'm not eating this damned baby slop!'

Sighing, Mr Brooks shook his head and turned to Sergeant Coulter.

'We're having a little trouble getting Barnaby to eat.'

A loud crash of crockery bore out this statement.

'Yes, it sounds as if you are,' said Albert.

Mrs Brooks, looking frail and wraithlike, came through the beaded curtains that separated the store from their living quarters.

'Oh, Sydney,' she cried, clasping her hands, 'you must come and help me. The child will starve, he's hardly swallowed a bite. I fixed Dickie's favourite supper for him and he won't touch it. And he's just thrown the sugar bowl at the wall.'

She turned to Albert.

'He's so highly strung. You have no idea, Albert. He's just like Dickie.'

She paused and looked quickly to Mr Brooks.

'Although Dickie never threw things,' she added in a gentle, bewildered voice.

No, not likely, not the ever-lamented Dickie. Sergeant Coulter rubbed his hands together.

'Perhaps I can persuade the little fellow to eat. I want to speak to him anyway. You two stay here.'

When he entered the parlour, he understood why Barnaby threw the sugar bowl.

Barnaby sat with his belligerent head lowered and his supper in front of him.

Dickie's favourite repast. A coddled egg, a bowl of bread and milk sprinkled with brown sugar, a cup of very weak tea, an apple peeled and cut into tiny pieces so that he should not tire himself unduly chewing, and a plate of arrowroot biscuits.

Sergeant Coulter sighed.

Barnaby looked up at the policeman, his expression one of outraged manhood.

Sergeant Coulter sighed again. Nursery food for a strapping, active child like this.

He put his finger against his lips.

'Shhhhh!' He said and leaned over the boy.

'Barnaby,' he whispered, 'eat it now, like a good boy. I'll speak to them and see you get some decent food tomorrow. Don't make a fuss tonight. It's been a long time since they had a boy around.'

Barnaby looked at him blankly, then at the food.

He shook his head.

Sergeant Coulter placed an arm on either side of the table and leaned closer to the boy.

'I thought you said you wanted to be a Mountie. The first thing you have to learn is to do what you're told.'

He leaned back.

'Eat it,' he said in a low, even tone.

Barnaby stared at him.

The hard eyes of the Mountie regarded him with detachment. Suddenly Barnaby smiled, a quick, cheerful grin.

'Okay,' he said and began eating.

'That's better,' said Sergeant Coulter, and the boy gazed up at him with adoring eyes.

'Now another thing, Barnaby. I don't want to hear any swearing from you in front of Mr and Mrs Brooks. Do I make myself clear?'

Barnaby nodded agreeably.

Sergeant Coulter walked to the beaded curtain, stopped and turned.

'Oh, yes, there's one more thing. You wouldn't happen to know who opened the bars of Mr Allen's sheep pen and drove all the sheep out, would you?'

'Nope,' said Barnaby Gaunt.

'Really?' said Sergeant Coulter. 'That's odd. You see, Mr Allen saw a blond boy running down the road after the sheep.'

'Did he?' said Barnaby.

'Yes, he did,' said Sergeant Coulter. 'And this Island isn't exactly overrun with little blond boys. As a matter of fact, you're the only one.'

'Am I?'

Sergeant Coulter nodded.

'You watch your step, young man.'

Sergeant Coulter was thirty feet from the store when that clear treble echoed again through the quiet dusk.

'No! I'm not having any bloody bath and I'm not saying any God-damned prayers!'

Sergeant Coulter paused momentarily, then walked on. He'd have to watch that boy. He had all the earmarks of a juvenile delinquent.

Unshriven, unrepentant and unwashed, Barnaby lay on his cot in the Brooks' parlour.

Mr Brooks held the flickering coal oil lamp high as he and Mrs Brooks gazed with awe at the sleeping child.

It had come to pass, even as Dickie had prophesied. Changed in corporeal form, perhaps, but here nevertheless, as he had promised them through the lips of the medium.

Slumber cast a spell of tranquillity on Barnaby's stubborn face. His cheek lay on one grubby hand, while the shadow of a smile played on his lips. Asleep he looked quite sweet-natured.

The voice at the séance had not sounded like Dickie's but as the medium had explained, Dickie was on too high an astral plane to descend personally, and he had to be relayed through the spirit control, White Deer.

White Deer had delivered the message as clearly as though Dickie had been in the room. Yes, Dickie was very happy on his astral plane, but it saddened him to see them grieving. Yes, he would comfort them.

CHAPTER THREE

They had never doubted it. And here was little Barnaby.

Mr Brooks turned to Mrs Brooks.

'I think, perhaps, that we had better not discuss this with Sergeant Coulter or Mr Rice-Hope,' he whispered.

Mrs Brooks nodded.

Everyone was entitled to his own beliefs, of course, even Sergeant Coulter. Albert had always had a hard, uncompromising streak in him, still, surely it had been unkind of him to refer to the medium, whom he had never even met, as a fraud. Or, to quote Albert's exact words, 'A bunko artist'.

Upon their return from the séance, which had taken place in the city, they had also confided in Mr Rice-Hope. The Reverend Mr Rice-Hope's attitude, like Albert's, had not been encouraging. Meek though he generally was, their minister had stated firmly that they lacked faith, and difficult as he knew it was, they must bear Dickie's loss as a test of their belief in life everlasting, as decreed by the church.

Only parents bereaved could understand fully that it was impossible for Dickie to leave them forever. They had had faith, of their own kind, and now their prayers had been answered.

As they blew out the lamp and tucked the covers about the sleeping child, they realised that the resemblance was uncanny. Nothing so commonplace or tangible as mere physical resemblance, but rather an indefinable aura, so unmistakable that to suppose the contrary would be absurd. Let Albert scoff; it could not be explained to the earthbound Sergeant Coulters of the world. Only those with extrasensory instincts could appreciate the likeness.

When Christie came down the ladder on the second morning she found another steaming platter waiting at her place.

Neither tea nor cornflakes were in evidence, but there was one new addition. Barnaby Gaunt sat contentedly in the rocking chair.

Seating herself, Christie smiled brightly at the goat-lady.

'Good morning. May I have my breakfast now, please?'

The goat-lady smiled back.

'You certainly may.'

Serene, Christie stared out at her fir tree.

The goat-lady poured herself a cup of coffee, and standing in the open doorway stirring it, she remarked on what a lovely morning it was.

Christie's face tightened.

'I'd like my tea and cornflakes now, please.'

'No tea. No cornflakes,' said the goat-lady. 'How is Mrs Brooks today, Barnaby?'

'Fine.' He eyed Christie's breakfast and licked his lips.

'Are you hungry?'

He nodded.

The goat-lady pointed to the table.

Leaning over, she placed Christie's plate before him.

'Oh, boy!'

The goat-lady noticed his table manners were curiously delicate for a child.

Every drop of canny Scots blood in her boiling, Christie watched him with narrowed eyes. Had not the goat-lady reminded her only yesterday that her poor overworked mother was paying for her board?

Unable to bear watching that boy putting her food into his mouth, she sprang to her feet.

'That's *my* breakfast!'

The goat-lady sat in the rocking chair that Barnaby had vacated and picked up her knitting.

'Oh, no. You only eat cornflakes and tea. Well, it's too good to throw to the dog, isn't it, Barnaby? And Christie doesn't want it.'

'I want it now,' said Christie, biting her lips.

'Too late.' She turned to Barnaby. 'What nice table manners you have.'

He looked up, surprised.

'Oh,' he said, 'my uncle is strict about table manners.'

'Well, as long as you enjoy your food.'

He looked surprised again. 'You mean I don't have to eat this way? You mean I can eat any way I like?'

'As long as you eat it, I don't care.'

Barnaby shovelled the ham and potatoes into his mouth. He finished them and the tomatoes and he drank the milk. Then, with an engaging grin, he turned to the goat-lady.

'Can I have the bread and jam too?'

'Certainly. More milk?'

His mouth was too full to answer, but he nodded.

When he had finished everything on the table, the goat-lady pulled a speckled blue coffeepot to the front of the stove.

'Like a cup of coffee?'

He smiled and nodded again.

It was too much for Christie.

'How come he gets coffee like a grown-up, and I can't even have my tea!'

'Because he likes my cooking.' The goat-lady paused and rewound the yarn which the cat had pulled askew. 'I used to be a cook, you know. It's nice to have someone to cook for again.'

A very sulky Christie watched Barnaby drink his coffee. 'I'm hungry.'

'Well,' said the goat-lady, 'it's only twenty-four hours till tomorrow morning.'

Christie glowered.

'I want some breakfast.'

'Cornflakes and tea?'

'No.' She gave in and pointed to Barnaby's empty plate. 'I guess I'll have to eat what he had.'

Without a word the goat-lady arose and cooked another breakfast. Christie ate until her shrunken stomach was tight and she felt almost ill, then she sighed.

'I can't finish it.'

'Give it to Shep. Maybe you can do better tomorrow.'

Again she put cookies in a bag and handed them to Barnaby.

'Now divide those evenly. And no quarrelling today. Go and play and have a good time. I've got a lot of work to do, so don't bother me for the next couple of hours.'

At the door Barnaby turned.

'Thanks,' he said. He and the goat-lady smiled at each other.

When Christie reached the bottom of the stairs, she paused and stared back at the goat-lady.

'You can curl my hair tonight,' she announced.

The two children followed the path they had taken the day before. They climbed the cedar fence and waved to the tall woman plowing, and again they stared fascinated at the bull, who surveyed his domain with murderous eyes.

He was grand champion and he knew it. For all the loving attention lavished on him, he remained, at the bottom of his mean heart, a sullen brute. A brute who ruminated by the hour, wondering how he could, with his polished black horns, impale his patron, Mr Duncan.

Once a year, at the end of August, sleek, shining and burnished like a pagan bull-god, he was shipped to the Exhibition. During his absence, the Islanders hung anxiously over their battery radios until reassured that he had won again. He was their one claim to fame.

Agnes Duncan stopped, tied the reins to the handle of the plow and walked over to the children. Red-haired, six feet tall and as strong as a man, she was held in eternal bondage by her father who had no intention of paying wages to a labourer as long as Agnes could put in an honest day's work.

'Hello,' she said shyly to the children. 'I heard you were here. How do you like the Island?'

'Fine, thank you,' said Christie. Both children smiled at her.

'I hope you won't be lonely.'

'I won't,' said Barnaby. He pointed to the bull. 'What's his name?'

'The Duke of Wellington, but everyone calls him the Iron Duke.'

'He's big, isn't he?'

Agnes Duncan nodded and smiled, then turned to look at the bull. The smile faded from her face. With the possible exception of her father, she hated the bull more than anything in the world.

'Would he hurt somebody if he got off that chain?' asked Christie.

Agnes looked over her shoulder, to her father, who was still painting the barn. She turned and leaned toward the children.

'Mark my words,' she whispered, 'mark my words, that bull will turn on him someday. He's vicious!'

'Agnes!' roared her father from the barn, 'get back to your plowing.'

'Yes, Father,' she called meekly. She nodded to the children and returned to the Clydesdales and the plow. Following the furrow, she looked longingly over her shoulder at the two children.

If *he* had not driven her only suitor, Per Nielsen, away, she might have two flaxen-haired children like that.

The big easygoing farm horses suddenly snorted and tossed their heads. Agnes spoke to them and they plodded on obediently, but their eyes rolled and their nostrils quivered.

Unlike Agnes, they were aware that a pair of eyes, the colour of grass under ice, were watching from a clump of bushes only ten feet away.

One-ear, the outlaw, was crouching in the undergrowth. He slavered and licked his chops as he looked past Agnes to the bull. He had killed a cow once and he very much preferred beef to venison, but he knew that unless he killed in his first spring, the bull would put up a savage fight. And furthermore, the crosseted Iron Duke was watched over as if he were a visiting diplomat.

One-ear sighed. There was already a price on his head; *they* had an unwritten law that cougars, hungry or otherwise, guilty or not, were fair game.

He lay like a huge house cat, his cool green eyes resting balefully on the quiet rural scene before him. Two children. He hadn't seen any on the Island before.

The Clydesdales began to tremble in real alarm, so, slinking on his belly, One-ear crawled deeper into the bushes until he came to a game path that led to the forest.

He flung himself down in his shady nook, a sob-like cough escaping him, and self-pity dimmed his frosted mint eyes as he brooded on his terrible history.

Wherever he went, persecuted. He placed his big head on his outstretched paws and blinked.

An old scar, as large as a man's fist, was just above the joint of his massive shoulder. People. *They* had done that. Next to dogs, he hated people more than anything in the world. Rotten to the core, all of them! Did cougars go after men with guns and dogs? Did forty cougars tree a man, wound him, and tear him to bits if they could?

He had committed the unpardonable crime and they had hunted him for four days, no food, no water and on the run. They trapped him up a tree on the edge of a ravine, and the dogs were waiting at the foot of the tree, barking, barking, barking.

His eyes became stony as he mused. After they had shot him, he fell a hundred feet into the ravine, on branches and rocks. Over and over he tumbled. The ravine was so steep that even the dogs could not climb down, and thinking they had finished him, they left him.

For three days he lay there, and if it had not been for a trickle of water near him, he would have died. He'd broken most of the ribs on his left side, and of course, he'd been shot as well. How he had suffered, every breath a torment. And then he got that awful cold in his lungs. It was, he reflected, a miracle that he had survived. On the fourth day he had managed to crawl out, but he could not hunt. After two weeks he was a hundred pounds lighter and every bone in his pain-ridden body could be counted. Even now, his ribs ached when it was damp.

It had been in January, with two feet of snow on the ground, and he had been dying of hunger. He hadn't eaten in three weeks.

There was a logging camp near by, so he went there at night, to the cookhouse, to see if there were any scraps about. Something hot and steaming was hanging on the porch rail, and, starving, he gulped it down. It was a dish-cloth. A wet dishcloth.

When the cook came out carrying a shotgun, One-ear was so weak the cook nearly outran him. The cook shot off his ear.

He stretched his right front foot before him. From that huge velvet paw sprang talons, two inches long and as sharp as razors. One was missing, caught in one of *their* traps. He'd had to bite it off at the root to free himself.

A piteous life, he thought moodily, blameless and piteous. Indignation choked him as he rose from his forest bower and lashed his long, black-tipped tail. Like an enchanted beast, he sprang into the bushes, looking for a nice plump deer.

L ADY SYDDYNS left a message at the store for
Sergeant Coulter to call at her home at his earliest
convenience.

He found her in her storybook garden, where the scent
of dianthus hung heavy and roses ruled. Though the air was
languid with the pulse of bees, a hummingbird darted about
in rapier haste, fearful of missing one blossom.

Surrounded by nymphs and plaster gnomes, Lady Syddyns
was pruning her prize bushes. She took off her floppy-
brimmed leghorn hat and switched on her hearing aid when
she saw Sergeant Coulter approach.

'Albert, how nice to see you. My, it's warm today. You
must stop for tea. How is your father, dear?'

Albert smiled.

'He passed away some time ago, Lady Syddyns. You
wanted to see me?'

'Why, Albert, I'm always happy to see you.'

She handed him her pruning shears and began brushing
leaves from the faded velvet dressing gown that was her usual
gardening costume.

'Where's my cane, dear?'

Seeing it hooked over the extended arm of a marble maiden, Albert handed it to her.

'My Bertha Alexanders are riddled, completely riddled. They won't win this year.'

She had not summoned him to discuss insects.

'You left a message at the store?' Albert repeated.

'Did I? Oh, so I did, so I did. It's my greenhouse, dear.'

She pointed with her cane.

'Two little children came into the garden yesterday. I didn't know there were any children on the Island, Albert. To whom do they belong? One had a catapult. My, my, they are high-spirited.'

Sixteen shattered panes of the greenhouse bore mute testimony to the nature of their spirits. Master Gaunt, Albert deduced, had recently passed by.

He sighed as he took out his notebook.

'I'll look after this.' He had a protective, proprietary feeling for his old Islanders, and Lady Syddyns was his favourite.

'I knew you would, dear.' She clicked off her hearing aid, smiled courteously, and went back to her pruning.

When he reached the gate, she called him.

'Oh, you mustn't go without one of my Star of Hollands. Such a year for aphides, but fortunately these have come through unscathed.'

Unconcerned with R.C.M.P. regulations, she pushed the rose through the button-hole of his tunic.

What a delightful old oddity she was, thought Albert, and he waited until he was around the bend of the road before removing the rose. He sniffed it wearily as he made his way home.

The old Sergeant-Major's cottage stood only a stone's throw from the high-tide line, with a short, overgrown path leading from the log-strewn beach almost directly to its door.

Grey shingles, weathered by the salt winds gave the two-roomed cottage a shabby air that was partly relieved by a scarlet trumpet honeysuckle vine.

Despite its worn appearance, the house was soundly built, for the old Sergeant-Major had raised it with his own hands, and like his son, he had been thorough.

It was a house with a face: two windows with the door between gave it the appearance of a pair of unblinking eyes separated by a nose. A dull, plain face and the only frivolous aspect of the whole scene was the gay honeysuckle, which held the little cottage in an embrace of jaunty green tendrils. Albert's mother had planted it when she came to the Island as a bride, and Albert watered it, pruned it, fed it and tied it with a secret tenderness.

Albert retired early, and at seven the next morning, his day off, he was awakened by a heavy pounding on the door. Still in his pyjamas, he opened it to find Mr Duncan.

Sergeant Coulter gazed at him in alarm, for, with his ginger handlebar moustaches quivering and his fists clenching and unclenching, the old man looked like a Viking berserker.

'Come with me!' he roared.

'What is it? What's happened?' asked Albert, throwing on his clothes.

Mr Duncan only sputtered and cursed, so Albert followed him silently. The old man sprinted with such agility that Albert, for all his youth, was breathless by the time they reached Mr Duncan's farm.

Pointing a finger at the Iron Duke, the old man wheeled on Albert.

'What are you going to do about this?'

Sergeant Coulter looked, closed his eyes and looked again. No, it was not some hitherto unknown bovine disorder.

The Iron Duke's sacred coat was covered with heliotrope-blue polka dots, the identical colour of Mr Duncan's barn.

'Well?' bellowed Mr Duncan, 'you know who did it, don't you?'

Sergeant Coulter's imagination did not have far to soar.

'I'll go down to the store immediately,' he said. He sighed. 'Where was the paint? Did you leave it outside?'

Mr Duncan pointed. The brush and paint were beside the barn door.

Sergeant Coulter walked over and looked in the doorway. Inside, Agnes Duncan was convulsed in happy, hysterical giggles.

'Isn't it the funniest thing you ever saw?' she gasped.

Albert wanted at least to smile, but he was too awed by the old man. He jerked his head warningly in the direction of her father. Agnes nodded, and still giggling, fled to the house.

Sergeant Coulter walked back to her father.

'I'll look after it, Mr Duncan. I'll call in later.'

Under interrogation, Barnaby denied knowledge of either the broken windows or the sullied Iron Duke.

'I see,' said Sergeant Coulter. 'Perhaps your little friend knows. I stopped in at Mrs Nielsen's on my way here, but there was no one home.'

'She's out, they're delivering the bread,' said Barnaby.

'I see. Well, I'll speak to her later. You run along now, I want to speak to Mr and Mrs Brooks.'

Barnaby got as far as the door, stopped and turned.

'Changed your mind?' said Sergeant Coulter. 'Care to tell me what you know?'

'I don't know anything,' said Barnaby. And then, with an insolent grin, 'You wouldn't want me to say I did it, if I didn't, would you?'

'I wouldn't like you to tell a lie, Barnaby.' Sergeant Coulter leaned against the counter and lit a cigarette. 'Still, you should know that Lady Syddyns saw you breaking the windows.'

'Maybe she's a liar.'

'Maybe. And,' Sergeant Coulter blew a smoke ring and gazed at it meditatively, 'and maybe there is blue paint on your hands.'

Barnaby raised his hands, stared and ran from the store.

When Sergeant Coulter rang the bell on the counter Mr Brooks, looking more than ever like Alice's rabbit, poked his white head through the beaded curtains.

'I'd like a few words with you please. It's about Barnaby.'

Mrs Brooks joined them.

'We couldn't help overhearing your conversation, Sergeant. I am sure there is some logical explanation. Barnaby is *not* a bad boy, please believe us when we say we know.'

'Perhaps not,' Sergeant Coulter stared at his boots. 'But, nevertheless he does these things.' He paused and gazed at the end of his cigarette. 'I think perhaps the best thing to do would be for us to hold a little meeting, and discuss Barnaby. You, Mrs Nielsen, Mr Duncan, Lady Syddyns. I'll see if maybe I can get Mr Rice-Hope to come over, perhaps he'll have some advice.'

The Brookses nodded meekly. Sergeant Coulter, in his official capacity, terrified them.

'Would this afternoon be all right?'

They nodded again.

'Very well. Two-thirty?' He touched the brim of his hat and left them.

At two-thirty that afternoon, they were all gathered at the store. Crime was unknown on the Island and the case of the Crown *vs.* Barnaby was an important incident in their lives. Even Mr Rice-Hope, the minister from the neighbouring island of Benares, made a special trip.

Mrs Nielsen volunteered the information that Christie had been present on both occasions. She offered to pay half the cost of the glass for the greenhouse, since she was being paid for Christie's board and the child was a small eater. She also suggested that Mr Duncan try paint remover on the Iron Duke.

Mr and Mrs Brooks, more disturbed by the stigma of the law than the amount of money involved, were only too glad to pay for the other half of the glass.

Mr Duncan, moustaches still bristling at the outrage suffered by the Iron Duke, had no comments to make except that he did not wish to find Barnaby on his property again. Then, mumbling darkly that certain persons were born to be hanged, he jammed his hat on his head and stalked out.

'Really!' Mrs Brooks reached for her digitalis. 'Really! I never would have expected Mr Duncan to take such an attitude. Why, that bull is dangerous and the child might have been killed. Sydney, did you notice he was only concerned with the bull? He didn't even mention the danger to Barnaby. That bull should be kept in a barn away from children.'

Sergeant Coulter stared down at her in disbelief. Not a word of censure to Barnaby for his actions. Merely worried that the little bastard was endangering his precious life.

'Now look here,' he said, 'I'm not satisfied about this yet. That boy is going to stay off Mr Duncan's property. And furthermore, it's all very well to offer to pay for the glass to replace Lady Syddyns's greenhouse, but someone has to install it.'

Mr Rice-Hope, the peacemaker, broke in.

'Sergeant, I will be only too happy to install the glass.'
He paused. 'It has occurred to me, Sergeant, that perhaps
the root of the little fellow's trouble lies in the fact that
he is separated from his uncle. Mrs Rice-Hope said the
same thing this morning. Children usually have a reason
for being naughty, and I think Barnaby is lonely and misses
his uncle.'

'No doubt,' replied Sergeant Coulter drily, 'but as a
policeman, Mr Rice-Hope, my duty lies in protecting the
possessions and property of the people of this island.
Whether he is lonely or not is quite beside the point. He
has to learn, and he will learn, that he can't get away with
this.'

Mr Rice-Hope, the gentle result of five generations of
clergymen, privately thought Sergeant Coulter was being
rather harsh about the whole affair. Obviously the boy
needed love, not discipline. Had not Gwynneth said so that
very morning?

'I was wondering,' he ventured, 'if I should write a letter
to his uncle, not complaining about the boy, mind you, but
merely explaining the circumstances. I think we should ask
his advice and inquire when he will be here. He really should
be kept informed about Barnaby.'

All agreed, and when the meeting broke up, Sergeant
Coulter stood at the counter thinking. The boy seemed to
enjoy giving a bad impression of himself. A means of getting
attention, no doubt. Sergeant Coulter shrugged to himself.
Maybe Barnaby did miss his uncle.

He saw the boy playing with a few marbles at the base of
the war monument. As he approached from one side,
Gwynneth Rice-Hope came from the other.

'My dear!' she cried, 'there you are!'

Sergeant Coulter blanched and secret gales lashed the rocky pinnacles of his heart.

But Gwynneth Rice-Hope's overflowing Christian love was directed to the boy at the foot of the monument.

Barnaby listlessly continued playing with the marbles.

Since he was not going to rise for her, she would kneel for him. Handling children was basically praise and love, praise and love.

'My,' she said as she sat beside him, 'that looks like fun.'

Barnaby eyed her without interest.

She glanced up, saw Sergeant Coulter, smiled and turned back to the boy.

'You're a really good marble player, aren't you, Barnaby?'

'No,' said Barnaby.

She was not discouraged.

'I've just been talking to Mr Rice-Hope, dear. He's going to write a nice letter to your uncle.'

The boy's manner changed. He watched her like an alert animal.

'Why, there's nothing to worry about, Barnaby. He's going to tell your uncle what a very, very good little boy you are, and how much everybody here loves you.'

Without warning, the boy sprang to his feet, almost exploding with rage.

'You - you - you stupid bitch!'

He kicked the marbles aside and ran away.

The policeman's face darkened. In a split second the disciplined Sergeant Coulter vanished and a very righteous Albert took his place. No one was going to talk to *her* that way.

He ran after Barnaby and Mrs Rice-Hope saw him collar the boy roughly. He shook him, and leaning down, spoke earnestly to him. The boy gazed up, nodded and walked slowly back to Mrs Rice-Hope with Albert at his heels.

He stood before her, staring at his running shoes. Finally he raised his eyes and said: 'I'm sorry I said that. I shouldn't have. I won't say it again.'

Mrs Rice-Hope tried to clasp him to her to reassure him of her never-failing affection, but he backed away.

'You're a very brave little boy to apologise,' she said.

Barnaby looked at her with surprise.

'Oh, that's okay,' he said with his sudden cheerful smile, 'Sergeant Coulter said he'd break every bone in my body if I didn't.'

With a startled glance at Albert, Mrs Rice-Hope left. When she reached the mission boat at the dock, she turned and gave a long look at the two who stood by the war monument.

She was profoundly shocked. At big, brutal Sergeant Coulter.

Sergeant Coulter, his expression sour, gazed down at Barnaby.

'Well, my little friend, you finally told the truth.'

His hand hovered over Barnaby's head as he took a deep breath.

'Now you get this straight! Any more of your didoes and you'll be off this island so quick it'll make your head swim.'

'Me?' Barnaby's face was innocent. 'Where'll you send me? Nobody but the Brookses wants me.'

That, Sergeant Coulter realised, was unfortunately only too true.

'There are things called reform schools, Barnaby. You just keep on at the rate you're going and you'll end up in one. Why did you swear at her? All she said was that they were going to write your uncle that you were a good boy. And what did I tell you about swearing?'

The boy shrugged. 'I forgot.'

'Why did you break all those windows? Why did you paint the Iron Duke? What gets into you, anyhow? Why do you do these things?'

'She told me to - Christie. It's her fault.'

'Yes, it's always Christie's fault, isn't it? I suppose if she told you to jump off the wharf you would. Barnaby, you're not even trying to be good.'

Barnaby backed away from him.

'I try but I can't.'

'No you don't.'

'But I do, Sergeant. Only I can't.'

'Why not?' Hands on hips, Sergeant Coulter leaned over the child.

'You wouldn't understand.'

The muscles of Sergeant Coulter's jaws tightened ominously.

'Don't tell me what I can understand. Why can't you be good?'

'My uncle likes me the way I am.' Barnaby's face had a guarded look.

Sergeant Coulter straightened up.

'I've had enough of your lying. As a matter of fact I've had quite enough of you. To date I've found you telling the truth exactly once. It's always somebody else's fault, isn't it? Don't give me any more of this nonsense.'

Barnaby mumbled something and raised his hands, palms up.

'What did you say?'

Barnaby kicked his toes in the gravel.

'I said I told you you wouldn't understand,' he replied in a loud, clear voice.

Sergeant Coulter swallowed and said nothing for a few seconds, then his face relaxed.

'Try a bit harder, Barnaby.'

'Okay.'

'Yes, sir!' snapped Sergeant Coulter.

'Yes, sir.'

Christie came bouncing toward them.

'Where have you been?' she asked Barnaby. 'I've been looking all over for you.'

She turned to Sergeant Coulter.

'Isn't he awful, Sergeant? Isn't he just awful? Agnes Duncan told me what he did. You're going to get it, Barnaby Gaunt!'

'Maybe he isn't the only one,' said Sergeant Coulter. 'He says you told him to do it.'

That was a great big fib and Barnaby was a liar, said Christie righteously. All she said was she bet Barnaby was afraid of the bull and he said he wasn't. And then she said that she bet the Iron Duke would look funny with blue spots, and she bet Barnaby was afraid to paint them on him and he said he wasn't.

And what about Lady Syddyns's greenhouse? Had she or had she not told Barnaby it would be fun to chuck some rocks at it?

Yes, she had *said* that. But she sure would never of gone and *done* that. Would her mother ever get after her if she did anything as bad as that!

Sergeant Coulter stared down at them.

'I'm warning you both. Any more nonsense and you'll be sorry. I mean it.'

As the children stood at the foot of the war monument watching the impressive figure disappear, their eyes were soft.

Suddenly Barnaby ran after the policeman.

'Sergeant Coulter!'

Albert stopped and turned.

'I'd jump off the wharf if you told me to.'

Sergeant Coulter gazed at the upturned face without emotion.

'That won't be necessary, Barnaby. Just try and behave for a change. And stop lying.'

He took two more paces.

'Yes, sir!' shouted Barnaby.

Sergeant Coulter wheeled as though he were on a parade ground.

But the child was not mocking him.

THE PAINT REMOVER had scarcely dried on the
Iron Duke's coat when Sergeant Coulter received a
summons from the crankiest spinster on the Island.

Murder had been done.

Albert glanced nervously at the twisted grey peach tree
which was still latticed against the southern wall of Miss
Proudfoot's house.

The little stinkers would pick on her. She spelled one
word, and one word only to Albert. Trouble.

During his own boyhood she had caught him with the
telltale juice of her stolen fruit still trickling down his chin.
After caning him mercilessly, she marched him, like a
Crusader with a captive Turk, to his father, who repeated the
thrashing.

Albert the man stood now, notebook in hand, towering
over his ancient enemy as he recorded the details of the
crime.

That morning, said Miss Proudfoot, she had put Fletcher
out for his usual airing. She noticed nothing untoward at
the time, as she placed him in the shade of her lilac bush.

Grotesque tears rolled down her leathery cheeks as she spoke. It was like seeing a lizard weep, and Albert was both awed and embarrassed.

After leaving Fletcher, she sobbed, she could hear him chattering, but as he always did that when he heard the birds singing in the garden, she thought nothing of it.

About ten minutes later, she heard other voices and decided to investigate.

Fletcher was gone, and that dreadful boy from the store was running down her garden path. Beyond him she saw the goat-lady's girl.

She chased them but had been unable to overtake them. A half hour later, having dressed herself suitably to go to the store and complain to Mr Brooks, she opened her door and found Fletcher on her doorstep. Dead.

Sergeant Coulter leaned down and picked up the ounce-light body of Fletcher. Even in death the eyes were glazed with fright, and the poor little feet with claws like cobwebs clutched for an absent perch.

He examined the bird carefully as it lay on the palm of his hand. Fletcher's feathers were ruffled, but there was no blood on him. The pathetic little beak was still open as if he had died with a shriek of terror on his lips.

Sergeant Coulter nodded in sympathy to Miss Proudfoot as he assured her he would investigate the matter immediately.

There would be another meeting at the store tomorrow, and in the meanwhile he would call on the goat-lady.

As he bade Miss Proudfoot good day, his face was sterner than usual. They had apparently outgrown their usual vandal pattern of behavior. This bore the sinister taint of sadism.

Christie, opening the door to his knock, took a quick look at the beloved Mountie and guiltily claimed sanctuary in her loft.

'Come in, come in,' said the goat-lady, her broad face amiable. 'Have some coffee.'

'I'm afraid this isn't a social call.' His eyes roamed around the bright kitchen as he seated himself at the table. The goat-lady's little house was the only one on the Island in which he felt comfortable. As he explained his mission and sipped his coffee, he saw a bright grey eye peeping down at him.

This time, he said, they had gone too far. They had killed Miss Proudfoot's pet, a little bird. It went beyond the realm of childish pranks.

The goat-lady beheaded her own chickens with heartless efficiency and privately thought there was something odd about elderly ladies who made pets of small inedible birds. However, she gave a sage nod, apparently in agreement, and she sighed philosophically as she remarked that children would be children.

The changeling face peering from the attic disappeared.

'Christie,' called the goat-lady, 'the policeman wants to talk to you. You come down.'

'No,' said Christie MacNab.

'Christie,' called the goat-lady, 'it's about Miss Proud-foot's budgie. What do you know about it?'

The head appeared at the top of the ladder again.

'Barnaby did it,' said his loyal little friend, without hesitation.

'Christie,' said Sergeant Coulter, 'I want to talk to you. You come down.'

'No,' said Christie, disappearing once more.

'Christie,' said the goat-lady again, 'you come down.'

'No,' replied a tremulous voice muffled by bedclothes, 'you come up.'

The goat-lady sat rocking and knitting.

'Looks like she's not coming down,' she said. 'Unless you want to go up and get her. More coffee?'

The dignified Mountie had no intention of dragging a screaming child bodily down the ladder.

He was getting in touch with Mr Rice-Hope again, he said, and another meeting was to be held in the store the following afternoon to discuss the children. Would she come?

Yes, of course she would.

Well, thank God there was one sensible, level-headed person on the Island.

'Now I'll have another coffee,' he said. 'This is the only place on the Island you can get a decent cup.'

When he rose to leave, he called up to the loft.

'Listen, young lady, you and your friend's shenanigan days are just about over. Do you hear me?'

There was no answer.

'Well, thanks for the coffee.' He carefully stepped over the tomcat on the porch and paused to pat old Shep's head.

The goat-lady stood in the doorway, her arms folded across her pillow-sized bosom, and an expression of tolerant amusement on her face.

Without turning, she called, 'You can come down now.'

'Has he gone?' came the piping voice from the attic.

'No, I haven't,' said Sergeant Coulter.

The old dog thrust his cool black nose into Albert's palm and tossed his head, begging for a caress. As Albert leaned down to him, there was a flurry in the doorway and a needle-toothed little bundle of rage flashed past the goat-lady.

The old dog took one look at Trixie and fled with his tail between his legs. Albert glared at the little dog and pushed it back into the house with the toe of his boot.

The tomcat, one foot poised heavenward like a ballet dancer as he groomed his bottom, paused with detached elegance, then calmly proceeded with his washing.

'Well,' Sergeant Coulter straightened up, 'I'll see you tomorrow at the store.'

The goat-lady nodded. He hadn't gone three feet when she called him.

'Sergeant,' she said, then paused and looked at him shrewdly, 'Sergeant, that boy - ' She stopped again, choosing her words carefully, 'That boy, he's not a bad boy.'

No, thought Sergeant Coulter, just a nice, clean-cut little sadist. He nodded and left her standing in the doorway.

When he reached the lane, he found Shep waiting, his half-blind, milky eyes pleading for a kind word.

Albert laughed and pulled the dog's ear affectionately.

'All right, old man, you can walk home with me.'

The dog's hindquarters were shaky from age and rheumatism, but he bounded gamely and happily by Albert's side.

As they passed Mr Duncan's fields, Albert paused, as he always did, to admire the mighty and again spotless Iron Duke. The tethered bull stared back with gloomy hatred, but the two great Clydesdales ambled up to the fence companionably.

Albert drew back. Despite his shining spurs and beneath the impeccable military exterior, he had a shameful secret. Not only did he not like horses, he detested horses.

He still remembered his R.C.M.P. training days in Regina, and his instructor, a powerful, bow-legged Prairie Ukrainian.

'You,' the instructor said without malice, and the banana-like finger tapped Albert's chest. 'You. We can get dozens of you. You don't count. But this horse,' and his eyes lit up. 'This horse, he's important.'

As was required of him, Albert eventually became a competent horseman, but his heart was never in it.

Now, he backed away from the two gambolling Clydesdales and continued his walk, with the old dog loyally keeping pace.

They had nearly reached the path that provided a shortcut across the Island, when Shep suddenly let out a howl of anguish.

Albert looked down at him in surprise.

'What's the matter, old-timer?'

The dog laid back his ears and, baring his blunt teeth, he stiffened and trembled from head to foot. Then, with an even more ear-splitting yelp, he raced back the road toward the goat-lady's house.

Albert watched the crippled old croup, with the twisted hocks, charging down the road. Shep's coat stood on end and his coward's tail was firmly tucked between his legs.

Albert shook his head in pity; the dog was senile and afraid of his own shadow. He was probably in pain and he should be destroyed, although Albert hoped he would not be called upon to perform the office.

He followed the path without turning around again.

Had he looked back, he would have seen, by the dusty side of the road, a large feline footprint. A print like a plaster cast, with the third pad of the right front paw conspicuously absent.

MISS PROUDFOOT presided at the meeting. With a regal nod to Lady Syddyns, she barely acknowledged the obeisance of Mr Rice-Hope and completely ignored the goat-lady and the Brookses.

She sat like an Australian bushranger, with her felt hat cocked aggressively on one side. Even in the heat of summer her sharp-cornered frame was decently attired in a heavy tweed suit, and her feet were encased in stout laced gillies.

Her father, long deceased, had retired to the Island with the rank of admiral, and her four brothers had been killed in the First World War.

She eyed Albert with disapproval. All the rest had been called upon to make the supreme sacrifice. Albert had been called upon to allow himself to be taken prisoner. He had clearly shirked his military duty by returning alive from battle, and but for him they would have had a perfect score.

As Mr Churchill had said, it was blood, sweat and tears, in the fields and on the beaches, and Albert had ruined the Island's unblemished record. It was inexcusable, a subtle, servant-class form of treason, but there he was, bold as brass, an example of the chaos the lower orders introduced when given too much authority.

Albert, on his part, squared his hat, his shoulders and jaw. He was determined that the tenets of British justice would be scrupulously observed, despite the whole bloody lot of them.

Mr Rice-Hope, with a glance at Miss Proudfoot, opened the sessions.

'We are gathered here today - ' he paused and began searching nervously through his pockets.

While he fumbled for the slip of paper he had written that morning, telling him why they would be gathered together, Albert closed his eyes.

Lady Syddyns, seeing the minister's familiar gesture and imagining herself to be attending either a wedding or a funeral, popped a peppermint in her mouth. With a smile she switched off her hearing aid, folded her hands on her silver-headed cane and dozed.

'Yes, here it is.' Mr Rice-Hope unfolded the paper. 'The children. Ah, yes. They have been, I gather, rather mischievous again and there have been some claims to - uh- '

He paused and looked at Sergeant Coulter.

'Damage,' said Sergeant Coulter.

'Yes, damage. And, let me see now, Sergeant Coulter has suggested that we all get together and discuss the - uh- '

Again he looked at Albert.

'The most sensible way of dealing with the situation,' said Albert.

Miss Proudfoot sniffed combatively.

Actually, said Albert, most of the damage had been settled. On behalf of Mr Brooks and Mrs Nielsen, he had purchased glass for Lady Syddyns's greenhouse, and Mr Rice-Hope had very kindly installed it, so that was all cleared up. The affair of the Iron Duke was closed. Mr Duncan had declined to attend the meeting and was prepared to forget the incident, *if* Mr and Mrs Brooks would assure him that that boy would stay off his property.

That left only Miss Proudfoot and the question of her bird unsolved.

'Only!' Miss Proudfoot was on her feet. Fletcher might be dead, murdered, yes, murdered, but she was still very much prepared to enter the field on behalf of his memory.

With the death-stand courage of saints, Mr Brooks now leaped to his feet. It had been an accident. A regrettable accident, but an accident nevertheless, and she was not imprinting the brand of murderer on that innocent child. He and Mrs Brooks were quite prepared to buy Miss Proudfoot another budgie.

Sergeant Coulter stood up.

'Just a minute,' he said. 'Mr Rice-Hope and I talked the matter over this morning. More than money is involved, Mr Brooks. This sort of vandalism can't continue.'

Mr Rice-Hope bravely took the floor.

He and Sergeant Coulter, after discussing the situation, thought a sensible solution would be for the children to work off the amount of money. Thus penalised, they would think twice before committing any more misdemeanors.

Sergeant Coulter leaned over and gently shook Lady Syddyns.

She switched on her hearing aid.

'Do you agree that the children should work off the amount of their indebtedness? Some light jobs, several afternoons a week, to keep them out of mischief?'

Lady Syddyns nodded.

'Keep them busy, keep them busy. Lovely children. Keep them busy.'

She switched off her hearing aid.

Sergeant Coulter touched her shoulder and pointed to his ear.

Click went the switch and Lady Syddyns was again in contact with the courts.

Did she have any suggestions?

Lady Syddyns turned her bemused old face to the ceiling and pondered.

Yes, she did. The graveyard. Sadly in need of weeding. She used to try to attend to Sir Adrian, but the walk from her house was long, and her roses took up more and more of her time. It was a bad year for aphides, consequently Sir Adrian was overrun with weeds.

Mr Rice-Hope looked pleased.

'An excellent suggestion, if I may say so, Lady Syddyns.'

He himself had long been distressed with the condition of the neglected little Island graveyard.

But now the Brookses objected.

It was child labour, cried Mrs Brooks. Surely the day was past when children were punished by a cruel society? It was child labour, child labour, nothing less. Up rose visions of tiny hands mangled in cotton gins and stunted bodies pulling carloads of coal from the bowels of the earth.

Little Barnaby had played a childish prank and they were willing to foot the bill.

An anxious look passed between Mr and Mrs Brooks. How could the others be expected to understand? How could they know how difficult it was to have descended from all those lofty astral planes? Small wonder the child was unpredictable at times.

And with the adamant stubbornness of the meek, they refused to budge an inch. They would pay, but that child was not going to toil in the fields.

Sergeant Coulter's patience was wearing thin. He took a deep breath, but before he could speak, the goat-lady, who had retained her usual unshakable calm, stood up.

'I must be going. I have the bread to deliver.'

'Just a minute,' said Sergeant Coulter. 'That's another job our little friends could take over. How about it, Mrs Nielsen?'

The goat-lady looked amused.

'It's fine with me. I'll speak to them on my way home. They're down by the war monument now.'

Sergeant Coulter had a satisfied expression as he watched that sensible body march from the room.

The Brookses were not so easily vanquished, nor were they giving in. They would write to poor little Barnaby's uncle.

Looking thoroughly uncompromising, Albert stood up.

Their attitude would not do, nor was the answer merely to purchase Miss Proudfoot another bird. She had rights that had been violated and the children were going to learn to respect those rights. Mr Rice-Hope had already written to Major Murchison-Gaunt regarding Barnaby. Furthermore, if they did not cooperate, he, Sergeant Coulter, would get in touch with the juvenile authorities, have the boy removed from the Island and placed in the custody of some responsible foster home until his uncle arrived to claim him.

Mr Rice-Hope, caught in the cross fire, but on Albert's side, nodded nervously.

Albert's determined face was enough to make Mr and Mrs Brooks realise he meant every word, and alarmed by this latest threat to their darling, they gave in.

Albert, pleased with himself in his Solomon's role, turned to Miss Proudfoot, but if he thought he had placated that lady, he was very much mistaken.

Miss Proudfoot was still bitter. It had taken years of love, patience and coaxing on her part to teach Fletcher to sing, and while they might recompense her for his 'real' value, indeed, they might even replace him with another budgie, nevertheless his passing left a void that nothing but time could fill.

And if those wicked children so much as set foot on her property again, she would write to her member of Parliament. There was still decency and order on this Island, although one could scarcely believe it with the present police administration. And as a taxpayer she felt it was her moral duty to see that decency and order were preserved. It was no wonder the world was in the state it was, and the Communists taking over.

And she was very disappointed in Albert's attitude. He simply did not seem to understand the seriousness of the crime, but she supposed he would wait until anarchy reigned supreme before taking a sensible stand and putting those children behind bars where they belonged.

Albert eyed her silently. The miserable old trout. Well, from a lifetime of experience on the Island, he knew that it was impossible to please everybody, but he had been just and firm. Secure in the knowledge that he had upheld the reputation of the Royal Canadian Mounted Police, he assisted Lady Syddyns to her feet.

Dudley Rice-Hope stood at the door, an awkward look on his pale curate's face.

'I hate to bother you further, Sergeant- '

'Yes, Mr Rice-Hope?'

It was, said Mr Rice-Hope, about Lady Syddyns's windows.

'I've had some trouble getting them to stay in. The ones in the sides remain propped up nicely, but the top ones seem to drop right through.'

Sergeant Coulter thought for a moment.

'It's probably the putty,' he said. 'If it dries too quickly, that could happen. If you lay the putty on a coat of wet paint it helps a lot. It makes it much easier to install the glass.'

Mr Rice-Hope looked bewildered.

'Perhaps,' Albert paused, 'perhaps, Mr Rice-Hope, I could finish the windows. Is the glass still at Lady Syddyns's?'

Dudley Rice-Hope flushed miserably.

'I'm very much afraid, Sergeant, that I have broken most of the glass.'

'I'll pick up more in Victoria on Tuesday,' said Albert. 'Nine-by-nine-inch, weren't they?'

Mr Rice-Hope nodded humbly. 'Be sure and give me the bill. I'm sorry you are being put to extra trouble, Sergeant.'

'It's no trouble,' said Albert, knowing that he would never give the bill to Dudley Rice-Hope. With the nameless waifs of southern Europe that he supported, and the local Indian children he insisted on showering with flannel vests and his many extra charities, Dudley's stipend was already strained.

And so the incident was closed, with big, brutal Sergeant Coulter buying the glass, paying for the glass and installing the glass, for all of which he received no particular thanks from his grateful Islanders.

BARNABY WAS an early riser, the earliest on the Island, and at dawn the goat-lady found him sitting patiently on her porch. With his head leaning against the carved post and old Shep cradled in his arms, he was waiting for his breakfast. The price was chores, which he performed cheerfully. He got the milk can out of the well for her, he watered Gudrun and he collected eggs. Then, eager and hungry, he sat in the kitchen while she started his meal.

When Christie, still in her nightgown, came down the ladder like a cross little princess, he was rocking noisily back and forth, usually carrying on a spirited gourmet's conversation with the goat-lady. Food was the one and only thing his uncle had taught him to appreciate.

Later in the morning he and Christie went back to the Brookses for a second breakfast of tea and toast. That fare might have been enough for the frail Mr and Mrs Brooks, but Barnaby looked upon it as a between-meal snack.

Mrs Brooks would have been alarmed at both the quantity and choice of foods Mrs Nielsen served, for Dickie had had a delicate stomach, but the goat-lady's meals were never left unfinished by Barnaby and now even Christie usually cleaned her plate.

They lived largely off the products of the sea and the Island. The children were particularly fond of oysters, and with watering mouths they watched the goat-lady dip the big, pearl-gray blobs, first in beaten egg, then in crushed cracker crumbs. Dropped into deep fat in the black frying pan, the oysters came out golden and plump. Sometimes the goat-lady baked them on fat slices of beefsteak tomatoes, seasoned with vinegar, salt, pepper and grated yellow cheese. While Barnaby and Christie hovered anxiously by the stove, the oysters were lifted from the oven with sizzling ebony edges.

They had oysters simmered in milk, topped with paprika and chives, and they had them in omelettes. They loved clams steamed in an inch of water, and scooping out the tiny insides with toothpicks, they dipped them in butter. The goat-lady's clam chowder was as thick as a stew, solid with bacon, new potatoes, sliced onions and halved tomatoes.

Oysters, clams, crabs or salmon, whatever the goat-lady cooked was good.

Each night the goat-lady washed Christie's blouse and cotton skirt and hung them on a line over the stove to dry. Each night she set Christie's hair in rag curls, and each morning as the children ate breakfast the goat-lady heated a flat iron on the stove and ironed Christie's clothing.

While Barnaby stacked the dishes and got water from the well, the goat-lady sat on the sofa with Christie at her feet, and undoing the rags she brushed Christie's hair until it stood out like a halo of fine, wheat-coloured silk.

With a satisfied expression she watched them going off. Already Christie was filling out, and the salt breezes had whipped a tinge of rose to her sallow cheeks. Why, the child looked almost healthy.

And the children, for the first time in their lives, were learning to play.

Each day brought new surprises and delights, and they soon knew the paths, fields and beaches of the Island. On the strange, fire-scarred mountainside they found ragged foxgloves rising bravely, and beneath cool ferns star-petaled trilliums winked at them. When they were thirsty they stumbled on secret icy springs. When they were hungry they found abandoned orchards where weary old trees were heavy with summer fruit, and along the lanes patches of wild blackberries, salmonberries and huckle-berries beckoned a passing child.

They pointed to the sinister floating eagles who shrilled from their airy heights at the two dots who were Barnaby and Christie.

'Listen!' said Christie, squinting against the sun, 'you'd sort of expect them to roar instead of making that silly little squeak.'

'Come on!' cried Barnaby. Life was too short for dawdling.

They had also, of course, their appointed judicial sentences to serve. They usually did the graveyard work before their second breakfast, while the bread delivery route was saved for the afternoon, when the bread was cool.

Surrounded by a drooping fence, the forsaken little grave-yard was so overgrown with weeds that the toppling crosses and monuments were hardly visible.

The aged of the Island could no longer tend the verdant, lively dead, and the children, leaping about the garter-snake-ridden paths, found pitiful glass jars filled with long-faded flowers. On the graves of the poorer the white crosses, made of wood, had rotted at the bases and tilted wearily in the heat and life of the rich soil.

With perspiring faces, Barnaby and Christie took a rest, sitting on the wobbly fence and gazing at the deserted tombstones.

And from the underbrush, a puzzled One-ear lay watching them.

'Well, come on,' sighed Barnaby, jumping down. 'We'll never get Lydia Buckingham done today if we don't get busy.'

Sergeant Coulter checked their work religiously any time he passed the graveyard, and sent them back for an extra stint if he thought they were shirking.

'Whew!' said Christie, looking at the task ahead of them.

They worked like coolies in the broiling sun. Barnaby took off his shirt and wrapped it about his hands to tug out the wild blackberry vines, while Christie pulled and carried armfuls of grass and ferns to the roadside.

It was hard work but finally they had Mrs Buckingham as neatly weeded as the day she was buried forty years past.

Christie sat on a tombstone, panting in the heat and looked proudly at their handiwork.

'That looks really good,' she said. 'I bet even Sergeant Coulter can't find anything the matter with that one. Let's quit now. My back's aching and it's too hot to do any more.'

'You better get up,' said Barnaby, 'you're sitting on Major-General Sir Adrian Syddyns.'

Christie leaped to her feet.

'I keep forgetting there are people under there.'

'Look, Christie!'

Barnaby was pulling ferns from a small white object.

'It's a little marble angel!'

They pushed the moss away and spelled out,

TO THE MEMORY OF OUR DARLING BABY
John Townsend
TAKEN TO JESUS, JULY 8TH, 1903

With his parents long buried on either side of him, there was no one left to tend or mourn little John Townsend. Saddened, the children knelt and stroked the angel's head.

'It seems funny to think of a baby dying, it's almost as hard to believe as that kids can die,' said Christie.

'Kids can die all right,' said Barnaby, 'but I can't understand a baby being born at all - if it's got to die it - I mean, it never got a chance to play or anything.'

Christie sighed. 'Well, he did die. Let's go. It's too hot to do any more today.'

'Oh, let's just finish the baby. I hate to leave him half done.'

'We can do him tomorrow. Come on, I'm cooking.'

But Barnaby stubbornly refused to go until he had finished.

As Christie sat watching him, her expression changed.

'You know,' she said in a very small voice, 'somebody's watching us.'

'There you are, John Townsend, your little angel looks much nicer now.' Barnaby patted the angel's head and turned to her. 'Who?'

Christie pointed to the large tombstone at the head of Sir Adrian Syddyns's grave.

'Behind there.'

A black-tipped tail flicked nervously at the edge of the tombstone.

Rushing over, the children found themselves looking into the large, cool green eyes of One-ear.

Like all cats, he was insatiably curious. What *were* they doing here? Believing the graveyard to be deserted, he often used it for sunbathing.

They were just as curious.

'It's a great big cat!' said Christie. 'What's he doing here?'

'It's a cougar, stupid,' whispered Barnaby. 'Isn't he beautiful? Don't frighten him.'

One-ear backed away from them. He had seen quite enough.

Christie stood rooted to the spot, but Barnaby advanced a step. One-ear gave a warning snarl, and turning, fled. With the stiff, high-rumped lope of the cougar, he cleared the graveyard in ten-foot bounds and disappeared through a hole in the thicket.

Barnaby turned to Christie.

'Come on!' he cried, and ran after the cougar. 'Hurry up or we'll lose him.'

Christie followed, but when they reached the dark tunneled break in the bushes, she stopped.

'Well, are you coming?'

'I don't know,' said Christie. 'What if he bites?'

'All right, stay here then!'

Without another glance at her, he dropped to his knees and began crawling through the hole. Christie took a deep breath and followed.

The tunnel led through thick underbrush for a hundred feet and emerged into a heavily wooded glade. A game trail, worn by generations of wild life, spiralled to the heart of the forest.

The earth beneath their feet was springy with years of fallen leaves. It was breathtakingly silent, even the birds were songless, and it was dim, for the sun filtered only fleetingly through the branches above.

The children had been warned to stay away from two places, a certain dangerous beach, and the forest. So this was the forest.

Between the great, moss-stockinged firs and cedars grew ferns, some six feet tall, and pale skunk cabbages, their broad leaves swaying like banners of evil, were as high as Barnaby. Devil clubs and salal formed impenetrable walls, and fallen, half-rotten trees wearied the children as they struggled on and over them.

'Let's go back,' said Christie, pausing. 'It's so dark and quiet here, and I'm tired. Let's go back. We aren't supposed to come here anyway.'

Barnaby waited until she caught up with him.

'Just a bit farther,' he coaxed.

They reached a sharp bend in the trail. Off the side was a shaded leafy alcove, One-ear's home.

He cringed on his belly, regarding them with raging suspicion. He was trapped in his own house, and in order to get away, he would have to pass either directly between, over or by them.

Neither child had ever had a pet. Christie's mother vowed animals were germ-ridden and invariably suffered some sad fate that broke the child's heart. Barnaby had once adopted a stray kitten which ended its life in a fireplace, following in the footsteps of an earlier, unfortunate Teddy bear.

To the children the sight of this great golden cat with the jewelled eyes and fur as clean and sweet as honey was like a vision from fairyland. Never had they seen anything so beautiful, and, as in the case of Sergeant Coulter, it was love at first sight again.

'Look at the scar on his side,' whispered Christie.

'Somebody must have shot him.'

One-ear was becoming more distressed by the minute. He knew from only too painful experience what would happen if he harmed them. The full complement of dogs, men and guns would be out again, and he had retired to this lovely little island to spend his declining years in peace. He cringed further in his bower.

As he took a step back, both children moved toward him. A muted snarl rose from his deep chest. A warning.

'He's only got one ear,' said Christie, as she held her hand out toward him.

One-ear hissed and spat like a demon, and the velvet paw, extended now to the size of a dinner plate, swung in the air before her. Another warning. Useless, of course.

He didn't dare hurt them. The wily, battle-scarred old warrior knew that if he tampered with the cubs of men once more, it meant death for him. It was an unforgivable crime, and *they* spared neither expense nor effort in hunting down the transgressor. Only by a miracle had he escaped the last time.

'Now be careful, you're scaring him,' said Barnaby turning to Christie. 'You'll get him upset.'

He nodded reassuringly to One-ear, 'It's all right, we won't hurt you.'

The cougar, fearful of attacking and unable to escape, bunched himself up in a miserable heap, his tail curled around his paws and his broad head lowered on his thick neck. His coat had a sheen like silk.

'Isn't he beautiful, Christie?'

Christie nodded. 'It looks like somebody shot his ear off too. Poor kitty.'

Barnaby, still mourning his own lost kitten, shook his head. 'How could anyone be so mean.'

One-ear watched them with cold-eyed fury.

'Now listen, Christie, we mustn't tell anybody about him, because they'll come and shoot him again. Not even Sergeant Coulter.'

Christie nodded.

'Look how pretty his coat is. See how it shines?' Barnaby slowly extended his hand toward One-ear.

The cougar, again panic-stricken, retreated until he reached a wall of solid bush. With ear flattened against his triangular skull and, hissing impotently, he regarded them with hopeless hate.

Barnaby's hand rested gently on the cougar's head.

'You see?' he said in triumph, 'I told you he wouldn't bite.'

One-ear had lost and he knew it.

Together the children patted his glowing coat, stroked his radar whiskers and caressed the stump of his ear.

Martyred, he squelched his eyelids together, but he sensibly, if resentfully realised he must suffer them.

And the children hugged him with delight because he was all theirs.

'He doesn't look too happy,' observed Christie.

'That's because he's hunted and nobody loves him. I know just how he feels. I'll always love him.'

'Me too,' chimed Christie.

'You? You don't know how it feels to have nobody love you, and to be hunted.'

'Who's hunting you? And I can love him if I want to.'

Bowed by a lifetime of vagrom misfortune, One-ear sighed in sulky despair and ignominiously capitulated.

8

SERGEANT COULTER sat in the police launch writing his weekly letter to Gwynneth Rice-Hope.

My dear:

Tomorrow is the second Friday of the month, so I suppose you and Dudley will be over to the church here. I'm off duty for the weekend, starting tonight, so I'll spend a couple of days at my father's old place. I'll be watching to catch a glimpse of you. I saw you in the real estate office at Benares last Tuesday, but you didn't look as if you saw me.

Things are fine on the Island. Do you remember when I was in the POW camp how you used to write to me about the gardens here? I never thought I'd be doing the same thing for you. Mr Duncan's corn looks very pretty. I walked by earlier, and the leaves or whatever you call them are bright green and already have little gold tassels. I finally found out what ails Lady Syddyns's roses. They haven't got afeedees, they have aphides. The hollyhocks are eight feet tall and the flowers look as if they are made of crepe paper.

The children are fine and have improved tremendously. It's just as I said all along, they merely needed a firm hand. It was nice of you to have them over for church last Sunday. Old Brooks told me about it. You must have been tired by the time you returned them here. My God, they're noisy. I know there are only two of them, but somehow they always manage to give the impression of a crowd, or maybe riot would be a better word. Of course, the Island has been so quiet for so long, it doesn't take much to liven it up. They're odd little beggars, though. They're doing a good job on the graveyard (I see to it) but on their own they have even put fresh flowers on one of the graves.

Naturally they picked Lady Syddyns's roses without permission. I wrung that out of them. Lady Syddyns doesn't know about it and I have no intention of telling her.

Brooks says the boy's uncle wrote he'll be here any day, flying over in his private plane. Maybe we'll have more peace now. He's wealthy, I suppose. Well, he won't find much company on the Island.

I'm on my way up to the post office to see if Professor Hobbs's book is here yet. He promised me an autographed copy. He was the one, I suppose I've told you a thousand times, who first got me interested in archaeology when I was in the POW camp. He taught a course in it.

Constable Browning is still reading indiscriminately; I never know what I'll find him busy scanning. The last book was How I Lived With Bright's Disease. I asked him if he thought he was coming down with it and he said no, but this fellow didn't know he was going to get it either. I'm only eight years older than he, but sometimes I feel like his grandfather.

Well, I must close. I hope to see you tomorrow. With my love, as always,

Albert

He folded the letter carefully and put it in his tunic pocket. As he walked up to the post office, he glanced at the war monument and the list of names.

Three mute and inglorious years in a POW camp. It wasn't his fault, they had been fighting a rearguard action and they had fought until they were surrounded and out of ammunition. Then, as ordered by their officers, they had smashed their rifles and surrendered.

He had been reported killed in action. What finished the old man off, was not that - it was the later news that Albert had surrendered instead. Forty years in the Indian Army, and he had never surrendered. Nobody else's son on the Island had surrendered either.

It was Dudley Rice-Hope who had written and told him of his father's death; he still remembered the phrases, the kindness, the genuine sympathy.

But it was she who had written to him after that. Knowing there was no one else to write to him, no one else who really cared whether he was a prisoner of war or not. Like her husband's, her first letter had been prompted by sympathy, but she had continued to write, week after week, month after month, year after year. She had knitted for him, and sent him food parcels. Her letters, innocent and loving, to a lonely eighteen-year-old boy. News of the Island, Mrs Brooks's heart condition, Dickie's death, Lady Syddyns's roses and rheumatism, the church bazaar, the fishing, Mr Duncan's new calf, Mr Allen's border collies and their prizes. Little things. Little things that had saved his sanity and made him love her. Irrevocably.

The children were having their second breakfast at the Brookses'. They sat sipping tea and munching toast and marmalade while Mrs Brooks opened her mail and Mr Brooks read the three-day-old paper.

'Have you ever seen a cougar here on our Island?' Barnaby asked.

Mrs Brooks put on her gold-rimmed spectacles.

'Good gracious, no!' she said. 'Sergeant Coulter would never allow a cougar on *our* Island.'

A happy glance passed between Barnaby and Christie. One-ear's presence was unsuspected.

'Those Russians!' Mr Brooks folded his newspaper and with the comfortable fierceness of old age declared, 'If they don't start behaving, we shall have to fight them.'

'Sydney,' said Mrs Brooks, handing him a letter and taking off her spectacles, 'read this.'

He read it, nodded and handed it back to her. They leaned over, whispering softly to each other for a few minutes. The children, oblivious to all except food, ate noisily.

Mrs Brooks looked fondly at Barnaby.

'Darling,' she said, 'we didn't want to disappoint you again, so we didn't say anything until we were absolutely sure, but we've just got a letter with wonderful news.'

Barnaby looked at her inquiringly.

'It's from your uncle, he'll be here any time now.'

Barnaby said nothing.

'Oh,' said Mrs Brooks, squeezing him, 'I know you're disappointed because he isn't here now, dear, and you have thought he was coming so many times. But this time he says he is sure, and you'll probably have to wait only a few more days.'

Barnaby did not look disappointed. He looked like the condemned prisoner whose last appeal has been denied.

'Can we go out and play now?' he asked.

'Of course, dear.'

Mrs Brooks leaned her faded cheek down for him to kiss. He brushed it with his lips and turned to Christie.

'Are you finished? Come on.'

Mr Brooks gave Mrs Brooks a proud glance as they watched the two children leave.

'Just like Dickie,' he said. 'Hates to show his emotions.'

As Sergeant Coulter came into the store, the children, barefooted and tanned and usually so ebullient, slipped past him. The girl smiled at him, but the boy, with a set face, walked on as if he hadn't seen the big policeman.

Sergeant Coulter shrugged. Kids. One day they climbed all over you with their sticky little fingers mucking up your uniform; the next day you were discarded, like some toy they had tired of.

He rang the bell on the counter and stared absently at a cobwebbed picture of the Queen hanging over the mail slots. That ought to be dusted.

'Good morning,' he said to Mr Brooks, 'is there a package here from London for me?'

'Nothing yet, Albert.'

'Is that you, Albert?' Mrs Brooks's quavering voice floated like ectoplasm from behind the beaded curtain.

'Yes, Mrs Brooks.'

'You must come in for a cup of tea; it's just freshly made.'

Sergeant Coulter suppressed a sigh. He dreaded going in that dim little parlour, a mausoleum to the dead Dickie.

He hated tea in the morning, but he could never think of excuses quickly or gracefully, so squaring his shoulders, he followed Mr Brooks to the back room.

Feeling three times his normal size and as though he were crammed in a doll's house, he perched on the edge of a delicate cane-bottomed chair.

'It's been quite a time since I've seen you, dear. How big and brown you are. Our own policeman. The only Island boy left. My, my, how proud your father would be if he could see you, Albert.'

Albert smiled and gripped his teacup as though it were alive. He always spilled tea when he visited the Brookses.

'How's the heart?' he asked politely.

Even before the death of Dickie, Mrs Brooks had had a heart condition, and she was never far separated from her bottle of digitalis.

'The same, dear, the same. It's a cross I'm used to bearing. I've learned to live with it.'

Like himself, Dickie Brooks had been born late in life to his parents, and his picture, with a look of startled innocence, gazed at Albert from the silver frame. How young he seemed. Of course, he'd been only nineteen. His face had a pure, untouched expression that made Sergeant Coulter feel guilty and old. Had he looked that guileless when he went overseas?

He dragged his eyes from the picture only to be confronted with a large seashell lettered with gold. Dickie had bought it overseas, on his last leave, which he had spent with his aunt at Brighton. Behind it, mounted on a stuffed heart-shaped cushion of white satin were Dickie's silver Sunday school attendance pins and his war decorations.

'We've had another letter from Major Murchison-Gaunt,' said Mr Brooks, lighting his pipe and settling down in his worn leather chair. 'He'll probably be here tomorrow.'

Sergeant Coulter looked at him vaguely for a minute.

'Murchison-Gaunt? Oh, Barnaby's uncle. That's nice.'

Dickie's last letter home was framed and hanging over Mr Brooks's chair. Sergeant Coulter didn't know where to look next until he noted with relief that the carpet was littered with comic books, two worn running shoes, a piece of bubble gum, some cereal-box plastic toys and a threadbare tennis ball.

'How are you getting along with the boy?' he asked.

'Barnaby?' Their old faces became alive, adoring.

'You have no idea how that child is blossoming, Albert.'

CHAPTER EIGHT

'Yes,' said Mrs Brooks, filling Albert's cup again, 'yes, he's such a dear little fellow. Just like Dickie was at that age.

She stopped, conscious of a warning look from Mr Brooks.

'And he's so happy.' She nodded to Mr Brooks, to assure him his message had been received. 'So happy. It's wonderful that Mrs Nielsen's little girl is holidaying here at the same time. They're together from morning to night, and they never seem to quarrel anymore.'

This was not entirely accurate.

Sergeant Coulter nodded but made no comment.

Just like Dickie. It was impossible, he silently decided, to find two people more unlike each other than Barnaby and the much-mourned Dickie. There was something tough, almost manly about Barnaby and, in his own self-contained way, Albert had grown to like the boy.

He finished his tea and stood up.

'Well, I must be going. Thank you so much.'

He passed the post office again, and although the letter was still in his pocket, he did not post it.

T HE BREAD, glazed and golden, was ready for delivery. The kitchen had cooled but still smelled deliciously of yeast, and Christie stood taking deep, appreciative sniffs. Barnaby, unusually silent, sat on the black leather sofa with Trixie in his arms.

The goat-lady put a clean linen cloth in a clothes basket and stacked the loaves carefully.

'Two for Lady Syddyns, two for Mr Allen, three for Mr Duncan, and remember, don't go up to his house, just shout at the fence, Agnes will come and pick it up, and two for poor Desmond. Don't forget poor Desmond.'

Each carrying a handle of the basket, they began their rounds. Their first stop was at Mr Duncan's, and following the goat-lady's instructions, they did not go up to the house, but stopped at the fence and shouted.

Next was Mr Allen. Neither he nor his border collies had forgotten the gum incident on the boat, and the collies slunk suspiciously at their master's heels as the old man carefully counted out pennies from a brass-topped purse.

And then on to Lady Syddyns. Wearing her faded purple velvet dressing gown and floppy-brimmed hat, she was, as usual, doctoring her roses.

She opened her arms to them and declared they must stop for tea.

Barnaby only smiled absently and did not answer, but Christie, pointing to the undelivered bread, declined with regret.

Surely next week then, said the old lady. They would have cucumber sandwiches and plum cake. She thumped both their heads affectionately with an insecticide sprayer, gave them each a rose and went on with her gardening.

The children were beginning to tire when they reached their last port of call, poor Desmond's.

Poor Desmond, the village idiot, lived in a shabby shack in the middle of the Island. He was their favourite customer.

At the age of four he had been stricken with scarlet fever, and never, said Mr Brooks, from that day to this, had his mind developed in any way. And they must always be very kind to him.

Poor Desmond had a flat back to his head, bad teeth, huge, gentle, lemur-like eyes and he was thirty-five years old.

Either because of a natural sweetness of disposition or from being so long isolated from his own age group, the four-year-olds, Desmond displayed none of the common failings of children. He never had tempers, he never pouted and he was trusting and generous, always sharing his meager ration of candy with the children.

Once his two older sisters had lived on the Island with him, but they had long since left. They had married well, had grown families of their own, and they were ashamed of poor Desmond. They supplied him with credit at Mr Brooks's store, where Mr Brooks chose his groceries for him, and in exchange for simple tasks such as woodcutting or gathering clams and oysters, the goat-lady gave him bread, butter and milk.

Christie and Barnaby had become very fond of him, although there were times when he was a nuisance.

All things considered, poor Desmond lived a simple and happy life, though occasionally the children had to drive him back with shouts and stones when, like old Shep, he wanted to tag along after them on their visits to One-ear.

When they entered the shack, they found Desmond seated in a chair, washing his socks in a bowl of soapy water.

'Oh, no!' said Christie. 'You're supposed to take them off first, darling.'

While she removed Desmond's socks, wrung them out and hung them over the doorsill to dry, Barnaby flung himself on Desmond's cot.

'I'll make lunch for you, Desmond. Won't that be nice?'

Desmond gave his random-toothed smile.

Christie rummaged through his food cupboard.

'Salmon. You love salmon sandwiches, don't you, Desmond?'

Desmond nodded, his trembling fingers happily brushing invisible spider webs from his face.

'No butter. Well, we'll just have to use that much more mayonnaise. You like mayonnaise, don't you, Desmond?'

Desmond beamed.

Christie opened the can of salmon, dumped it in a bowl and threw the empty can out the door.

Barnaby sat up.

'You are not supposed to do that. Sergeant Coulter says so. Desmond will get rats. You're to put them in a card-board box and Sergeant Coulter will take them over to his place and burn them.'

The lordly Sergeant's merest whim was law, and retrieving the can, Christie continued her work.

'Come on,' she said to Barnaby, 'the sandwiches are ready.'

'I'm not hungry.'

He turned his face to the wall.

Christie looked at him suspiciously.

'You sick?'

'No.'

She and Desmond stuffed sandwiches into their mouths.

'I think we'll have a glass of milk, Desmond.'

She went to the cupboard and took out the milk jug.

'Phew!' she sniffed. 'This is sour.'

She poured it out the front door.

Barnaby raised himself on his elbow.

'I told you, you can't do that.'

'You can't pour milk into a cardboard box, stupid. Desmond, you better go to the goat-lady's tomorrow and get fresh milk. Oh yes, Mr Brooks says you're to go to his place for your bath and shave tomorrow, too.'

The goat-lady always put a little treat for Desmond in with the bread.

'Oh, goodie,' cried Christie, opening a brown paper bag. 'Molasses cookies. You going to have one, Barnaby?'

He shook his head and turned his face to the wall.

'What's the matter with you, anyway? You've been acting funny ever since this morning.'

Barnaby did not answer.

'I think I'll make us a cup of tea. You love tea, don't you, Desmond?'

Desmond nodded.

Barnaby sat up again.

'You can't light Desmond's stove while the fire season's on. Sergeant Coulter says he'll burn down the whole damn Island.'

Christie's mouth became prissy.

'That's swearing, Barnaby Gaunt, and you know it isn't nice.'

'That's what he said.'

Christie pondered for a minute. 'Well, that's different.'

She swept the crumbs off the table onto the floor, and otherwise busied herself tidying the place.

Barnaby had his face to the wall again. Puzzled, Christie sat on the edge of the cot. There was a camaraderie between her and Barnaby; next to her mother, the goat-lady, One-ear, Shep, Desmond, and of course the incomparable Sergeant Coulter, she liked Barnaby more than anyone.

'What's the matter, Barnaby?'

He sighed wearily and shook his head.

'Is it because your uncle is coming?'

Barnaby had always been strangely disinclined to discuss his uncle.

He turned his face to her.

'Yes,' he said.

'Don't you love your uncle?'

Barnaby sat up, trembling.

'I hate him!' he said fiercely.

'But why?'

'Because. He killed Rodney, and he'll kill me too.'

'You ought to go to the police,' said the sensible Christie. 'Why don't you tell. Sergeant Coulter?'

'It's no good. He wouldn't believe me. You'll see. Nobody believes me.'

He gave a hopeless sigh.

'I told Mr Robinson, the lawyer, and he didn't believe me. He called me a confirmed liar. And he said even if Uncle did kill Rodney, I was too big to make a fuss over a thing like that. He says my uncle is a very fine man, known for his philosophy.'

'What's that?'

'When you give money away and you don't have to. I told the headmaster of the school, too, and he waved some papers in my face and said, 'Barnaby Gaunt, I've got a file here on you with the names of four schools you've been expelled from.' Then he said my uncle was a long-suffering, patient man who had done his best by me. I'm bad, Christie, bad. Everybody says so.'

'Oh, you are not.' Christie yawned. 'You always try to make things worse than they are. Who was Rodney and why did your uncle kill him?'

'Listen,' said Barnaby earnestly. 'I am bad. And you know why? Because of him! I'll tell you something nobody would ever believe.'

'What?'

He leaned over.

'He beats me.'

'Oh, go on,' scoffed Christie. 'Lots of kids get whipped. My mother slaps me hard if I'm bad.'

'You don't understand! He only whips me if I'm good! If I'm bad he gives me presents. He's crazy and nobody believes it except me. It's the truth, Christie, he only beats me if, I'm good.'

He paused and added mournfully, 'I don't get beat very often.'

Christie sat staring at him. She was a shrewd little person. 'Who was Rodney?'

Barnaby blushed and turned away.

'All right for you,' she said. 'Just wait till you want me to tell you something.'

He turned to her and she saw he was close to tears.

'Oh, stop being such a crybaby!'

'You don't care,' he said. 'Nobody does. Nobody loves me. I'm just like One-ear! And Rodney was my Teddy bear. I loved him! More than anything in the world. My mother gave him to me when I was a baby. *He* told me. Rodney had real fur, real brown fur, and a little box inside of him played music, and his eyes were glass and opened and shut when you put him upside down. I loved him and I couldn't go to sleep without him. *He* knew it! He burned Rodney in the fireplace, right in front of me. He said, 'I got him, Barnaby, I got Rodney and I burned him. He's dead. You remember that. You wait, Barnaby, you wait!' '

'Oh, he didn't! That's awful!' Christie was horrified.

'I'll be next! He's going to kill me. I know it!'

'But why?'

'Because of the money, don't you see? He's not my real uncle. He added my aunt's name to his after they were married. When my aunt died, she left the money to me, ten million dollars. It's in a trust fund, for me, and when I'm twenty-one I get it, and he gets what they call the interest off it until then. If I die before I'm twenty-one, he gets it all.

'You don't know how awful he is, Christie. He does things - awful things- '

'What kind of things?'

Barnaby's face went red and he turned away.

'I can't tell you. They're too awful.'

Christie shrugged.

'Once, though, Christie, we had a lady living with us. We had lots of ladies living with us. Housekeepers, he called them, but they never stayed long. I liked this lady, she was good to me. I liked her a lot. She came to me in the middle of the night, and she said she was going away, right then. She was crying and she put her arms about me and said, 'You poor little boy, you poor little boy.' You should of seen what he'd done to her!'

'What?'

'I won't tell you. She said she wanted to take me away with her but she couldn't. She said she couldn't go to the police about me because he had her number, whatever that is. She said I must try and get away from him as soon as I could, even if it meant being poor and hungry. She said he was a devil, and if he didn't kill me, he'd ruin me.'

'He sounds awful.'

'What'll I do, Christie? What'll I do? I'm so frightened.'

Christie sat thinking, her eyes narrowed and her mouth a prim little line.

'Well,' she said finally, 'stop being such a baby, to begin with. If he's as bad as you say, and mind you, Barnaby Gaunt, I'm not saying I believe everything, because you always make things worse than they are, but if he's as bad as that, there's only one thing *to do*.'

'What's that? What'll we do, Christie? I'll do anything!'

'We'll just have to murder him first,' said Christie.

Barnaby looked at her with awe and admiration as she sat calmly swinging her legs over the edge of the cot.

'I never even thought of that,' he said. 'I never even thought of it. You *are* my friend, Christie, and I won't forget it, and when I get the money, I'll give you a million dollars.'

'Okay. Come on, let's go home now. I'm thirsty. We'll start figuring out how to do it tomorrow.'

THE GLEAMING PLANE circled the Island harbour like a bird of prey. It swept to the water, making a smooth landing, and taxied to the float beside the wharf.

Mr and Mrs Brooks hopped about their little parlour in happy agitation. Who knew? If they made a good impression on Barnaby's uncle, he might even let them have Barnaby next summer. They hardly dared hope.

'Sydney, you and Barnaby go down to meet Major Murchison-Gaunt, while I tidy up,' cried Mrs Brooks, hastily swallowing her digitalis.

Mr Brooks, tiny and erect, with Barnaby in tow, walked down to the wharf to meet Uncle.

Sergeant Coulter, off duty and in civilian clothes, relaxed on the porch of the store. Watching.

Uncle, wearing dark glasses and impeccably dressed in white flannels, ascot tie and crested navy blazer, sprang lightly to the wharf.

'Major Murchison-Gaunt? This is indeed a pleasure.'

Uncle and Mr Brooks shook hands heartily.

Mr Brooks reached behind and gently dragged Barnaby to the fore.

'And here's the young man who's the cause of all the excitement. I'll leave you two alone, while I go back to the store. You will come up for tea, won't you Major? Mrs Brooks is looking forward to meeting you.'

'My dear Mr Brooks, I feel I have imposed on you enough.'

Uncle's voice was soft, indeed, delightful, with its public school accent.

'Not at all, not at all,' Mr Brooks patted Barnaby's shoulder fondly. 'We'll be waiting for you.'

Barnaby, left alone with his uncle, offered a grubby hand to Major Murchison-Gaunt.

'How do you do,' he said.

The old, cheerful, wicked Barnaby had been spirited away, and in his stead was left a small automaton.

'Barnaby, my dear little fellow,' Major Murchison-Gaunt embraced the child affectionately. 'Are you well? Have you been happy here?'

'Yes, Uncle.'

'My, my, how you've grown. Well, how kind it was of the Brookses to look after you. And you like it here?'

'Yes, Uncle.'

'I'm so glad, Barnaby. Now, we mustn't keep Mr and Mrs Brooks waiting. I must thank them again. Shall we go up?'

'Uncle?'

'Yes, Barnaby?'

'Uncle, may I stay with them, for the summer, at their place behind the store, instead of at the cottage?'

Uncle looked sadly down at his little nephew.

'Barnaby,' he said in a hurt voice, 'don't you want to be with me?'

'Yes,' said Barnaby faintly, 'only I thought maybe you wouldn't mind if I stayed on with them.'

'Well, we'll see. You know I want you to be happy. I'll go up and have a talk with them now. I was going to try to cancel my lease on the cottage, as I have a great deal of unexpected business to attend to in the city, and I'll be able to fly over only occasionally.'

Barnaby's face was very white.

'Oh, let me stay on for the summer. Please, please! I'll do anything you say, only let me stay!'

'But my dear little chap, it isn't entirely up to me. I'll have to see what Mr and Mrs Brooks think about the idea. You run along and play while I talk with them.'

Barnaby's gaze rose to his uncle's face, but stopped at the razor-like mouth. He didn't dare contemplate the eyes behind the dark glasses.

Uncle's eyes were quite mad.

Uncle, of course, knew this, which was why he always wore dark glasses.

As he walked away, Barnaby took a deep breath and exhaled slowly. Uncle had not changed.

Christie, who had been hiding behind the war monument watching the meeting, now came forward and waved for him to join her.

'Did you see him?' he whispered when they met.

'No, not really. I was too far away. Come on, let's go up to the old church, it's quiet there, we can talk and no one will hear us.'

Sergeant Coulter, although off duty, automatically and unconsciously noted height, age, weight, build, colour and mannerisms. Six foot one, forty to forty-five, weight two ten to twenty, build muscular, complexion florid, hair fair and very curly. He recognised the army carriage. Sergeant Coulter was impartial, but Albert hated army officers. Uncle, he decided, was a very natty dresser, his clothes skilfully cut to disguise the animal bulk. Savile Row or Bond Street, Albert thought sourly. But something was out of place. The hard eyes of the Mountie swept over Major Murchison-Gaunt again. The hands. Tailoring couldn't disguise them. Powerful, hairy hands which dangled in a restless manner, like paws longing to walk.

No, Uncle was not one of those toothbrush-moustached, spindly, regular army officers whom Albert detested. Uncle looked like a tough customer, a gentleman, of course, but as tireless and strong as a wolf, a mixture of country squire and ex-commando.

Uncle, Mr Brooks and Sergeant Coulter all met on the porch of the store.

Mr Brooks introduced Major Murchison-Gaunt and Sergeant Coulter.

'Army?' said Uncle in surprise.

'Royal Canadian Mounted Police.'

'I had no idea the law was represented here. Many desperadoes?' asked Uncle jovially.

'Sergeant Coulter lives on the Island,' explained Mr Brooks. 'He's an Island boy. He drops in twice a week officially, not that we give him much extra work.'

'That's a nice plane you've got,' said Sergeant Coulter. 'De Havilland Beaver, isn't it?'

Major Murchison-Gaunt nodded.

'We mustn't keep Mrs Brooks waiting, she's so anxious to meet you, Major. Do come in. Albert, you will join us for tea, won't you?'

Albert looked absent-mindedly at Mr Brooks.

'Why, yes, thanks,' he said.

Mrs Brooks was delighted to meet Major Murchison-Gaunt.

'We can't tell you how much pleasure it has given us having Barnaby here,' she said. 'He's an orphan, is he not? He has never mentioned his parents, and of course, we've never asked him.'

'My dear Mrs Brooks, let me begin by trying to thank you for all you have done for the boy. Yes, Barnaby is an orphan. He is now. I owe you an explanation for not being here to look after him, but the truth of the matter is I have been in Europe. Handling the funeral arrangements and settling the estate of his mother.'

Major Murchison-Gaunt paused, then continued,

'I hardly know where to begin. The whole thing has been such a tragedy. First, I must ask you not to repeat a word of this to the child. You'll certainly understand why as I explain.

'You see, Barnaby believes he was orphaned in his infancy. As a matter of fact, his father did die then. But his mother passed away just three weeks ago. In a mental hospital in Switzerland. Naturally I don't want the boy to learn this.'

Shocked glances passed between Mr and Mrs Brooks; even Sergeant Coulter looked impressed.

'That poor child,' whispered Mrs Brooks.

'He is indeed.' Uncle paused reflectively, then gave them a quick glance. 'No doubt you remember the Gaunt case? It made international headlines about ten years ago.'

Mrs Brooks's hands flew to her face.

'Oh, no, you mean Barnaby- ?'

Uncle nodded.

'Gaunts?' said Mr Brooks. 'The biscuit people?'

Those black-and-gold tins marked 'By Appointment' were known all over the British Empire.

'Yes,' said Uncle.

CHAPTER TEN

'I don't recall the case,' said Sergeant Coulter.

'I thought you in particular would, you know, Interpol and all that.' Uncle sighed. 'Well, my wife and Barnaby's father were brother and sister. After Barnaby's birth, his mother, Claire, suffered a very profound depression - postnatal something or other, the doctors call it.

'My wife and I had rented a villa in Italy, on the Gulf of Spezia, and we suggested that poor Claire and Robert and the baby should visit us. We hoped that perhaps cheerful company, and boating and sports and that sort of thing would snap Claire out of this depression of hers. Her doctor thought it was an excellent idea.'

His listeners leaned forward anxiously.

Uncle sighed again.

'Unfortunately, what we, and even her doctor, thought to be a temporary derangement, proved to be a deep-seated psychosis. We were naturally alarmed by her condition, but at that time we had no idea of the seriousness of it.'

Uncle paused, unable for the moment to continue.

Mrs Brooks refilled his teacup, Sergeant Coulter lit a cigarette, and they waited expectantly.

Uncle took a deep breath, once more in control of his emotions.

'I'm sure you must all remember now. While in the acute maniacal stage, in the middle of the night, she fatally stabbed my brother-in-law Robert. And if it hadn't been for the child's nurse and myself hearing his dying screams, she would have killed the baby - yes, little Barnaby. We reached her only just in time to prevent a second murder.'

His audience sat stunned.

'She couldn't stand trial, of course. She was committed to a hospital for the criminally insane, but five years ago I managed to have her transferred to a private clinic.'

Uncle rubbed his hands wearily over his face.

'My wife and I adopted Barnaby. I even added the name Gaunt to my own, so the child would have the feeling of security.'

'And is your wife in Europe now?' asked Mrs Brooks.

Life was almost insupportable to poor Uncle.

'My wife was killed in a car accident six months later, Mrs Brooks.'

'Oh, my dear' cried Mrs Brooks.

Uncle took out a silken handkerchief and blew his nose.

'Dying and leaving me was the only unkind thing Maudie ever did in her life,' he said hoarsely.

'My dear Major,' said Mr Brooks. Even Sergeant Coulter looked affected.

Uncle Sylvester, momentarily overwhelmed by the appalling mortality rate of his family, raised a hand briefly to his dark glasses.

Sergeant Coulter blinked. He could have sworn the fellow had hair even on the palm of his hand. But that, of course, was impossible.

'One learns to live with tragedy,' said Uncle bravely. 'Barnaby is all I have left, the only link I have with my dear Maude. So now you understand how deeply I appreciate your kindness to him.'

'Anything we can do for that child is a privilege,' said Mrs Brooks, reaching for her digitalis.

Oh, that Dickie should always follow such a dark star!

'He's so happy with you. I was talking to him on the dock. The little rascal wants to stay with you for the summer.'

Uncle gave a courageous laugh.

'He and I have always been so close, but do you know, I hardly think he has missed me at all. You must have been very good indeed to him.'

'Children are often cruel, but they don't mean to be,' said Mr Brooks. 'Our boy Dickie, who had the most thoughtful disposition in the world, couldn't wait to get overseas, even though he knew how lonely we'd be.'

'Maudie and I never had a family,' said Uncle sadly, 'although we wanted one. So you see, Barnaby is doubly precious to me. I adore children.'

He did indeed. Several little girls to whom he had taken a fancy had vanished into thin air.

'Which brings me to another problem,' Uncle went on. 'I had intended to spend the summer here with Barnaby, but I find now that business commitments make this impossible. The best I can do is to fly over a couple of times a week, so I suppose I must keep Barnaby in the city with me.'

'Not at all, not at all,' cried Mrs Brooks eagerly. 'We'd love to have him for the summer, Major. He is such a dear little boy. I know this must sound selfish, but, you see, Major, we lost Dickie, our only child, in the war. Barnaby is so like him in some ways.'

Mr Brooks looked at Albert and cast her a nervous glance.

Uncle stood up.

'My dear Mrs Brooks, and here I have been burdening you with my own private sorrow.'

'Not at all,' said Mrs Brooks, daubing her eyes, 'we share a common bond in Barnaby.'

Uncle pondered. Barnaby's welfare was a matter of prime concern to him.

'I am wondering if it would not perhaps be unsettling for him to be shuttling back and forth between us.' Uncle sighed again. 'But you see, I must be a bit selfish myself. If I could, perhaps, have him over to the cottage, say, one evening a week?'

'Of course, of course,' cried Mr and Mrs Brooks. Sergeant Coulter, with a monumental effort, stifled a yawn.

Uncle took out his chequebook and wrote two cheques. 'This is for Barnaby's board and any incidental expenses.' He handed it to Mr Brooks.

'Why, this is far too much,' said Mr Brooks.

'Tut, tut,' said Uncle. 'Knowing he is getting love and affection is worth a great deal to me, sir.'

He handed Mr Brooks the second cheque.

'And this is for your church. I received a very kind letter from Mr Rice-Hope. The real-estate people told me that services are held on Benares, and I don't know if I shall be able to attend, but if you would be kind enough to give him this on my behalf- '

Mr and Mrs Brooks looked at each other in wonder.

'You are a very good and kind man, Major Murchison-Gaunt.'

'Not at all,' said Uncle modestly.

'Barnaby and his little friend Christie have been over to Benares to church,' said Mrs Brooks with a certain pride, for Barnaby's religious life seemed to have been neglected.

Pleased, Uncle chuckled.

What, did they actually mean to tell him that the little devil had voluntarily attended services?

Why yes, said Mrs Brooks, he and the little girl liked to. As a matter of fact they spent a lot of time in the old church on the Island. Mr Rice-Hope didn't mind, as long as they didn't touch anything.

Little girl? How sweet. Oh, yes, there was one more thing.

Uncle, in an ecclesiastical manner, piously folded his hands over his paunchy, iron-muscled gut.

'I feel I should tell you,' he said, 'that Barnaby has had a little trouble in school. No, I suppose I had better be honest and say schools. Just plain high spirits, you understand, although one of his masters had the effrontery to suggest that perhaps there was some taint in the boy. I took him out of *that* school in a hurry! I'm a great believer, Mr Brooks, in environment. But just to be on the safe side I took Barnaby to Zurich, to a psychiatric clinic for children.'

Uncle paused and looked around proudly.

'Well sir, the most eminent doctors in Europe gave Barnaby a clean slate. Naturally, being orphaned so early there was bound to be some slight emotional problem; for instance, Barnaby *does* tell lies. But I ask you, now, what healthy, normal boy doesn't?'

Uncle stood up again, dwarfing Mr and Mrs Brooks.

'That boy is as sound as a dollar,' he said.

Sergeant Coulter, who believed that a prompt clip on the ear was worth a thousand child psychologists, also stood up.

'I must be going, thank you for the tea. Glad to have met you, Major.'

'Do come again, soon, Albert. We love to see Dickie's friends.'

When Sergeant Coulter had gone, Uncle turned to Mr and Mrs Brooks. 'Fine-looking, upstanding chap. Men like that are the backbone of the British Empire.'

Mr Brooks smiled proudly.

'Sergeant Coulter was in a prisoner-of-war camp for three years.'

Uncle, about to light a cigar, started slightly and turned to Mrs Brooks.

'Excuse me, Mrs Brooks. Does cigar smoke bother you?'

'Oh dear me, no,' cried Mrs Brooks. 'I think they smell so much nicer than pipes. I've often wished Mr Brooks smoked them.'

Uncle lit his cigar and turned to Mr Brooks.

'How very interesting,' he said. 'Do you happen to remember which camp he was in? You see, I was a POW myself.'

'What an extraordinary coincidence,' said Mr Brooks. 'As a matter of fact, I don't remember. You must ask Albert the next time you see him.'

'It was Silesia,' said Mrs Brooks. 'I remember because I always get it mixed with Siberia.'

Uncle exhaled slowly.

'Ah,' he said. 'I'm afraid we wouldn't have run into each other. I was in Colditz. No, I don't think I'll discuss it with the good sergeant. It was a very distressing period of my life, which I must say I prefer to forget.'

Mr and Mrs Brooks quite understood.

'And now, Mr Brooks, if you'll just open the cottage for me, I'll get settled in.'

THE LITTLE LOG CHURCH, chinked with white mortar, stood on top of a grassy knoll, surrounded on three sides by trees, the fourth facing the ocean.

The interior was dim and smelled of lemon-oil polish, dust, incense and age. Mrs Rice-Hope had just decorated the altar with fresh, cream-coloured gladiolas, which looked incongruously vital and alive in the prism shadows cast by the stained-glass windows.

The children sat in a back pew, flanking poor innocent Desmond, who nodded dully in the almost stupefying quiet.

The children loved the little church; it was such a pleasant, peaceful spot in which to plan a murder.

A great weight had been lifted from Barnaby's mind by Christie's very sensible suggestion, but, as is usually the case, the little assassins had difficulty in deciding on the technical details of the murder.

They sat quietly discussing and discarding ideas, while poor Desmond, as harmless as a time bomb, dozed between them.

They sighed, for it was not easy. It was very simple to decide to commit a murder, but an entirely different and difficult task to execute one.

They racked their brains, going over every movie and TV plot they had ever seen.

Victims could be run over, but alas, they could neither drive, nor did they possess a car. Christie rather favoured drowning Uncle, but Barnaby assured her the Major was a powerful swimmer.

Knives were discussed at great length, but Uncle, a black-belt judo man and ex-commando, would easily disarm them. Pitfalls and bear traps were out, it might take months before he accidentally trod on one, and they had only till the end of the summer.

'Well,' said Barnaby, 'there's one good thing, the time he's really dangerous is when the moon is full, and it's only in its first quarter now.'

'What does that mean?'

'The moon's got four quarters, in the first it's just a little thin line, but it gets fatter and fatter all month and when it gets to the last quarter, it's a full moon.'

Barnaby had become an expert on lunar phases.

'You're sure it's okay now?' asked Christie.

'Pretty sure. He told me so himself, he says, 'Watch out for the boogeyman the next full moon, Barnaby, maybe we'll catch you then.' I've watched him and he's worse then, a lot worse.'

Having exhausted all other possibilities, they reluctantly concluded that shooting was the only foolproof method. Reluctantly, because they didn't have a gun.

'We'll just have to get one, somehow,' said Christie.

'I know!' said Barnaby, 'Sergeant Coulter! Why didn't we think of that before!'

CHAPTER ELEVEN

Their beloved sergeant did have a gun but, as Christie pointed out, he always wore it strapped around his waist. They agreed sadly that the chances were negligible that they would be able to spirit it away from him without his knowledge.

And they had a very healthy respect for Sergeant Coulter.

'Wait a minute,' said Christie. 'Lady Syddyns's. There's a big room across the hall from the living room. It's got books all over one wall, and I'm sure I saw a bunch of guns hanging on the other wall.'

What could be simpler. They had an invitation to tea, they would pay the old lady a courtesy call and check the situation thoroughly.

A shadow fell across them, and both children started.

Sergeant Coulter stood in the doorway, looking down at them.

'Hello,' he said casually, glancing past them to the altar. When he saw the fresh flowers, he sighed. He had missed her.

'Mr and Mrs Rice-Hope have gone, eh?'

'Yes, half an hour ago. She put them there. They're nice, aren't they? He said we could sit here, any time we wanted, as long as we didn't touch anything.'

Sergeant Coulter nodded and turned away.

'She's pretty, isn't she?' said Barnaby.

This time it was Sergeant Coulter who started.

'Who?' he snapped.

'Mrs Rice-Hope.'

The Mountie's bronzed face flushed darkly.

'Mr Brooks wants you. Run along, both of you.'

Reluctant to part with him, they stood shuffling their feet and nudging each other.

'You tell him,' whispered Barnaby.

'No, you.'

'He won't believe me, you know that.'

'Well, what is it this time?' Sergeant Coulter could look forbidding when he chose.

Barnaby stood silent, so, talking a deep breath, Christie began.

It was about Fletcher Proudfoot. They were sorry they killed him, they hadn't meant to.

They had heard him singing 'Rule Britannia' in Miss Proudfoot's garden. They never knew birds could talk, so they sneaked in to have a look at him.

He was so pretty, with those green and blue and yellow feathers, and he put his head on one side and called himself a dear little birdie.

All they wanted was to take him out and play with him for a minute. They had just got him out when they heard Miss Proudfoot, calling and asking who was there.

They were afraid of her, that's why they ran away, but they didn't have time to put Fletcher back in his cage.

They didn't know what to do with him, so Barnaby shoved Fletcher down the front of his shirt.

When they finally stopped running and took Fletcher out, he seemed dizzy and staggered around in a circle. Then he fell over on his back with his little feet in the air and his mouth open.

They waited for him to get up and speak. He didn't and they were afraid he was dead. They carried him back to Miss Proudfoot's but Miss Proudfoot had taken the bird-cage inside, and again they didn't know what to do with Fletcher. Finally they put him on her front door step and again they ran away.

Sergeant Coulter stood staring over their heads.

'You didn't deliberately hurt him?'

'No.'

'Why didn't you tell me this before?'

'I didn't think you'd believe me,' said Barnaby.

'And you didn't ask me,' said Christie.

Sergeant Coulter put his hands on his hips and leaned down to them.

'This is just another example of what happens when you don't tell the truth and don't do what you are told. You are not to go on other people's property, and you are not to touch anything that doesn't belong to you.'

They nodded.

'Don't you understand,' he explained, 'Fletcher died of fright. Tiny birds are delicate. Even the warmth of a person's hand is enough to upset them, and being shoved down the front of your shirt-'

His finger tapped Barnaby's chest, and he stopped himself only just in time from implying that Fletcher was important and Barnaby wasn't.

' ... Don't you realise that being shoved down the front of your shirt was enough to kill him? He probably suffocated from heat and fright.'

The children looked sad.

Two pairs of loving eyes stared up at him.

'All right,' he reached in his pocket and took out a package of gum. 'Here. Now beat it and see if you can stay out of trouble for the rest of the afternoon.'

He turned and walked slowly down the steep rock path. Old Shep, sleeping on the thyme- and wild-violet-strewn bank, awoke, ran to his side and thrust his cool nose into the policeman's hand. Albert paused briefly, stroked the dog's grizzled head and walked on.

The children watched the broad shoulders disappear around a bend of the road, then, scuffling their feet listlessly in the dust, they started for the store.

They both agreed it was a pity it was so easy to kill poor little Fletcher Proudfoot, whom they liked, and so difficult to do away with Uncle, whom they didn't.

'I wonder why Sergeant Coulter's face got so red when you said Mrs Rice-Hope was pretty?'

'Oh,' Barnaby peeled the package and shoved his two and a half sticks of gum in his mouth, 'I guess he thinks it's sissified for a Mountie to like girls.'

'What else could he like, silly. He couldn't very well like boys. I wish he'd buy spearmint instead of peppermint gum. I hate peppermint.'

'Give it to me then.'

Christie took the gum out of her mouth and handed it to him, watching with uncritical eyes as he managed to get the whole five sticks in his mouth.

She burst out laughing.

'You look like a chipmunk!'

Linking arms companionably, they ambled back to the store.

Sergeant Coulter's own speedboat, which would take him to R.C.M.P. headquarters, was tied up at the float.

He smiled as he climbed on board, relieved that the death of the bird had been accidental. Their other pranks could be dismissed, but Fletcher had seemed inexcusable. The children were still a nuisance of course, but the boy wasn't quite the little monster he had appeared.

It was a shocking thing about the mother and with a family history like that, it was small wonder there was something odd about the child.

CHAPTER ELEVEN

Sergeant Coulter had escorted prisoners to the hospital for the criminally insane, and even now the memory of it made him sweat.

Drunks, murderers, forgers or con men didn't faze him, but the thought of *them* made his flesh creep.

One could almost believe in full moons, witches' Sabbaths, black masses and silver bullets for the hearts of werewolves. The crimes some had committed were almost inconceivable, and yet they could not be brought to trial. Detained at Her Majesty's pleasure. It had a fine medieval ring to it.

Well, he was a policeman, not a psychiatrist, and as long as people didn't break the law, they didn't concern him.

Probably the uncle was right and Barnaby was as sound as a dollar. And for all the child was, orphaned, he was fortunate in having such a devoted uncle. Being custodian of that boy was not a job Sergeant Coulter coveted.

Uncle's first night at the cottage was uneventful. He was weary from much travelling, and before the sun had set he was sleeping the sound sleep of those without conscience.

After dozing late, Uncle arose but did not breakfast. Punctilious, he puttered around the already spotless cottage, arranging things precisely.

Then he changed his clothes, donning a white silk kimono. He did some judo setting-up exercises, plus a few of his own specialties, such as flinging himself feet first against the wall, doing a back flip and landing neatly on all fours. He could now reach a height of six and a half feet. Seven was his goal.

At four o'clock in the afternoon he started preparations for dinner. In the corner of the kitchen was a large box of groceries he had brought from the city. He liked cooking for himself; he liked living alone. It was hideous having to eat in restaurants while travelling.

He was a good cook and he planned his meal carefully. He lit the kitchen range, put the baron of beef in the oven, and while it was cooking made the Yorkshire pudding. He liked his pudding fluffy; a soggy pudding ruined his meal. As he stood dreamily staring out the window and stirring the white sauce for the cauliflower, he remembered with indulgent self-forgiveness that he had forgotten the grated cheese.

He made his own French dressing; the secret was not too much vinegar - restaurants never got it right. The lettuce was soaking in a bowl in the sink. He got a clean dish towel, dried each piece individually and tore it into bite-sized pieces by hand. One should never cut lettuce, for it bruised it and spoiled the flavour absolutely. He peeled and halved the potatoes, then left them soaking in cold water for a few minutes. They browned much nicer that way.

He really didn't care too much for vegetables but, as he admitted to himself with a wry smile, they kept the old pelt in good condition.

He wasn't a dessert man at all and he attributed his flaw-less teeth to the fact that he never touched sweets. That and heredity, of course.

He was neither a glutton nor a gourmet - simple, perfectly prepared foods were to his taste - but, like One-ear, he ate enormous meals every day or so. The ten-pound roast would provide him with two meals. He followed no regular meal hour pattern; when he was hungry again, he ate again.

Leaving his dinner in the warming oven, he lit a fire in the cobblestone fireplace in the living room and prepared a small table tastefully.

CHAPTER ELEVEN

At last he settled down with his dinner, picking daintily until he had finished.

He had brought his own brandy, cigars and Turkish coffee. When the thick coffee was brewed, he sat sipping it from a tiny brass cup, happy and content. He was replete.

It was too early for a prowl, so holding his expensive cigar in one large hirsute hand, he leaned back, as fond old memories crowded in on him.

Have to have the boy over soon and start the treatment again. At the time of Claire, medical authorities said it was impossible. Couldn't be done. But having read ancient cabalistic treatises and studied rare documents of demonology, he had known better. Unfortunately he was not in a position to write a paper on it. Could he do so, they would be forced to admit he had been right. He was always right. Why, the psychiatrists had even coined a word for it not too long ago - brainwashing.

It worked differently with each individual of course. Would have taken years with old Maude, for instance. Had to expedite matters there. It had gone off beautifully with Claire.

It had been easy with her, foolish, spiritless little creature with her migraine headaches, always complaining that Robert and Maude didn't understand her.

Oh, Sylvester, clasping her helpless little hands, I really do think my headaches are milder since you hypnotised me. Do you really, my dear? That's extraordinary. It usually takes four or five sessions, you know. Perhaps we'll try again tonight, if you feel it helps you.

Started out as a parlour game. Damn clever, that.

A parlour game in that haunted villa. By George, he had had fun haunting that place at midnight.

A delightful spot, rather damp, heavy with miasmas and departed spirits. Place was filled with happy memories, ideal for a neurotic hypochondriac like dear Claire. Silly little ass.

Shelley and Mary Wollstonecraft Godwin stayed there, Mary brooding on *Frankenstein* and Percy seeing the ghost of little Allegra Byron floating through the gloomy halls and beckoning from the misty waters. Percy had drowned practically in the front yard.

Foolish, spineless little creature. Now your eyelids are heavy. You are getting very tired. You are nearly asleep. Now you are asleep.

Your headaches are getting worse. They are blinding you. They are maddening. They are driving you insane.

Six times in the deep trance stage would have been enough - she was an ideal subject - but he'd given her a dozen, just to make sure.

Your headaches are worse. They are maddening. They are driving you insane. It's Robert's fault. His and Maude's. They hate you. They are giving you the headaches. You are going insane. You hate them. Tonight you will get the knife. Tonight you will do it. While he's asleep. After him, the baby. You will remember nothing when you wake up. You are insane.

By God, what a silly thing she was. She hadn't done it, of course. Broken down at the last minute and he had had to finish the job for her. But she thought she had, and her mind had certainly got pranged when she believed she'd nearly butchered the baby too.

Still, he musn't take all the credit. Never would have worked so well if she hadn't been neurotic to begin with, and the hauntings and postnatal depression had been pure gravy, what with Maude and Robert pooh-poohing her vagaries.

No one to turn to but big, strong, kind Sylvester.

Of course, he had had no idea it took these bloody loonies so long to die a natural death. Thought she'd just curl up and fade away in a few months. Ten years, instead. Been carried away after he'd done in Robert. Had to be so careful. Really impetuous about leading Maude to her Maker. Still, things had worked out very well, except for that damned nurse. Fortunately she had no family. Never even been missed since, as far as he knew. Nonetheless, couldn't be too careful.

No, it would have been too difficult with Maude. Nothing but bloody murder would do for her or Robert. Hadn't the imagination of a hinny. No wonder they simply adored horses. Natural affinity. No fools when it came to money though. Close-fisted and hard. That's how the old man had made it and that's how they hung on to it. And baby makes three.

Too bad the boy wasn't like Claire. Just like Maude and Robert. A real Gaunt, stubborn and hard as nails. He would have to work overtime on the boy. Maude had been a tough nut too. Had to use a wrench on her, even after pushing the bloody car over the cliff to make sure.

Good old Maude. Live dangerously, she always said. Proud of driving a car and riding a horse like a man. Horsey bitch. Ah, those lovely winding, dangerous mountain roads.

Courting Maude. What sport. Come into the garden, Maude, and by God, she had. Ogling each other like a couple out of Tennyson. With that face, how she honestly believed a man could marry her for anything but her money. And those pit-pony legs. Ugh!

He'd given her her money's worth, by George. No one could say he hadn't helped her to live dangerously.

CHRISTIE HAD TWO BLOUSES. The one she was wearing was clean, having been washed the night before, and her best one was drying in the sun on a gooseberry bush, for that afternoon the children were going to tea at Lady Syddyns's.

The goat-lady was busy canning while the two children sat on the black leather sofa, cuddling Trixie and Tom.

The goat-lady paused in her stirring, gazed at Barnaby critically and sighed. His face was reasonably clean, but the rest of him was, as usual, grubby. Though the Brookses loved him, he still looked like an orphan.

'Take off your shirt, you're going to have a wash.'

When he demurred, she merely threatened to cut off his breakfast. Tamed, he followed her.

She filled a basin and took him to the porch. And stripped to the waist, he was scrubbed mercilessly. His cheeks glowed, his ears were a stinging scarlet, and his yellow hair stuck out and shone like the down of a young duck.

When the goat-lady was satisfied he was clean, she washed his shirt and hung it next to Christie's.

The Islanders were discreetly snobbish and the goat-lady had no intention of letting her charges go in a grimy condition.

Lady Syddyns might be aged, deaf and slightly befuddled, but invitations from her were important, even if they were, much to Miss Proudfoot's horror, usually extended to the wrong people. Why, she even had Albert to tea.

Lady Syddyns was distantly related to royalty and therefore above reproach. However, as Miss Proudfoot stated to an embarrassed Mr Rice-Hope, who also received the occasional invitation, plainly only certain inferior persons would take advantage of the old woman's dotage by accepting.

'Now both of you mind your manners when you're there. Don't talk with your mouths full and say thank you. And above all, don't touch anything. Her house is full of antiques and you're sure to break something if you do.'

The children nodded but a secret glance passed between them. They fully intended, when the old lady's back was turned, to lay rude hands upon a gun, if they could.

The goat-lady returned to her stirring and the children to the black sofa, where they sat sniffing and savouring the spicy odours. Clutching the patient little animals, they tilted their noses to catch the tantalising smells of vinegar, onions, cinnamon and cloves.

'And no matter what you may have heard, don't say a word about Sir Adrian. She got her hearing aid only two years ago, and she was deaf as a post for forty years before that, so she missed a lot. The rest of us weren't so lucky.'

The children nodded again, their eyes fastened on the glass bottles that always seemed to be bubbling and gurgling in the big blue-and-white enamel preserving kettle. The goat-lady canned almost daily for the winter when Per, her fisherman son, would be home.

She pointed to half a dozen jars of tomatoes on the table.

'Take those down to the cellar for me. After, you can go and hunt for mushrooms in Mr Duncan's field beyond the fall rye. Go along by the road, though, so he won't see you. He won't pick them and there's no point in letting them go to waste. You aren't expected at Lady Syddyns's until three, so you can take a picnic lunch if you want.'

'Oh, boy!' said Barnaby.

'Why doesn't Agnes pick the mushrooms?' asked Christie.

The goat-lady sniffed.

'Her old man won't allow her that far off by herself. Afraid she might meet someone.'

'Who?'

'A man.'

'What man?'

'Oh, any man,' said the goat-lady. 'Take those down like I asked you to.'

A trap door in the goat-lady's bedroom led to a stone-lined cellar, where, on long shelves, the glass bottles were stored.

The children were fascinated by the cellar. Regimented on the cobwebbed shelves was the harvest of the Island, emerald bread-and-butter pickles, tiny white onions, sliced cucumbers, sweet gherkins, pale, garlicky dills and brick-coloured chutney laden with crystallised ginger.

The Island produced fruits and vegetables with an almost tropical abundance, and the children never tired of turning and examining the jars.

Beets, peas, beans, asparagus and tomatoes came from the goat-lady's garden. Plums, strawberries, apples, pears, peaches, raspberries, blackberries and mushrooms were gathered from deserted fields and orchards.

A big crock of sauerkraut, with a stone on the lid, reeked delightfully in a corner, mingling with the scent of hams, hanging from the rafters.

Jewelled jams, translucent jellies and big bottles of berry wines winked in the faint light. Row after row of squat jars containing salmon, girdled with shining skin in silver belts, gleamed like pink marble. Jars of venison and duck, from Per's last fall's hunting, looked sinister and muddy, although the children knew from experience that they tasted delicious. Pickled eggs floated in purple beet juice, chillies and relishes and gnarled brown pickled walnuts stood ready for the goat-lady's table.

It was a dim, subterranean gourmet's delight, which the children left reluctantly, for, when they weren't thinking of murder, their thoughts usually dwelt on food.

Upstairs, the goat-lady handed them two baskets, one for the mushrooms, the other containing their lunch.

'What's in it?' asked Barnaby.

'Oh, don't tell, Auntie,' begged Christie. 'Let's save it for a surprise, Barnaby.'

Barnaby agreed. Christie loved surprises, which was fortunate.

Each swinging a basket, they left, dancing down the country lane.

They paused on their way to climb Mr Duncan's fence and shy a few rocks at the Iron Duke's sleek behind. In the distance they saw Mr Duncan with his back to them, so they felt safe to stick their tongues out and thumb their noses.

Bob and Bill, the giant Clydesdales, came thundering to the fence, their hairy feet making the earth tremble.

As gentle as puppies, they slobbered on the children's outstretched hands with velvety noses and nudged and butted each other as they sought the lumps of sugar the children offered them.

When the children reached the field they found that the daisies had pitched their bright camps between the buttercups and mushrooms.

The children worked gaily, tossing mushrooms and toadstools alike into the basket.

'Auntie can sort them later,' said Christie.

Barnaby looked at the half-filled basket.

'There's nearly enough here. Let's eat, I'm starving.'

From the lunch basket Christie took out a chequered tablecloth and spread it under an old, moss-covered walnut tree. Then, with their mouths watering, they unwrapped their lunch from the white linen napkins.

'Gee,' said Barnaby, 'egg and lettuce sandwiches, apricot jam tarts, sugar cookies, and oh, look, a bottle of raspberry vinegar! I wish I could stay here all the time. You ought to see what they feed you at boarding school.'

'Mmmm,' said Christie, shoving half a sandwich in her mouth, 'my mother cooks good. Not like this though. Auntie's the best cook in the world. Things like the sour cream and chives in these sandwiches, my mother wouldn't think of something like that. Open the raspberry vinegar, I'm thirsty.'

Despite its name, the drink was not sour; it was a non-alcoholic wine made by the goat-lady just for them, and she stopped the fermentation by adding a minute part of vinegar. It tasted and smelled like liquid raspberries and it was the children's favourite beverage, given to them as a treat.

'Christie,' said Barnaby leaning back, 'you talk about your mother sometimes, but you never talk about your father. Where's your father, Christie?'

'MacNab?' Christie shrugged vaguely. 'In the city. He doesn't live with us.'

'MacNab? Why do you call him MacNab? Why don't you call him Daddy, like other kids with fathers do?'

Christie hooted with derision, and instead of answering only shoved another sandwich in her mouth.

'What's he like?'

Christie thought for a minute, then, 'He doesn't count. Pass me the bottle.'

Barnaby did, and sat surveying her as if he had just seen her for the first time.

'Doesn't he love you?' His voice was gentle.

'Of course he does. He's my father, isn't he?'

'Well,' Barnaby persisted, 'do you love him?'

Christie looked at him with wonder. The thought had never occurred to her before.

'Yes, I guess I do,' she said. She shrugged again. 'Maybe I do, maybe I don't. I don't know why I should love him, he's never done anything for me or my mother. Like she says, he's a drunk, and he hasn't drawn a sober breath for fifteen years.'

Barnaby was shocked.

'You shouldn't talk about your father that way.'

'Well, that's what my mother says, and she ought to know. What would happen to the child if she didn't work like a slave? Does he think shoes for the child grow in beer parlours?'

'What child?' asked Barnaby.

'Me, of course. That's what my mother says and she's right. My mother is always right.'

'Don't you wish he lived with you?'

'Certainly not!' Christie was appalled. 'The only time I see him is when he turns up on my birthday and at Christmas, with presents. Drunk.'

'Nice presents?'

Christie reflected for a minute. 'Yes, I guess so. But like my mother says, I wouldn't have a stitch on my back if we had to rely on him. Two days a year she says he thinks he can buy the child's affection with expensive gifts. She wouldn't so much as have shoes on her feet, and who's to pay for her education? That's me she's talking about.'

Barnaby was fascinated with the thought that people actually had two live parents.

'Tell me about your mother later,' he said. 'Tell me more about MacNab now.'

'Well, he sings when he's drunk and sits me on his knee.'

'What does he sing?'

'Oh, 'The Big Rock Candy Mountain,' and 'Abdul Debulbul Ameer' and 'When the Work's All Done Next Fall, Mother.' My mother gets mad when he sings that. She says winter, spring, summer or fall, no one will ever catch that man working.'

'I don't like your mother,' mumbled Barnaby.

'Barnaby Gaunt!' Christie was horrified that her saintly mother should be criticised. 'Don't you say a word against my mother. She works so hard for me. And I'm going to go to university. She says so. Then, if I ever get stuck marrying a drunk like MacNab, I won't have to work in hospitals. I'll be a teacher and able to go back teaching. My mother says so.'

'I still don't like her. I kind of like MacNab, though. Give me another sandwich and tell me more.'

'They're all gone. Let's start on the tarts. No more to tell. That's all. He's always promising he'll quit drinking. Going on the wagon, and straightening out. My mother says that man will straighten out when a snake does, and nobody ever stopped drinking in a beer parlour.'

She sighed and looked at Barnaby quizzically, then continued.

'He's kind of nice, though. He never gets mad about anything. My mother does because she's got to work so hard. When MacNab does work, he's a longshoreman and he makes good money. My mother says we could of had a lovely home and money in the bank and she'd be twenty years younger if he weren't a drunk.'

'What's he look like?'

'Like me. My mother says it's sort of a pity, but she'd rather I looked like him than was like him. I'm just like her in everything else. She says so.'

Barnaby took a swig of raspberry vinegar and sat staring over the quiet, daisy-strewn meadow.

'Christie,' he said finally, 'why don't they get a divorce if they don't live together, then maybe your mother could marry again, and you could have a real family, with both a mother and father, like other kids.'

Christie pondered gravely before replying.

'Well,' she said, 'they can't get a divorce. My mother says that the one thing she can say for MacNab is he's never looked at another woman since the day she married him. She could have him put in jail for not supporting the child, that's me, but she says the disgrace isn't worth it, and he wouldn't earn any more money in jail than out. She says at the rate he's going he'll end up there anyhow, and no one is going to say she helped put her child's father behind bars.'

'Your mother—'

'My mother is *always* right. She's Highland Scotch, not like MacNab, he's only a Canadian. She says her family never forget a friend or forgive an enemy. Or maybe it's the other way around. Come on. Let's go.'

She sprang to her feet and began prancing through the meadow, leaving Barnaby to pack up the baskets.

'You come back and help!'

But Christie only laughed teasingly and ran away.

Looking like a brace of timid and very clean angels, Barnaby and Christie knocked on Lady Syddyns's front door.

The old woman, dressed now in a yellow silk tea gown, with a string of amber beads swinging from her neck to her hips, opened the door almost immediately.

'Come in, children, come in. I'm very pleased to see you.'

Her withered, diamond-laden old hands caressed their shining heads as she drew them in.

'And how is Mrs Brooks?' she asked Barnaby.

'Pretty good,' he replied, 'but her heart bothers her sometimes.'

'Glad to hear it, glad to hear it,' she said, and then remembered to switch on her hearing aid. 'Well, I hope you're both really hungry.'

Although the children had been in her hall, they had never seen her drawing room.

They stepped back four generations when they entered it, and looked about them in wonder.

Christie had spent all the years she remembered in that clinically colourless apartment, while Barnaby's life had been lived in starkly efficient boarding schools and starkly modern hotels.

This room was as nostalgic and lovely as an old Victorian valentine and the children turned beaming faces to Lady Syddyns.

'Oh, it's so pretty,' sighed Christie.

Barnaby sniffed the air like a young, curious animal, for a potpourri of roses and beeswax drifted about him. He smiled.

'It smells nice here,' he said politely.

'I'm glad you like it,' said Lady Syddyns. 'I'll show you around later. Now sit down while I prepare tea.'

The children, realising it would be rude to appear too anxious to see the gun collection, seated themselves shyly on the edges of two chintz-covered sofas before the white marble fireplace.

'Isn't it lovely?' whispered Christie, when the old lady had left them.

Barnaby nodded.

They stared at the rug, a pale, silky Oriental carpet which shone as though woven on a fairy loom.

'Look,' said Barnaby, pointing, 'a piano.'

Standing before the French doors, the piano was about three feet high, square, and almost as big as a pool table.

Made of gleaming lemonwood, it stood on massive, carven legs.

The French doors were open, and from the terrace a large hairy hand which had pushed the drapes aside, disappeared.

'I never saw one like that before. Look at all the elephants on top,' said Christie. She arose and stared at them curiously, a herd, carved from ebony and with ivory toenails and tusks. The largest was two feet high and his companions marshalled down to one half the size of Christie's thumbnail.

Delighted, the children gazed about the room which was filled with curios and antiques.

'You know,' said Christie, 'when I've got my million dollars, I'm going to have a house like this.'

She looked at Barnaby with affection. 'I'll have you over for tea,' she added magnanimously, 'and you can eat all the cake you want.'

From his gilt frame over the fireplace, Major-General Sir Adrian Syddyns, K.B., O.B.E., gazed icily down at them.

'Look, I wonder who that is?'

'It must be Sir Adrian,' whispered Barnaby. 'That's a Bengal Lancer's uniform he's wearing, and Mr Brooks said he got to be a knight killing innocent blacks in India.'

During his retirement on the Island, Sir Adrian had not been beloved by the other Islanders.

He had been a young man, and an exceedingly handsome one, when the portrait was painted, and the children stood spellbound by that overbold, hawk-nosed visage.

The sculptured lips had an arrogant sneer, and it was easy to imagine that Sir Adrian had not endeared himself to twice-born, haughty Brahman princes or self-indulgent Mogul Maharajas.

'I don't like him,' whispered Barnaby, staring at the portrait.

'Me either.'

They gazed rudely back. Stubborn, bullet-headed, yellow-haired Barnaby, only three generations removed from stolid Yorkshire plowmen, could be as uncompromising as Sir Adrian.

Christie drew her mouth into the smallest possible mean little purse and deliberately turned her back on Sir Adrian.

She may have been the daughter of an ineffectual alcoholic, but on the distaff side a host of ragged, unforgiving Highland chieftains, no novices at arrogance themselves, whispered insistently that she was as good, if not better than any Sassenach soldier.

Lady Syddyns, bearing a large silver tray, returned. She glanced up at the portrait.

'That's Sir Adrian, my late husband.'

She put the tray on an inlaid table, then held out her hands to the children.

'While the tea is steeping, I'll show you some of the things Sir Adrian and I collected. We lived in India for many years.'

The tour included endless tales of Government House balls and hill stations, of Simla and Poona, of Afghan warriors and the indefatigable Sir Adrian.

The children smiled politely at the carved sandalwood chests. They played reverently with the ostrich plumes and fan which had been Lady Syddyns's when she was presented at the court of Queen Victoria. They feigned interest in brass jars, lacquered trays and jade chessmen.

The stories would have been fascinating at any other time, for the children could almost feel the heat from fierce Bengal skies as they exchanged secret and dismal glances. The unsolved problem of the gun still loomed before them.

Only when Lady Syddyns finally led them into the hall and pointed to a sword hanging on the wall did they prick up their ears like a pair of fox cubs.

'His dress sword, the very one you saw in the portrait.'

She lifted it down and let the children handle it. It was, Barnaby decided regretfully, far too heavy for him to wield on Uncle.

Six more steps and they were in the library, their eyes sparkling and their fingers itching, for here before them were leopard skins, spears, assegais, bows, arrows. And guns, guns, guns!

Elephant guns, tiger guns, big guns, little guns, slender guns, fat double-barrelled guns, antique flintlock guns, guns dating from the Crimean War, the Afghan wars, the Sudanese wars and the Boer War. There were handmade guns from the Khyber hills, chased with silver; there were hunting guns with carved stocks and dueling pistols with ivory handles.

'Oh, Lady Syddyns,' cried Barnaby with delight, 'they're beautiful!'

Then a sobering thought struck him.

'Have you got bullets for them?' he asked with a disarming smile.

'Oh, my goodness, no,' said Lady Syddyns. 'I'd be afraid to have a loaded gun in the house, my dear. What if it went off? Besides, these guns are all so old that they haven't made bullets to fit them for years and years and years.'

Barnaby hid his despair. He was an intelligent boy with a mechanical mind, and he knew that every different-sized gun fired a different-sized bullet, and they couldn't be interchanged. And there were *no* bullets for *any* of these lovely guns.

'You're hungry,' declared Lady Syddyns, noticing their resigned expressions, and she dragged them back to the drawing room.

The children looked with awe at the huge silver tray and the Crown Derby tea service. A plate was heaped with cucumber sandwiches, the bread paper-thin, and the crusts cut off.

The crustless bread struck Christie as the height of elegance.

The old lady looked at the serious little girl.

'Would you like to pour?'

'Could I?' Christie bounced up and down on the edge of the sofa with excitement.

Smiling, the old woman pointed to the tray. 'I would be delighted if you would. Barnaby, you may hand the sandwiches.' Christie laid a silver apostle spoon beside each of the eggshell china cups, and with the air of a duchess, poured.

'Milk and sugar, Lady Syddyns?'

'One lump, please.'

Christie had trouble with the sugar tongs but finally managed and graciously handed Lady Syddyns her tea.

'Milk and sugar, Barnaby?'

Barnaby looked puzzled.

'You know I take both.'

Christie gave him a furious look and unceremoniously dumped his accustomed four lumps in with her fingers.

Barnaby passed the cucumber sandwiches.

'Take two,' he said to Lady Syddyns. She did.

Christie began refilling the teacups, and, although there was no breeze, the drapes stirred slightly.

Suddenly the magnificent china teapot, so beautifully coloured with blue and gold and maroon, slipped from her fingers and smashed to a hundred pieces on the silver tray.

The pupils of Christie's eyes were enormous and the muscles of her jaw and mouth quivered.

The old lady looked at her in alarm.

'My dear,' she said, 'you mustn't worry because you have broken the teapot, it isn't important. As a matter of fact, I have far more teapots than I need.'

She sat next to Christie and placed her arm about the child's trembling shoulders.

Christie sat silent and motionless.

'Now, now,' said Lady Syddyns, 'I'm an old woman and soon I'll be going and I can't take my teapot with me.'

She stood up.

'I'm going to make fresh tea and I shall be back in a minute.'

When she had gone, Barnaby thrust out his truculent lower lip.

'For Pete's sake, what's the matter with you? She said it was all right.'

Christie sniffed and gave him a very odd look.

When Lady Syddyns returned, she was bearing a silver teapot.

'I'd like to see you break this,' she said with a chuckle as she rapped Christie on the head with her diamond rings.

Christie rose to the occasion with a faint smile and finished pouring the tea. Lady Syddyns chatted on and kept the conversation from being a strain, but Christie was subdued for the remainder of the visit.

As they were leaving, the old lady gave them each a present, a snuff-box for Barnaby and a tiny silver vinaigrette for Christie.

In her garden she cut them an armful of her most beautiful roses, and as she kissed them goodbye she made them promise they would visit her again.

They nodded gratefully, then walked slowly down the dusty lane.

When they were around the bend of the road, Barnaby turned to Christie with a scowl.

'Why did you have to make such a fuss about breaking the teapot? You never even said you were sorry, just sat there with that funny look on your face.'

Christie handed him the armful of roses and leaned against a tree.

It was a shockingly pale, frightened little girl who stared at Barnaby.

'I saw him,' she said tonelessly.

'Who?' asked Barnaby.

'Your uncle. He was looking in through the French doors, just behind the piano. You and Lady Syddyns had your backs to him. He took off his dark glasses and laughed. His eyes! I've never seen anything like them! And then he rolled them way up, till only the whites showed, just like Little Orphan Annie.'

Barnaby sat down suddenly, the roses spilling from his arms.

He was speechless for a few moments, then: 'Yes, that's what he does to scare me. Now you really believe me about what he's like?'

'Yes, but why? Why? And why me?'

Barnaby lowered his head. 'He's after you too now.'

Christie picked up the roses.

'The sooner we kill him the better,' she said. 'Come on, we'd better be going. Mr and Mrs Brooks and Auntie will want to hear all about how it was at Lady Syddyns's. Don't say anything about me breaking the teapot.'

'Okay.' Barnaby lowered his head again, then looked up at her and touched her arm lightly.

'I'm sorry, Christie.'

Christie took a deep breath.

'It isn't your fault,' she said. 'You couldn't help it that he married your aunt.'

They were silent as they walked home.

13

'SERGEANT!'

Mr Brooks was calling from the porch of the store.

'Sergeant, your package from London came in on yesterday's boat!'

Sergeant Coulter changed his stately military pace and
almost ran to the store. When Mr Brooks handed him
the parcel, the Mountie's face broke into a pleased, boyish
smile.

'Thank you,' he said. 'It's a book written by a friend of
mine, an archaeologist. We were POWs together.'

Mr Brooks watched the policeman walk toward the dock.
How like his father Albert had become.

Mr Brooks remembered Albert and the old Sergeant-
Major coming into the store when the top of Albert's head
barely reached the counter. The little fellow would look
longingly at the gum and horseshoe all-day suckers and
then turn silently to the old Sergeant-Major. The old soldier
would shake his head. They were as poor as church mice,
eking out a frugal living on the Sergeant-Major's Imperial
Army pension.

Mrs Coulter died when the boy was four, but the old soldier kept Albert neat, and his black, steel-capped boots were polished even if they had holes in the soles.

He and Dickie were the same age, or had been, although one never would have guessed it. As Mrs Brooks said, Albert had always been so big for his age.

Mr and Mrs Brooks had not lived behind the store then, but in their own cottage, the one that Major Murchison-Gaunt rented now.

And Dickie had been alive.

The two boys had never been close, but somehow they had always been together, because they had both, even then, been odd men out.

Many of the boys were sent back to the old country for schooling, but Albert and Dickie belonged to the social strata that attended the village school. It was used to store fire-fighting equipment now.

He remembered Albert calling for Dickie on the way to school, knocking timidly on the door, too shy to come in, and Dickie, with a jam-smeared face, seated at the kitchen table, eating his breakfast.

Albert was always early.

When he was finally coaxed in, Albert stood staring tongue-tied down at his shining boots, although he answered politely enough when spoken to. The old Sergeant-Major brought him up well.

Mr and Mrs Brooks encouraged Albert to be with Dickie; that way Dickie was not teased so mercilessly by the other boys.

Perhaps they had tried too hard to shield their boy, but they had done what they thought was best; and in the end, what difference had it made?

But Dickie had been safe enough with Albert. Even then Albert seemed to have the policeman's instinct for law and order, for protection of the weak. He wasn't aggressive, but there was a hardness behind his shy exterior, and boys who pushed him around were beaten by Albert, who then wiped his hands on the seat of his patched trousers and went quietly on his way, making neither friends nor enemies. A lonely little boy who walked dutifully beside the tall old Sergeant-Major, the Punch-cartoon Sergeant-Major, with his ramrod back and waxed pointed moustaches. A self-contained man, like his son, somehow cut off from the rest of humanity, wanting but unable to make contact or small talk.

Sergeant Coulter paused when he reached the war memorial. A forlorn figure was sitting hunched on the granite step, its pointed chin on its knees and its shoulders looking pathetically small.

'Hello,' he said. 'What's your trouble?'

Christie turned her pixie face to him, the big grey eyes disconsolate.

'I haven't got anybody to play with.'

'Where's your little pal?' The Mountie, in a rare mood of companionship, sat down beside her, his precious book laid carefully across his knees.

'He's visiting his uncle until tomorrow morning. Did you get a present?'

'Yes, a book.' He wondered what to say next.

'Well,' he said finally, 'it's going to be a real scorcher today.'

The wise, black-lashed grey eyes looked at him without comprehension.

'Your name's not there.' She jerked her thumb to the marble shaft at her back.

'I know,' he replied drily.

'Were you in the war?'

He nodded. Now it was beginning, the third degree kids always gave you if you treated them like human beings.

'Did you kill anybody?'

'Of course not,' he lied.

Her eyes were unbelievably clear.

'I bet you did.'

He didn't answer her. Instead, he took out a package of cigarettes and, absent-mindedly, nearly offered her one.

She was now conducting the interrogation in earnest.

How many? Did they cry? Did you cry? What did it feel like? You know, killing people. With a gun? Do you ever think of them now? Do you suppose they are in heaven? Did Germans go to heaven? The same one as us?

'I don't know, I forget. I don't know. Maybe.'

'How come?'

'How come what?'

'You know, how come you didn't get killed like everybody else?'

'Just sheer luck,' he replied. 'Whether it was good or bad, I can't say. Maybe I hadn't suffered enough and fate spared me for you and his lordship.'

'Who's that?'

'Barnaby.'

She liked that little joke and laughed heartily, then, mumbling, she prepared to pull out the pin in the grenade.

'What did you say? I can't hear you.'

'Oh,' she was vague, 'just about what Mrs Rice-Hope said.'

He leaned toward her, his eyes only a few inches from her face.

'Well, what *did* she say?'

Her eyes were innocent.

'We had tea at Lady Syddyns's. I bet you didn't know that, did you?'

'No. What did she say?'

'I bet you don't know what else we did.'

Sergeant Coulter replied, not unnaturally, that no, he didn't.

'We had tea with Mr and Mrs Rice-Hope at Benares. Barnaby and me. Last Wednesday. We had chocolate cake.'

'Yes, yes.' He was impatient.

'How did you know we had chocolate cake? Barnaby ate six pieces and then he threw up and Mrs Rice-Hope put a cold cloth on his head.'

Sergeant Coulter tried to possess his soul with patience. He hated questioning juveniles. If you looked sideways at the little bastards they burst into interminable tears. Tears that made sympathetic old magistrates cast cold eyes on big cruel Mounties.

'What *did* she say?'

'Oh, you mean about you?'

He swallowed hard.

'Yes.'

'About you being handsome?'

'I don't know, do I, until you tell me?' He gritted his teeth.

'I'll bet you did. Kill people in the war.'

'What about me being handsome?'

'She thinks you are.' She gave him a delightful smile. 'I do too.'

'Did she say that?'

Christie nodded.

'But why?'

'Because I asked her. I said, "Mrs Rice-Hope, don't you think Sergeant Coulter's handsome?" '

He leaned closer. 'Yes?'

'That's what she said. Yes. He's nice too, don't you think? He's got awfully thin legs, but he's nice. He took us swimming. She hasn't.'

'Hasn't what?'

'Got thin legs.' She paused for breath and pointed to the plane. 'What kind of plane is that?'

Sergeant Coulter's head was reeling. If she ever fell afoul of the law, he fervently hoped to God it would never be his lot to question her.

'It's a De Havilland Beaver. Did Mrs Rice-Hope say anything else?'

'Yes. Do they cost a lot of money?'

'Yes,' said Sergeant Coulter. 'What else?'

'How much?'

'Oh, I don't know,' he sighed wearily, 'about eighty or ninety thousand dollars, I guess. Did she say anything else?'

'Yes, but it's a secret. I'll tell you another secret though.'

She beckoned him down and whispered.

He straightened up.

'What did he do?'

She whispered again.

'What do you mean! Now look here, you quit this. He can take off his glasses if he wants. And if you don't want to look at him, don't.'

She shrugged.

'All right. I won't tell you any more then. But the aeroplane and all the money is really Barnaby's and when he gets the money he's going to give me a million ... '

She stopped and put her hand over her mouth.

'Don't tell Barnaby I said anything.'

'Don't worry, I won't. I've got to be going now.'

As he took a step she put her hand on the holster of his gun.

'Don't touch that!' he said sharply. 'Now or any other time.'

She nodded.

He should never have sat down and started talking to her. The golden head was bouncing by his elbow.

'I don't, do you, Sergeant Coulter?'

'Don't what?' he said irritably. It was like trying to get rid of a friendly puppy.

'I don't like Barnaby's Uncle Sylvester.'

'You run along home now,' he said.

'Okay. He's a real wicked uncle.'

He stopped.

'Now look here, it's not nice to say things like that about people. You remember what I say, and run along now.'

She turned and ran back to the store. From the porch she waved to him in a friendly manner.

He shook his head as he strode back to the launch. Kids! Well, it served him right for starting the conversation. They were all the same.

And then a pleasant glow suffused his body. *She* thought he was handsome. Oh, the little girl wasn't bad. Imagination too lively, that's all. Still, she shouldn't tell stories like that. Saying Barnaby's uncle had done something awful, he had taken off his long pause glasses and she had seen his long pause eyes. Innocent men had been sent to prison because little girls started nasty rumors.

She was right about Dudley. He was a damned nice fellow.

Albert felt honourable liking Dudley Rice-Hope. It helped balance the scales and the incontestable fact that he was in love with Dudley Rice-Hope's wife.

He wondered, on his way to Benares, if he would catch a glimpse of her there.

The police launch was cutting past the arbutus point, and looking up, Sergeant Coulter could see the Brookses' cottage. He lifted his binoculars and swept them in an arc over the place. Everything seemed in order. Uncle, Barnaby, sitting on the front porch. Uncle waved, then, as if prompted, Barnaby did. Sergeant Coulter raised a hand in greeting.

That evening he began his weekly letter to her, the precious book unwrapped and at his elbow, and the soft slap, slap of the waves against the hull making him feel contented and drowsy.

The little girl told me today that you said you thought I was handsome. She doesn't always stick to the truth, but in this case, I hope she has.

I finally got my copy of Fascinating Fragments of Etruscan Pottery *from Professor Hobbs. He wrote an inscription to me in it. It's a wonderful book, with marvellous colour illustrations. Speaking of Hobbs, by the way, I must write to him. Brooks tells me that the boy's uncle was at Colditz. Hobbs was finally sent there from our Stalag. I don't suppose the name Colditz means anything to you, but that's where they sent the bad boys, mostly officers, but in Hobbs's case they made an exception. The veteran escapers and the ones who wouldn't accept discipline, or, as the Jerries called them, the incorrigibles, were sent there. Hobbs, being an archaeologist, just had to dig. Force of habit, I suppose. He dug himself out of our camp four times before they sent him to Colditz. Even Hobbs couldn't dig himself out of that place. It was supposed to be escape-proof, a huge medieval castle set on a rock mountain, walls twenty feet thick and all that sort of thing. I'd like to have a chat with Murchison-Gaunt about it, but old Brooks says he can't, the Major, that is, bear to speak of it. Well, he's not the first POW to feel that way. When we were liberated by the Americans, some of us were taken as witnesses to view the concentration camps. I still can't speak of that.*

I'll close for now and maybe read a chapter of the book before turning in. By the way, I'm sorry the boy threw up, the greedy little hound.

With love,
Albert.

As usual, he folded the letter carefully and put it in his pocket, next to his heart. Then, like a miser with his gold, he opened the book.

Constable Browning raised his mild eyes from the police radio and looked over his shoulder. At his own elbow was a book, *Beekeeping in the Argentine*.

'Say, that looks interesting, Sergeant,' he said. 'Can I have a look at it?'

'It's not something to be taken lightly, like your damned beekeeping or Bright's disease. Where do you get those crazy books, anyhow?'

'Oh, at the library. Mrs Rice-Hope's a volunteer worker, and she puts aside the interesting ones for me.'

That, of course, was different. He would have to read some of those himself.

He opened the book and pointed proudly to the inscription.

'To my dear friend, E. A. Coulter,
with kindest regards from
Percival Hobbs.'

'See? It should be A. E., of course. He's a professor and he wrote this book. We were together overseas. You know, archaeology is really fascinating, it's like detective work. Hobbs is busy now trying to decipher the Etruscan language. It's never been broken. It's like decoding, only much more difficult.'

He flipped through the book and stopped at two full-page colour illustrations.

Two magnificent terracotta Etruscan warriors, with raised weapons, stood on guard.

'You see these boys? They're in the Metropolitan Museum of Art in New York. The statues are over seven feet high. I've got a month's leave coming in September, and I'm going there to see them. Next year I hope to get to Rome, maybe help Hobbs on a dig. I've never been in on a field party, but he says I'm welcome.'

The young constable looked impressed.

'That's really something, isn't it? I guess you know pretty well all there is to know about these Etruscans, eh?'

'I know quite a bit,' said Albert modestly. 'All from books, of course. Hobbs taught a course in archaeology in the prison camp, and he says I'm a born archaeologist. You need the same qualities as a policeman, he says, patience, intelligence and persistence.'

'That's us,' said Constable Browning blithely, 'we always get our man.'

Sergeant Coulter gave him a reproving glance. Archaeology was hardly a subject for levity.

The nasal, staccato voice of the police radio cut in.

'Gale warnings all through the straits,' repeated Constable Browning. 'I wonder if it will bring rain? We could do with some.'

The door of Uncle's cottage was open, and Constable Browning stood hesitant, wondering how to announce his presence.

A soothing voice, soft as the summer breeze, wafted on the silent evening air.

'You are very tired, Barnaby. Your eyes are heavy. You can't keep them open. You are falling asleep, Barnaby. Soon you will be asleep.'

Puzzled, Constable Browning reached in and knocked on the open door.

Uncle, clad in his white silk kimono, padded around the corner, appearing so suddenly that Constable Browning took a step back.

'Good evening, Constable. I didn't hear you coming up the path. Come in, sir, come in.'

Constable Browning's tolerant eyes fell upon Barnaby, sitting drowsily by the fireplace.

'Hello, Barnaby.'

'Stand up when Constable Browning addresses you, Barnaby, and say good evening.'

Without effort, Uncle lifted Barnaby to his feet.

'Good evening, Constable Browning,' said Barnaby.

'Really, Constable, children these days- ' Uncle sighed and patted Barnaby's head. 'He used to have very nice manners.'

Constable Browning smiled at the sleepy little boy, then turned to his uncle.

'We didn't know if you had a battery radio here and we just got a storm warning. They're expecting gale-force winds all down the straits. We're protected here, but Sergeant Coulter thought you might want to put an extra anchor on your plane.'

'Thank you, Constable. Thank you very much indeed. May I offer you a drink for your trouble?'

'No, thank you, Major.' The young Mountie touched the brim of his hat politely. 'Goodnight, sir.'

Barnaby sat in a high-backed winged chair before the cobblestone fireplace. His uncle sat opposite him, reading.

'Uncle, can I get some new running shoes soon?'

Uncle peered over the top of his book and down to
Barnaby's shoes.

'Good heavens, boy, you do need them, don't you?'

Barnaby's running shoes were too short and he had slit
the rubber toes for comfort.

'I'll pick you up a pair when I'm in town. What size?'

'Five.'

'Very well.'

Uncle went back to his book.

'May I go to bed now, Uncle?'

Uncle looked up absently.

'Are you tired, my dear?'

Barnaby nodded.

'Perhaps you'd like a glass of milk and a biscuit before
retiring, Barnaby?'

Barnaby looked confused.

'I - yes - no - no, thank you.'

'Come now, Barnaby, indecision is the hallmark of a
mediocre mind. Now, Barnaby, think carefully. Would you
like a glass of milk and a biscuit?'

'No, thank you, Uncle.' Barnaby rose and got as far as
the door.

'Oh, Barnaby, come here.'

Barnaby returned and stood before his uncle.

'My dear boy, you haven't said goodnight. Sometimes
I fear I'll never make a gentleman out of you, Barnaby.'

Barnaby said goodnight and got as far as the door again.

'Oh, Bar-na-beeee.'

Barnaby stopped and turned.

'Yes, Uncle?'

Uncle crooked a finger and Barnaby returned.

'Barnaby, I was always taught to shake my father's hand when I retired.'

Barnaby, who knew Uncle's little games only too well, extended a trembling hand. He had never yet won a set with Uncle.

'That's better, my boy.'

He got to the door again.

'Bar-na-beeeeee!'

Barnaby took a deep breath and closed his eyes.

'Did you say you did or did not want milk and a biscuit?'

'No, thank you.'

Uncle smiled. 'They're on a tray beside your bed. The milk will be drunk and the biscuit will be eaten.'

'Yes, sir.'

Barnaby was shaking when he reached the door.

'Barnaby.'

'Uncle, *please!*'

Uncle's voice was no longer soft.

'*Come here!*' he roared.

Barnaby returned.

'Barnaby, you seem to have forgotten Rodney. Poor Rodney. Do you remember Rodney, Barnaby? Poor, poor Rodney. We don't want any more regrettable accidents, do we, Barnaby? And we won't have any, if you do what Uncle tells you.'

His voice was soft and mocking.

'Goodnight, dear boy.'

Unable to believe the game was over, Barnaby stood with bowed head.

'Oh, by the way, Barnaby, you must bring your little friend over some time soon.'

Barnaby's face went scarlet and his hands clutched convulsively.

'She's my friend!' he shouted. 'You never let me have friends. I never had one before. You can't have her! She's mine!'

Uncle was amused.

'I do believe you are jealous, Barnaby. Oh, by the way, you really don't have to have the biscuit and milk, I was only ragging you.'

The wretched child clung to the doorway.

'Oh, just one more thing, Barnaby. Mr Brooks tells me you have been a very good boy since you came to the Island!'

Barnaby screamed and ran to his bed.

'Don't forget your biscuit and milk, dear.'

Chuckling, Uncle went back to his book and his favourite author, the Marquis de Sade.

Constable Browning rubbed his eyes and yawned. He was tired and puzzled.

Sergeant Coulter looked up from his book.

'What's the matter? Coming down with Bright's disease?'

'Constable Browning didn't laugh.

'Sergeant,' he said, 'that Major's a queer duck. There's something creepy about him. I heard him telling him that he was tired and sleepy and couldn't keep his eyes open. He kept repeating it.'

It was Sergeant Coulter's turn to yawn.

'First of all,' he said, 'who was telling who?'

'The uncle was telling the boy. It didn't sound natural, somehow.'

'Browning,' said Sergeant Coulter, stretching, 'look at your watch and tell me the time.'

'Five after ten.'

'All right. What time was it when you were at the cottage?'

'I'd say about a quarter to.'

Sergeant Coulter smiled and stood up.

'It sounds like a reasonable statement to make to a child, this time of night, doesn't it?' He slapped his constable on the back, then, 'You know, you're young yet and new at this game. You'll find, after a few years, that you develop a certain instinct, a sort of sixth sense, about people and things and situations. I'm telling you this for your own good. You've got to have facts. When you are called upon to give evidence in real cases - well - you'd look pretty silly making a statement like that in court, wouldn't you?'

The next day Barnaby was spiteful to Christie and insolent to Mr Brooks.

'Upon my word, I don't know what's got into that boy. I hope he's not coming down with something. Do you think he looks feverish?' said Mr Brooks.

'It's the heat,' said Mrs Brooks, fanning herself. 'It always made Dickie cross. Barnaby should have a nap in the afternoon. Although he looks like a strong child, he really isn't, and he tires easily.'

But when Uncle climbed into his plane and flew to the city for the week, Barnaby was restored to health and good spirits and he apologised to Christie.

Christie looked into his eyes and spoke one word.

'Uncle?'

Barnaby nodded.

There was no more to be said. She understood.

IT WAS BACK to the old grind, the quest for firearms, for Barnaby and Christie. The afternoon, they decided, would be given over to serious business, but after their morning chores they allowed themselves a treat. They would visit their dear One-ear.

One-ear, snoozing peacefully in a ferny dell, heard them before he saw them. Their shrill laughter went through his eardrums like porcupine quills. Pursued as if by the furies, he sought an avenue of escape, but too late, for they were upon him.

'There he is! Did you miss us?' yelled the boy. They flung themselves upon him as if he were an old log.

He settled down moodily, laying his huge flat head on his paws.

'How are you, dear?' The girl gave him a smacking kiss.

Dirty, sticky, dreadful little creatures.

Had he been capable of speech he would have informed them that he felt terrible. His ribs ached, his shoulder was stiff, his missing claw throbbed and he had a pain right below his heart.

Not that anybody cared.

There was also the matter of his nerves. He hadn't slept a wink for two days, just dropping off when they barged in. He had had to force himself to eat lunch, even though it had given him heartburn.

If the dogs or that monstrous police sergeant didn't finish him, his own overwrought, delicate constitution would.

'You'd better watch out, Sergeant Coulter will be here tomorrow,' shouted the boy, who was sitting astride him as if he were a pony.

Why did they have to shout?

The boy flipped over One-ear's head and knelt before him, looking into his mouth.

'Gee, he's got big yellow teeth!'

'That's because he doesn't brush them,' yelled the girl. They shrieked with laughter.

'Quick! Christie, look! I've got my head in the lion's mouth, just like at the circus!'

One-ear gagged with disgust and snarled.

Even his snarls amused them, and they went into more gales of laughter.

When the girl took hold of his tail and draped it about her shoulders, he sprang to his feet with a roar.

She was not frightened.

'I know somebody who's grouchy today,' she declared archly.

'Did you hear what I said about Sergeant Coulter?' asked the boy, rubbing his cheek against the cougar's shoulder.

One-ear turned and yawned rudely in the boy's face.

He sat down squarely, his massive paws splayed. Had they known the fate of the little Indian boy, the author of all his misfortune, they would think twice before taking their liberties.

But no. They would not be frightened. That horror of a boy would only want to know if he'd tasted different from white people, and the girl, with playful reproach, would, as usual, call him a great big naughty kitty cat.

Traps, dogs, guns, hunger, and now in his declining years *them*. The eternal outlaw blinked back the never distant tears. He sank onto his belly and closed his eyes. If he couldn't eat them, he could at least ignore them.

They took it as a sign that a rest was in order for all. They had been running and jumping in the morning heat and now they were tired. Sleepily, they flopped down on him, the boy's head leaning nonchalantly on his shoulder, the girl using his paws as a cushion. They fell asleep almost immediately.

He tried to slide his paws out from under the girl, but she stirred in her slumber, and flinging a slender golden arm carelessly, she bopped him on the end of his flat, tender nose.

He lay immobile so he would not disturb their rest; they were not quite so bad when they were asleep.

They snored sweetly and quietly.

One-ear held his head erect until his neck felt strained, then, sighing, he put his chin delicately on the girl's chest and tried to catch a nap himself.

Fifteen minutes later they woke up and bounded to their feet, completely restored.

'Goodbye, One-ear! You watch out for Sergeant Coulter!'

'Race you down the path!'

They were gone. He'd have to start sleeping in trees, he thought with despair. At his age.

He growled hopelessly and sharpened his razor talons on a handy cedar, ripping the bark off in huge shreds.

And the children, racing merrily through the forest trail, stumbled and almost stepped on the remains of One-ear's lunch.

Horrified but fascinated, they came closer to have a good look.

'Ugh!' said Christie, turning away from a cloud of big blue-bottle flies, 'poor One-ear. I don't know how he can eat anything so awful!'

Barnaby shook his head in sympathy.

'I guess,' he said sadly, 'if you get hungry enough you can eat anything.'

'Well, I'm sure I couldn't get that hungry,' said Christie. 'Come on, let's go. It makes me feel sick.'

'Me too.'

They raced to a stream and were having a cool drink when they were startled to see a large-eyed doe tiptoe to the water.

The animal lowered her beautiful head and sipped daintily. Huge ferns waved gently about her narrow brown brow, and at her trim hooves, trilliums, like white stars, dotted the mossy carpet of the bank. The sun, dappling though the trees, twinkled on the dark waters and the doe's nostrils quivered delicately, as though she were a permanent, but sensitive, living part of the forest landscape.

Then, catching their scent, she moved her nervous ears back and forth in alarm. With two huge springs, she disappeared like a wood nymph.

The children hardly dared breathe in their wonder.

'That's the prettiest thing I ever saw,' whispered Barnaby.

'I could have watched it all day,' said Christie in a hushed voice, 'if only it hadn't seen us.'

It was the sister of One-ear's lunch.

They loved One-ear, and they believed that all One-ear needed to complete his happiness was to accept and return their love.

CHAPTER FOURTEEN

Like the woman enraptured of the drunkard, they were convinced he would change. They would transform him.

One-ear would give up his evil ways and bizarre eating habits. He would, in short, reform, adoring them as they adored him, and he would wax fat on a lovely diet of cinnamon buns and candy, drinking raspberry vinegar ins-tead of blood, and they would all live happily ever after.

With the stubborn blindness of love, they simply refused to believe otherwise.

On his part, One-ear detested them more heartily each time he saw them, and the thought of their gummy little hands and licorice-laden breaths made him wince.

Poor Desmond, who had been driven off earlier with stones and shouts, was invited to join the children in their afternoon pilgrimage to the little church.

They sat, as they always sat in church, quietly and seriously.

It was no use, Christie reported, even trying to get Sergeant Coulter's gun. The same, she imagined, went for Constable Browning's.

Barnaby sat gnawing his lower lip.

'You know,' he said finally, 'we don't have to get the guns they wear around their waists. There are guns on the police launch.'

Christie brightened.

'Yes,' he continued, 'there's a locker there with big guns in it on the launch. Once, when I was on the wharf, I looked in and I saw Constable Browning cleaning them.'

He paused, his face saddened.

'Then he put them back in the locker and locked it with a big padlock.'

Disgruntled, Christie sagged against poor Desmond.

'Well, that's out.' Then she had one of her ideas.

Only last week Barnaby had fixed Mrs Brooks's old phonograph which had been silent for twenty years. He was remarkably adept with anything mechanical. Christie, who was all thumbs, looked upon it as a form of magic.

'Listen,' she said. 'It's easy. You'll just have to learn how to pick locks. Mr Brooks has a drawer full at the store. You had better start practising now. Get a hairpin; that's how they do it in the movies.'

Barnaby agreed to start that very afternoon.

Ah, but there was another problem.

Sergeant Coulter, he said, always left the launch when it docked at the Island. But, and it was a big but, Constable Browning stuck to the boat like a barnacle.

'Well, we can't murder him too,' said Christie.

He was not in a class with their wonderful Sergeant, but the children were fond of gentle Constable Browning. Besides, he was bigger than Sergeant Coulter or even Uncle.

'I know!' Barnaby was radiant. 'You fall off the wharf. Constable Browning will have to jump in and save you. While he is, I'll pick the lock and get the gun and some bullets. We'll have Desmond standing right there on the wharf, and I'll hand him the gun and he can hide it in the wharf shed. Then, at night we'll sneak down and get it and put it in a safe place.'

Christie thought for a minute and then turned to him with an alarmed scowl.

'I'm not going to fall off any wharf! I can't swim.'

'You'll have to,' said Barnaby. 'I can't because I'll have to pick the lock. You're too much of a dummy to learn.'

He paused and added reassuringly: 'There's nothing to worry about. They give people medals for jumping off wharves and saving kids. I'll bet Constable Browning would love to.'

Christie remembered Uncle's blazing eyes, like peepholes into hell. Anything was better than falling into his hands, and reluctantly she agreed.

Suddenly Barnaby shook his head and leaned on Desmond's other shoulder. There were times when it seemed as if every man's hand was against them.

'It's no good,' he said, his lower lip thrust out.

'Why not?'

He leaned across Desmond and looked her straight in the eye.

'Christie, even if we do get the gun, and even if we do kill Uncle, what's the use? If Sergeant Coulter finds out, he'll hang us.'

An awful vision of a noose swinging from a handy tree and Sergeant Coulter standing at the foot of it, looking very cross indeed, flashed before Christie's eyes.

'Well, what are we going to do? We can't just sit around and *wait* for Uncle to kill us.'

Sensing her distress, poor Desmond turned his empty, lucid sweet stare upon her.

Christie rubbed her head affectionately on his shoulder and then nearly leaped from the pew. She had another idea. Clapping her hands together, she cried,

'I've got it!'

'What?' asked Barnaby.

'*We'll blame it on Desmond!*'

Barnaby looked at her with honest admiration. There were times when she seemed almost inspired.

'I never would of even thought of that. Golly, that's a wonderful idea!'

They skipped all the way back to the goat-lady's, holding Desmond's hands between them.

They helped carry milk, bread, butter and fresh garden vegetables over to his shack for him. Nothing was too good for their friend, poor Desmond.

The next afternoon as they stood on the wharf watching the police launch dock, Barnaby turned to Christie.

Picking locks was, he said, as easy as pie.

Poor Desmond was posted beside the shed as arranged, and it was a pair of contented little conspirators who smiled innocently at Sergeant Coulter as he strode up the dock.

In the launch they could see Constable Browning lounging and reading a book.

Things went like clockwork, although at the last minute Christie balked at jumping and Barnaby had to push her.

He marked the spot by pointing his finger at the rising bubbles and then ran for Constable Browning.

Constable Browning threw down his copy of *Astronomy Made Easy* and raced to the dock edge.

'Where! Where!' he shouted.

Barnaby looked stupidly at the water and then at his finger. The bubbles were all gone.

He pointed in the general direction and began to scream.

Fully clothed, even to his hat, the Mountie dived and Barnaby watched the flashing spurs disappear into the murky depth. The hat came up and presently Constable Browning followed.

Barnaby was now hysterical. He pointed to the left.

'Over there, I think,' he sobbed.

Like a military Undine, and this time not empty-handed, Constable Browning surfaced again.

Sergeant Coulter arrived in time to haul his dripping constable and a sodden, yellow-haired bundle onto the dock.

When Christie regained consciousness she was half-covered with a blanket, while two panic-stricken, scarlet-faced, sweating policeman performed the Holger-Neilson method of respiration.

She brought up buckets of foamy, bitter brine, and was finally carried, her head rolling listlessly on Sergeant Coulter's shoulder, to the store, where Mr and Mrs Brooks immediately put her to bed.

She spent the night in Barnaby's bed, while Barnaby slept in her little carved cot at the goat-lady's.

Just before she was tucked in finally for the night, Barnaby leaned over and whispered: 'Bad luck! It wouldn't have worked anyway. I got into the boat okay, but it was a combination lock.'

Christie looked at him fiercely.

'Listen!' she hissed, 'The next time somebody has to fall off the wharf it's your turn.'

The next day she still felt rather ill, and leaned shakily on Barnaby's shoulder as they left the store to play.

Sergeant Coulter was waiting for them.

'I want a word with you, sonny.'

'Me?' said Barnaby.

'What were you doing on the launch yesterday?'

'The police launch?' asked Barnaby.

'That's right. I saw you as I was running down the wharf.'

'Oh, then,' said Barnaby. 'I was looking for a life jacket to throw to Constable Browning, in case he couldn't swim.'

The Mountie nodded and patted Barnaby's shoulder. It was a sensible thing to do. The boy had his wits about him.

But their session with Sergeant Coulter was not over.

'You are both to stay off the wharf. You understand? And don't either of you ever set foot on that police launch.'

He took each of them by an arm and led them to where there was a view of Uncle's cottage.

He pointed across the little cove.

'You see those pilings away over there? About a quarter of a mile from the beach at the foot of the cottage?'

The children nodded.

'There are only a few dangerous places on the Island. That's one of them. It's called Death Beach. You don't go there, you don't go on the wharf, and you don't go in the forest. Okay? You understand?'

They nodded.

'And we don't go on the police launch,' added Christie.

Sergeant Coulter looked at her quickly to see if she was being cheeky, but she was merely making a statement.

'Good kids.' Sergeant Coulter patted their heads and gave each of them a nickel.

The bit about the police launch was rather redundant, for, as Barnaby later remarked, it was impossible to get on the launch unless they went on the wharf.

They had already been to the forest many times, so they ignored that particular piece of advice.

And it had never occurred to them to go to Death Beach. It was too close to Uncle's cottage for comfort.

They recalled vaguely that both Mr Brooks and the goat-lady had warned them never to go near it.

Now they were curious about Death Beach and stood for a long time staring across the water. What a sinister name!

There was a steep cliff crowned by twisting, peeling arbutus trees. At the foot of the cliff they could see an old rowboat, turned upside down and looking like a dead whale.

In the water were four rows of pilings, standing out like rotten teeth. On the rest of the beaches of the Island the waves pounded regularly, but on Death Beach they swirled and eddied, and there was a dull boom-boom resounding over the waters as a loose log pounded against the pilings. Past it they could see Uncle's cosy cottage.

They asked Mr Brooks about Death Beach.

Yes, he said, Sergeant Coulter was quite right to remind them they must never go there. It was the most treacherous spot on the Island. The pilings were the remains of a jetty that had been built many years before by one of the first settlers on the Island. Why he had picked that spot nobody knew, except that the water was so deep there perhaps he thought large boats could anchor.

It had always been called Death Beach. Even the Indians had called it that in their own language, long before the white man came.

There were strange riptides and currents in the waters of Death Beach and they must never, never, never go near that beach.

ONCE, to the Pacific Coast Indians, the passages of water between the islands had been like the canals of Venice. Through them the giant, lynx-eyed aristocrats, the Haidas, had paddled a thousand miles south in their sixty-foot war canoes, on slave-raiding sorties.

At one time they had all passed through here, Nootkas, Songhees, Kwakiutls, Salish, dressed like Homeric heroes in their barbarian regalia. With their proud helmets of cedar and copper, tasseled with ermine, their capes of sable and mink, their garments of cedar bark-cloth dyed in harsh primary colours, and their ceremonial robes of dog hair woven with the tufts of the mountain goat, they had paddled through the bright straits, and sometimes they stopped.

On the very beaches where the children now played so innocently, the warriors had paused to gorge themselves on tyee salmon. Their dugouts, bearing their haughty clan crests, the emblems of the raven, the otter, the killer whale, were dragged up to the beach, while their owners prepared for feasting.

On these beaches they had dug pits, piled them with stones and heated them until they were white hot. They set out their five-foot wooden cooking vessels, carved with beaked thunderbirds, and filled them with water. Then they dropped the hot stones in and boiled their repasts, ungutted salmon, clams, mussels, venison and berries. Their sauce and their favourite delicacy was the foul oolichan oil, which no white man could stomach, and which they relished like manna.

When they were gorged, their drums began a muted, ominous roll. The warriors recited tales of their greatness, their victories in war and their transient glory.

Here, in their potlatches, the symbolic belittling of their friends and enemies by their generosity, they had broken their priceless copper disks, burned their Hudson's Bay blankets, smashed their rifles and joyfully impoverished themselves. Here, with stone clubs they had dispatched their slaves to shame their guests by their largesse.

Here they had been and from here they departed, their tenancy leaving no more mark than an army of ghosts. Only the abandoned goddess D'Sonoqua stood deep in a forgotten village in the forest, carved from the living cedar, her mighty arms outstretched for children.

Only three generations ago the Indian reigned where now Barnaby and Christie played. Two children, innocent of mankind, past or present, children who delighted in finding agates and tiny pink shells and purple starfish and clam holes which spurted like naughty subterranean fairies.

Two children who wandered, happy, brown and busily plotting murder with an insouciance that would have appalled the former savage tenants.

And here, Uncle, from his rocky cliff stronghold, licked his chops and leered as he watched them through high-powered field glasses.

Had they any chance against a wily old pro like Uncle?

If Sergeant Coulter had known more, he would have said no. But both Uncle and Sergeant Coulter underestimated them. Barnaby would never give in and Christie MacNab was a worthy protagonist for any uncle.

Forewarned by her mother, *she* was one little girl who would never be lured into parks or vacant lots. The promise of twenty-five cents or a stick of candy would have been lost upon her. Her strength was as the strength of ten because her heart was pure, because she did not like Uncle and because, in her own uncomplicated way, she rather wanted a million dollars.

The children had several distinct advantages. For one thing, there was no point on the Island from which they could not hear Uncle's plane arriving or departing; consequently they always knew when he was in residence.

Also, their very inexperience helped, for they were not bound by any preconceived principles on the method of murder. The gun, they knew, was the most sensible approach, but they had no personal preference. Had it been feasible, it would have made no difference to them whether hemp, cold steel or poison were used to dispatch Uncle, as long as Uncle was dispatched.

Uncle, backed by a lifetime of experience, had marked preferences. He despised the contrivances he had been forced to use in the past, such as hypnotism, stabbing and monkey wrenches. He was too cunning to stick to the same pattern, but he pined for the days of yore. The supple weighted piano wire had been more than satisfactory during his commando days and as far as he was concerned it still was. Of course, things had to be arranged with finesse, one simply did not go about leaving strangled bodies in one's wake, but then, he was a master in covering his tracks.

There was also the element of chance, and Barnaby and Christie's flip of the coin was just as likely to be heads as Uncle's, as was proved only a few days after their abortive attempt on the police launch.

It was a burning hot morning, and they sat on the step of the war memorial, gazing at the glittering water, still disgruntled over their failure.

A trim yacht, flying the American flag, sailed up to the dock.

The wheels of the gods were beginning to grind.

There was not a soul about, Sergeant Coulter was not expected until the next day, Mr and Mrs Brooks were having their morning tea in the dim little parlour behind the store, and the children were quite free to wander about.

As a party of half a dozen hunters streamed from the yacht onto the wharf, a look passed between Barnaby and Christie. A look of pure telepathy, and Operation Police Launch, a failure, was scrapped.

Without a word Christie slipped silently into the shed on the dock and Operation Yacht began.

'Hey, sonny, is this Benares?'

The party, laden with fishing rods, shining gun cases, binoculars, cameras and valises, filed up to the sturdy boy who stood smiling a welcome to them.

'No, sir,' said Barnaby. 'Benares is four miles southeast.'

'Oh. Well, we'd better pack up again.'

The speaker, a tall, distinguished-looking man, turned to Barnaby again.

'Is there any place I can get cigarettes here?'

'Yes, sir. At the store.' Barnaby pointed it out. 'I'll get them for you, if you like. Are you staying at the lodge at Benares?'

How delightfully polite these Canadian children were. The tall American decided he would have to have a word with his own son when he got home.

'Yes, we are. We've been doing some big-game hunting in Alaska, and we're stopping off for some fishing on our way back.'

Barnaby beamed.

'I hope you catch some. Mr Brooks, he runs the store and I stay with him, he says we have the best salmon fishing in the world. Have you got your bait yet?'

'No.'

Barnaby smiled again.

'Oh, you must get it from Mr Brooks. He has fresh herring bait. And if you get it from Mr Brooks you can fish on the way to Benares. Mr Brooks knows exactly where the salmon are running this morning.'

The tall man laughed and, rumpling Barnaby's hair, asked him if he was in the herring-bait business.

Seeing not a soul about except the boy and being honest men themselves, they left their guns, rods arid cases on the wharf as they accompanied Barnaby to the store.

Ten minutes later, bearing cigarettes and bait, they waved goodbye to the charming, helpful boy who had never been out of their sight for a moment.

Barnaby and Christie danced a gleeful little jig in the village square. Alone, unaided and with no trouble at all they had accomplished what they had expected to be the most difficult part of their mission.

Barnaby decided that after dark he would sneak out of bed, go to the shed, get the gun and hide it in Desmond's shack.

The next morning even Christie awoke early, so eager was she to see the precious prize.

Barnaby got down on all fours and dragged the gun case from under Desmond's cot. With reverent hands he laid it upon the unmade bed, while Christie peered over his shoulder.

Desmond sat unnoticed at the table, his luminous eyes forlorn because he thought they had forgotten to bring him his little treat.

Barnaby unbuckled the ammunition pouch on the side of the case.

'Whew!' He counted the bullets. 'Look, Christie, nine of them. Aren't they big?'

Next he took out the gun. Christie leaned forward to put her hand on the shining barrel, but Barnaby took a step back.

'Don't touch it, stupid. It might be loaded.'

He laid the gun upon the bed and sat looking down at it for a long time. Then he put his hand out and touched the polished walnut stock almost shyly.

'Isn't it beautiful, Christie? I'm going to practise taking it apart now.'

It looked like any other gun to Christie and she turned to poor Desmond.

'Oh, darling,' she said, seeing his crestfallen face, 'you thought we forgot to bring you something nice. Well, we didn't. Look, Desmond, a coffee cake Auntie baked yesterday. We'll put raspberry jam and peanut butter on it and it'll taste even better!'

Singing 'The Big Rock Candy Mountain' she began to prepare their snack.

Barnaby, dismantling the gun and memorising each piece as he did so, turned irritably and told her to shut up.

Christie shrugged and offered him a slice of coffee cake, covered with nuts, raisins, icing, and now peanut butter and jam.

But he was too fascinated by the gun to be interested in food. Lovingly, almost gloatingly, he looked at the parts on the bed, his sharp eyes noting the shape and contours of each piece. Then, confidently and unerringly, he reassembled the gun and turned proudly to Christie.

'I did it. Give me a slice of coffee cake now. I'll practise some more later, then tomorrow, or Thursday, when I'm sure Sergeant Coulter won't be here, I'll try firing it. Just once, to make sure. There are only nine bullets. That'll leave me eight. I can't take a chance of wasting any more or anyone hearing the shot. Give me a bigger piece than that, you and Desmond are one ahead of me. Isn't it beautiful? I'll take it up on the mountain to fire it. That way if anyone hears it, they won't know where the sound is from. Bigger than that, don't be such a hog!'

They sat cramming food into their mouths and feeling very much at peace with the world.

Barnaby, earlier so tense and bad-tempered, was now mellow.

'Christie, what do you want to be when you grow up?'

Christie took a bite out of her last piece of cake, thought the better of it and handed the remainder to poor Desmond. She had eaten too much and she felt sick.

'Rich, I guess.'

'No, I mean besides that. I'm going to be rich, but I'm going to be something else too. I'm going to be a Mountie.'

Christie wiped peanut butter from poor Desmond's chin and turned to Barnaby.

'You won't be rich unless you kill your uncle. And don't forget, you've got to give me a million dollars. I'd like to be a Mountie too, but I suppose girls can't. I think I'll marry Sergeant Coulter instead.'

Barnaby jeered. 'He won't marry you, silly.'

Christie tossed her head. 'You don't know everything.'

'I didn't say I did,' said Barnaby, settling back. 'Tell me more about MacNab.'

'Nope.'

Her mouth was set in that prim little line he hated.

'Why not?'

'Because you won't tell me any more about Uncle.'

Barnaby flushed with anger.

'You wouldn't like to hear any more.'

'I would too.'

'Well, you can't.'

There were times when it was useless to argue with him and Christie knew it. She cleared off the table, then pointed to the gun, which she didn't like.

'Put it away so I can make Desmond's bed.'

'Okay, but hurry. We'd better get a couple of graves done today.'

As Christie straightened the bed an unlovely thought struck her. She turned and stared at Barnaby for a few seconds, then at poor Desmond, who was dozing with his head on his arms.

'You know,' she said, 'if we blame the murder on poor Desmond, maybe Sergeant Coulter will hang him instead of us.'

Barnaby thought that over for a while.

'Well, it's either him or us,' he said with a sigh.

Christie agreed.

They took poor Desmond to the graveyard with them. He was afraid of the little garter snakes that slithered between the paths among the graves, so he sat on the rickety fence with his thumb in his mouth, watching them with gentle, unquestioning eyes.

It was a lovely morning, not so unbearably hot as it had been lately, and when the three left the graveyard the children sniffed the fragrant air happily.

Christie, holding poor Desmond's hand, looked up at him.

'Don't you worry, Desmond. You'll be an angel, of course.'

The ever-agreeable Desmond nodded.

'Do you think, Barnaby,' Christie turned to him, 'do you think Auntie will make a raspberry pie for dinner?'

'No. She baked this morning, and she doesn't bake twice the same day and she didn't bake one this morning. I guess he will be.'

'Will be what?' Christie had dropped Desmond's hand and was skipping after a butterfly.

'An angel.'

Barnaby suddenly burst into roars of laughter.

Christie stopped and turned.

'What's so funny?'

'Gee, Christie, can't you just see poor Desmond with long golden curls and a halo?'

They laughed until their sides ached. Poor Desmond laughed with them, although he didn't know why.

WHILE THE CHILDREN kept themselves busy, Uncle had not been frittering away his time. Far from it, for Uncle had taken an extraordinary interest in gardening. He had bought a big shiny shovel from Mr Brooks, and had spaded up a twenty by twenty plot at the back of the cottage.

He had also purchased two dozen rubbery, listless tomato plants which lay prone in the sun, like guardsmen fainting on parade. Occasionally, when Uncle happened to think of it, he threw the odd bucket of cold water on them.

They were not important, for Uncle's real interest in horticulture lay deep in the gloomy heart of the forest. A pit, six feet deep, five feet long and three feet wide.

Uncle was returning from Mr Brooks's store, where he had had to purchase a new shovel, having broken the shaft of the original in his enthusiasm for his work. He met face to face with Sergeant Coulter who was on his way to his father's cottage for the weekend.

Sergeant Coulter was weary from a day of giving evidence in court. It had been a particularly grisly murder case, and the hours of following the testimony and keeping mentally and physically at attention had left him exhausted.

Sonny Gitskass Charlie, a youth of nineteen, was charged with patricide.

He had hacked his father with an axe and when he was through with his parent he had hacked up the floor.

His half-white mother had fled earlier, taking her younger children with her to hide in the bushes.

His aged grandmother, through an interpreter, testified that when she had barricaded herself in the bedroom Gitskass had tried to break down the door with his axe.

By the time Sergeant Coulter had been called in the father lay dying. The father insisted he had provoked his drunken son and that the youth had acted in self-defence.

Then, at the old lady's prodding, he had admitted he had begged Gitskass not to kill his grandmother. His exact words were, testified Sergeant Coulter, 'I said, Sonny, don't you chop your grandma.'

In the witness stand, Sonny Gitskass Charlie stood sullen and unconcerned. He declared his grandmother was a liar, he had never attempted to kill her, and that he had murdered his father in self-defence.

Sergeant Coulter felt certain the father had lied to protect his son. He believed the old woman, but he had no proof, and the grandmother had heard but not seen the crime.

She was the daughter of a Nootka chief, and when she took the stand she pointed an accusing finger at her grandson. Through her interpreter she declared that Gitskass was just like his great-grandfather, insane and a murderer. He had, she said, killed her favourite son, and since she had sixteen other grandchildren, she could well spare Gitskass and she hoped the law would hang him.

When Sonny Gitskass was led from the courtroom hand-cuffed to two Mounties, he turned his monolithic face to Albert and muttered softly: 'You lie. So does the old woman. I'll get you, horseman.'

The merciless slanted eyes chilled Albert to the bone.

He silently agreed with the old grandmother, Sonny Gitskass was as nutty as they came. For his own future peace of mind, he hoped very much that they would hang Sonny Gitskass Charlie.

When Uncle paused before him, Albert sighed. He was really in no mood to talk, but politeness forced him to stop and smile.

'Nothing like a bit of hard work when you reach forty,' Uncle boomed heartily, patting the shovel. 'Keeps the old waistline down. Ah, but I see you don't have to worry about that yet, Sergeant!'

Sergeant Coulter nodded and eyed the wicked Uncle. Major Murchison-Gaunt with his deep chest looked to him to be in exceedingly good shape. Not an ounce of fat on him, and Albert was an expert in judging such matters.

Albert looked at the brilliant, cloudless sky.

'We could certainly do with some rain,' he ventured. 'It's hard on the gardens.'

'Ah, yes,' Uncle agreed. 'But what a delightful spot this Island is, rain or no rain. Forests, the fields, gardens ... the cottage looking out over the sea ... chambered nautilus and all that. Why, do you know, I put crumbs on the veranda and the squirrels and chipmunks come right up and eat out of my hand. Tame as kittens, cheeky little rascals.'

Albert smiled and nodded.

'Yes, they're cute, aren't they? I had one for a pet when I was a boy.'

He stared at Uncle, and he had a peculiar sensation as he did so. People very often did. It was the thought of the eyes behind the dark glasses. Albert decided it was because Uncle could see him and he couldn't see Uncle. It put him at a disadvantage, somehow.

'My, my, it is warm,' Uncle drew his silken handkerchief from his pocket, shook it and mopped his gleaming brow. A carmined fluff of chipmunk fur floated like down and landed on Sergeant Coulter's immaculate sleeve.

Albert plucked it off absently.

'Yes, it certainly is.' And having exhausted his conversational store, he bade the Major good day.

'Good day, my boy, good day.'

Jolly old Uncle Sylvester strode briskly up the path, whistling 'The Teddy Bear's Picnic'.

When he reached the top of the path he turned and saw that the Mountie was out of sight.

He smiled.

Just plain luck about the girl being on the Island. So much more logical, two children drowning instead of one. Mischievous kiddies, they had already been rescued once, and he'd see they were rescued once again. The third time, they wouldn't come up. Not that they were really going to drown, of course. Bodies had a way of washing back on shore, and it was important that these bodies should never be found.

He was setting the stage carefully. The Islanders would remember them as naughty children who insisted on playing around dangerous waters.

If it had been only Barnaby, even that stupid policeman might put two and two together. This way it very logically added up to five. Claire, Maude, Robert, Barnaby and little what's her name.

Uncle sighed. It wasn't all beer and skittles. He would still continue to get the interest, but since the bodies would never be found, he'd have to wait seven years for the bulk of the estate.

And certainly he had had no idea when he'd picked out this lonely little island, that that idiot officer of the law was an Island boy with an almost pathological affection for his native heath. As a matter of fact he'd always understood that Mounties were posted far from their stamping grounds. They had a reason, he supposed, R.C.M.P. always did, so he'd heard. He sniggered. They probably had Miss Proudfoot tagged as a red spy and the homespun sergeant was keeping her under surveillance.

Nevertheless, the real-estate people had said no electricity, no church services, no doctor. He had assumed that, except in cases of emergency, the police would never visit the Island.

Fortunately one could almost set one's clock by the sergeant.

Well, back to work. He was extremely interested in the transplanting of the huge ferns in the forest. If the root system was not disturbed, the beds dug deeply enough, and if they were watered frequently, they transplanted splendidly.

And the way they grew! Six weeks after putting them on the grave, he probably wouldn't be able to find it himself.

Yes, a great man for gardening was Uncle.

If you go down in the woods today,
You're sure of a big surprise.

He had always liked that song.

Reaching his father's house, Albert first checked the honey-suckle vine. The earth about the roots seemed cracked and parched but the foliage was healthy. He got a rake, and using the handle as a probe he poked deep holes in a circle about the stem. Drawing up buckets of water from the well, he slowly filled the holes until the soil turned from ashgray to black.

It was nearly dusk, he had not eaten since ten o'clock in the morning and, entering the cottage, he looked about absently for something to provide him with a dinner. Opening the cupboard he scanned the meager supply of food and took out a tin of pork and beans.

He had half a mind to eat them cold, to save himself the trouble of lighting the stove, but he decided that that would be slovenly. He would heat the beans and make himself a cup of tea like a civilised man.

Soon a fire was roaring in the stove, the beans were bubbling and the kettle boiling. The room was stifling from the long daytime sun and a mirage of dancing air hovered over the kitchen range.

He opened the windows and the front door which faced directly on the ocean and thankfully breathed in the sea breeze, then, seating himself at the table, he ate without haste or relish. Food did not mean a great deal to him; his father had been an indifferent cook and as a boy Albert's favourite meal was canned corned beef with boiled cabbage and potatoes. It was still his preferred dish.

He lit a cigarette with his tea and leaned back, conscious of the frugal pleasure the old man's house always gave him. The room was almost as it had been the day his father died, for, like his father, Albert was not given to changes.

CHAPTER SIXTEEN

The old man had lived in barracks for so many decades that the two-roomed cottage had a military starkness, unrelieved by ornaments or pictures. It never occurred to Albert to add any.

The books on the windowsill mirrored father and son, half a dozen prim Victorian novels, including *East Lynne*, which had brought a secret dimness to Albert's eye. There were a few classics, *Cranford*, *Pride and Prejudice*, *Vanity Fair*, and a Bible which neither father nor son ever bothered to open. Completing the library were Albert's expensively bound and well cared for books on archaeology, plus a handful of volumes that might be expected to interest a policeman; books on ballistics, forensic medicine and dermatography. At the end of the row was a dog-eared, much thumbed little book, Palgrave's *Golden Treasury* of verse. It was bound in soft red morocco and had belonged to Albert's mother. Albert knew most of the poems by heart.

On a spindly bamboo table stood an ancient Victrola from which a large black horn rose like a mute plea for sound. Beneath was a stack of phonograph albums filled with red-labelled records, as thick as piecrusts.

As was his habit, Albert wound the machine and picked out his favourites. The records were all ones his mother had brought to the Island. Albert had never purchased any new ones and saw no need to. Caruso, Madame Melba, Harry Lauder and John McCormack were soon pealing out over the silent beach.

He closed his eyes as the nasal, quavering tenor's 'Believe Me, if All Those Endearing Young Charms' floated on the soft night air. It moved him deeply each time he heard it.

Thou wouldst still be adored, as this moment thou art,
Let thy loveliness fade as it will,
And around the dear ruin each wish of my heart
Would entwine itself verdantly still.

She was hardly a ruin yet, as a matter of fact she enjoyed robust health and was only two years older than himself, but to him the words were strangely apt in some mystic way.

When he had played the records and done the dishes, Albert looked around the cottage in dismay. There was, as usual, nothing to do.

The science of fingerprinting had always fascinated him, but when he took down the book on dermatography he found he could not concentrate.

His mind and body usually worked in concert, mental exhaustion bringing physical fatigue, but tonight his brain felt like a wet sponge while his body was charged with alert, nervous energy.

He decided to go for a swim, but after getting into his trunks and wading gingerly over the barnacled rocks, he almost changed his mind. The water was tepid and not the least refreshing.

One look back at the lonely little cottage made him wade farther. After a few minutes the soothing buoyancy of the ocean relaxed him and he swam on and on.

It was not until he reached an icy patch of water that he realised how far he had travelled. The light in the cottage was distant, and he knew he was at a point nearly two miles from the shore, where the current was strong and the ocean deep and cold.

Now he was weary, and he cursed himself for a fool. He floated on his back, resting for a few minutes, then began the tiresome swim home. He had not gone a half mile when fatigue forced him to rest again. He was a strong swimmer, and not a man who panicked quickly, but he felt a certain uneasiness as he saw the oil lamp, so tiny, and looking just as distant as it had when he turned back to shore.

The brief respites he took did not seem to replenish his strength, the tide was changing and he felt as though he were harnessed against it. He was appalled, after floating for the fourth time, to find that his arms and legs seemed even more leaden, but at least the cottage was closer.

When he was within half a mile of the beach he suddenly doubled up with an excruciating cramp. The icy stretch after the bathtub temperature of the shore waters had been too much.

When the pain had passed there flashed before his eyes death certificates and visions of the drowned bodies he had seen. And he who had so recently lectured the children on the dangers of water now remembered the old adages of swimming too soon after eating, going beyond one's depth and overtaxing one's strength.

He knew he was in trouble and he prayed he could make the short distance without another crippling seizure. The cottage was very near now, but he was dismally aware that he could as easily drown fifteen feet from the beach as two miles out at sea.

His strength was nearly gone but he gauged the situation and distance calmly. If he did drown, he decided, it would not be because he lost his head.

Finally, gasping and with his limbs trembling uncontrollably, he felt bottom under his feet. Without the water to support him he found he could not stand, and he crawled on his hands and knees to the beach. He reached it none too soon and gritted his teeth as he doubled over with another cramp. When it had passed, he managed to get to his feet and stagger to the cottage.

Never had he been so spent. Once, while taking cover in a ditch during the preliberation death marches, he had realised wearily that his limbs would no longer obey him, and he had said goodbye to his beloved Island of cranky inhabitants, wild roses and deserted fields.

His youth saved him then, but he felt now that he could not take another step if his life depended on it, and stumbling through the stifling cottage he fell heavily on the iron army cot.

The warmth of the room faded and was ousted suddenly by a chill, nippy and unseasonable. He looked around in wonder; he was no longer in his father's cottage, but in a strange room. A very strange room. It was unfurnished, the floor was of broad planks and the ceiling oppressively low for a man of his height, but standing up he realised he was not as tall as he had thought, for there was still ample headspace. Yes, there was no doubt about it, he was shorter. As his eyes swept the room, he knew with certainty that something was not right, but observant as he was he could not find the missing detail.

He walked to the lone window, and found himself staring out over an old city, familiar and yet unfamiliar. The streets were narrow and twisting, most of the houses were low, but the landscape was periodically broken by soaring spires and towers. A foot of snow on the streets logically accounted for the chilly air.

Then, from some distant quarter of the city, he heard the faint, long-drawn call of the town crier, 'Beware, beware, there are wolves in the streets.'

CHAPTER SIXTEEN

Staring into the street below him, he saw a lone citizen running. The man looked up and waved as if he knew Albert, then he disappeared. Feeling lost and frightened, Albert leaned his head against the window, only to find it was glassless and he nearly lost his balance.

As he clutched the sill for support, he heard the first howls of the wolves. They were approaching and, although he was frightened, he was fascinated.

The pack flashed into sight, yelping, snarling and obviously hungry, driven from some winter retreat to forage in the city. Their coats were glossy, their bodies well padded with muscle, and their saffron eyes gleamed in the winter dusk.

They were racing toward the house that sheltered Albert, when the leader suddenly wheeled and disappeared down a side lane, to be followed by the rest of the pack. All but one.

Albert heard a scream, the scream of a man beset by wolves, and he knew it was the man who had waved to him.

One wolf had not followed the pack. It stood, staring straight at Albert, fixing him with its blazing eyes. Albert stepped back, and only just in time, for the wolf suddenly hurled itself at the house, trying to leap high enough to gain a foothold on the window.

Horrified, he saw the snarling face appear, with the hairy paws hooked over the sill, and he heard the beast's hind feet scrabbling against the side of the house as it sought a purchase to vault into the room.

Hastily looking for a means of escape, Albert now knew what was not right about this room. It had no door.

He began to tremble, but sank back with a sigh when he saw the wolf fall into the street.

He sighed too soon, for once more he saw that vision at the window, and this time he could have sworn that the wolf, with an unalterable prescience, had left its pack to single him out.

Again the wolf lost its foothold and slid back. Rushing to the window, Albert knew that his only chance was to stand guard and cast the animal down before it could gain entry.

Except for their evilness, the blazing eyes were without expression, and the lips drew back over a set of teeth that made the snow in the streets seem grey.

Some ancient instinct warned Albert that a creature of unbelievable malignancy and almost human awareness was weighing him, holding him spellbound as it prepared to spring again.

Dream or no dream, he had had enough, and he willed himself awake.

The room was black and he was unable to orient himself. He could not decide which end of the bed he was lying on or where the door leading to the kitchen was. It was imperative that there be light, and he stumbled about blindly until he found the open doorway.

Once in the kitchen he got his bearings and, with shaking hands, lit the oil lamp. The familiar shadows, the homely furniture reassured him, and with a sigh he sank to a chair, breathing deeply. After a few minutes he rose, lit the now cold kitchen range and put the kettle on for tea.

Sighing again, he sank back in his chair.

It was only a dream. It was not possible. His hands trembled as he lit a cigarette.

No, that was not the answer. The other thing, which he still dreamed of, had not been possible either, or so he had thought.

But it had been because he had seen it, and if that were possible it was impossible not to believe that one lived in a generation of monsters. Perhaps they weren't new to this age. Perhaps they had always existed, elementals who formed basis for folktales and medieval superstitions. But how could one reconcile them with a civilisation of television and electronics?

Nevertheless, the six million had gone into cushions, lamps and crematoriums, proof that demons could roam the earth, and Albert had no intention of forgetting them.

Dawn found Albert standing in the doorway watching a fine sunrise. The ocean already had the glassy, still look which forecasts a long hot day, while birds carolled quarrelsomely and the sharp odour of rotting kelp and seaweed wafted from the beach.

It was reassuring to know the sun could be counted on to rise regularly, that nature's laws were immutable, despite night fantasies to the contrary. The fear seeped away and he was again logical Albert, carefully assessing an unusual nightmare.

That day in court had been more unnerving than he was willing to admit. Then, having been in a state of complete exhaustion, so much so that he had not even bothered to take off his wet bathing trunks, he had forgotten to close the front door. When the kitchen fire died out and the cool night breezes from the ocean struck his half-nude body, the stage had been set for a winter scene. The undoubted fright he had received by foolishly swimming too far, coupled with his physical state, was enough to account for the rest.

Why, even the glassless window of that dream-room made sense. He had repaired Lady Syddyns's greenhouse, and the incident, though minor, still lurked in his subconscious mind.

The wolf with the blazing subhuman eyes was merely the phantom of a shocked, overtired brain.

He felt much better when he had all the pieces fitted into such a reasonable pattern, and he dismissed the subject from his mind.

AT MIDNIGHT a strangely worried Christie awoke. She lay in her little troll-ridden bed sighing with the big fir tree and grieving for poor Desmond, who was so soon to join the angels.

When Barnaby called in the morning, Christie was very quiet throughout breakfast and all the way to the graveyard.

They worked diligently, for they no longer resented their enforced labour. Indeed, it gave a purpose and orderliness to their lives which they found increasingly necessary.

The pattern of nature had become unbalanced, and the children felt it. Uncle's presence was proof enough.

In its primeval state, forests covered the Island down to the beaches. Man had come, logged, cleared the land and planted crops. Only a vestige of the once mighty forest remained, and a cigarette, dropped by a careless smoker had, two years before, reduced it even further.

One half of the mountain was a desert of grey trees, acre after acre of a quenched inferno. The blaze had been so quick and so intense that the trees were not charred. They had died almost instantly, and now stood with their barkless limbs entreating the sky for mercy, silver skeletons on a silent cratered landscape. And the silence was not the hushed cathedral silence of the living forest, but rather an eerie lunar stillness, as though the air itself could no longer carry sound. Apart from the few fireweeds and ragged foxgloves it supported, the very earth of the ravaged mountainside seemed dead.

In clearing the land, man had killed off nature's euthanatic surgeons, the predators. The deer, overbreeding, were stunted and weak, so that even the children sensed in the appearance of One-ear something logical and necessary.

After clearing the land, man had abandoned it, and soon the bush, the wild bush, blackberry, salmonberry, salal and the useless alder, crept like a gigantic serpent across the fields, strangling out all other life; and the seedlings, borne by the winds to replace the dead forest, were smothered.

Their work done, Christie sat on Sir Adrian's tombstone, her chin in her hands and her eyes pensive.

'What's the matter?' asked Barnaby, sitting beside her.

'I don't know. Sometimes it hardly seems worthwhile. By the time you get one end done, the weeds are nearly out of hand at the other end.'

Barnaby chewed a piece of grass, then turned to her.

'That's not what I meant. What's really the matter?'

Christie poked at the grass with a piece of twig and said nothing.

'Well, what is it?'

She sighed and said, 'We can't do it.'

'Can't do what?'

'Blame Desmond.'

Barnaby's face darkened.

'It was your idea. It's him or us. Why can't we?'

Christie opened her mouth, closed it, and said nothing.

'Why not?' Barnaby persisted.

She looked sad, for the vision of the tree, the rope and poor Desmond refused to budge.

'My mother wouldn't like it,' she said.

Barnaby jumped to his feet. His eyes were cold and he kicked Sir Adrian's tombstone.

'That's not fair! It was your idea!'

Christie sighed again.

'Listen,' she said, 'it would be like we hanged old Shep.'

'Who wants to hang old Shep? What are you talking about? I like old Shep.'

Christie nodded.

He sat down again, and this time it was he who had his chin on his hands.

'Yes,' he said after a long pause, 'I see what you mean. I like Desmond too.'

It was unthinkable. Poor Desmond must and would be spared. They were distressingly sane; remorse, which clever Uncle Sylvester could never feel, dinned in their ears with the persistence of an unanswered telephone.

Barnaby rose, kicked Sir Adrian once more and leaned his cheek on the headstone.

'Gee!' he said, 'why does everything always have to go wrong for me?'

Christie patted his shoulder.

'Nevermind. We'll think of something else.'

They went over to poor Desmond's and sighed at the sight of that beautiful, useless gun. Sadly they wandered down to the store.

'There must be some way out,' said Barnaby. 'We can't always have such rotten luck.'

They sought refuge from the world under the counter of the store, where they sat eating licorice whips and thinking.

When Christie had finished hers she licked her fingertips fastidiously and turned her sticky face to Barnaby.

'What about One-ear? Couldn't we take him to Uncle's cottage some night and have him kill Uncle? I'll bet he could do it easily.'

Yes, one blow of that mighty paw could break the neck of a stag.

'But suppose he doesn't want to?'

'He'll have to want to. We'll make him want to.'

'How?'

Christie thought for a long while.

'I don't know,' she said.

Barnaby stared into space, chewing the last of his candy.

'You know,' he said, wiping a trickle of black saliva from the corner of his mouth, 'I've got an idea. They train dogs for hunting and killing. Maybe we could train One-ear. The last school I was at, there was a boy that had a German shepherd dog. He trained it so it would sit and run and fetch, and it only bit people he told it to. We'll teach One-ear to be like that.'

It seemed like a sound idea to Christie and she nodded encouragement.

They were interrupted by Mr Brooks who came in bearing a sixteen-pound salmon he had just caught.

'Barnaby?'

Barnaby came out from behind the counter, followed by Christie.

'Golly, isn't that a beauty,' said Barnaby, reaching out and stroking the fish.

'I'm going to cut some steaks off it for us. Do you think you could carry the rest over to Mrs Nielsen for canning? It won't keep in this heat.'

'All right,' said Barnaby.

Mr Brooks took the salmon onto the porch, cut the steaks from it and wrapped the rest in newspaper.

'Are you sure it isn't too heavy? It must weigh a good twelve pounds still.'

No, no it wasn't too heavy. They could manage. Yes, they knew it wouldn't keep in the heat and they would go straight to Auntie's with it.

Like two little Red Ridinghoods and carrying the big fish wrapped in newspaper, they promptly made a detour to look for One-ear.

They took a short-cut through the silent, dead forest. It filled them with awe.

Barnaby, carrying the fish, began lagging behind.

'It *is* heavy,' he finally admitted.

'I'll carry one end, and you take the other,' offered Christie.

But that didn't work. The damp paper fell off, making it even more difficult to hang onto the slippery fish.

If they had a knife, they could cut it in two and each take a half, suggested Christie, but of course they didn't have a knife, so they struggled on, becoming wearier each step.

They did not find One-ear, instead, he found them. He had been strolling absently through the corpse-like trees when he had caught wind of the salmon.

He stepped smartly along behind them and surprised them at the edge of the forest, where, innocent and unconcerned, he led them to his bower.

They flung the fish down and threw themselves on either side of him. He graciously allowed them to caress him, his lazy eyes on the salmon.

'Now then,' said Barnaby, sitting up, 'we've got to get busy and train him. He's got to learn to follow us, and to come when we call, and later we'll sick him on things and teach him that.'

He stood up and walked a few paces away.

'Here, One-ear. Come here. Good boy. Come here!'

One-ear yawned.

'He doesn't understand,' said Christie. 'Go on, One-ear, go to Barnaby. You've got to learn to do what we tell you.'

One-ear stretched, yawned again, and then peeked slyly out of the corner of his eye at the fish.

Christie stood up.

'He doesn't get the idea. Maybe I can help.'

Sinking her hands into the loose fur of his neck, she heaved and panted as she tried to drag him to his feet.

With only the slightest hint of irritation, he sat up and shook himself violently.

Christie was flung on her knees a yard away.

Angry, she sprang to her feet and pointed an accusing finger at him.

'You quit that, One-ear!'

With a show of penitence, he lay down meekly.

Barnaby sighed as he saw One-Ear stretch out again. Walking around the cougar, he took hold of One-ear's tail and tried to heave him up from the back end.

One-ear gave a tiny, bored snarl and, carefully keeping his claws sheathed, he turned and cuffed Barnaby across the shoulder.

Barnaby spun in a circle and fell on his face six feet away.

Winded, he stood up. After breathing heavily for several moments, he went to the fish and picked it up. Turning to Christie he said.

'It isn't going to work. He won't do anything we tell him. He won't stand up, fetch, or follow, and never will.'

He looked at One-ear reproachfully.

'Come on. We might as well go.'

A smirk began curling one corner of the cougar's lips as the silly boy stood holding the fish right under his nose.

With a quick flick of his claws, One-ear flipped the beautiful salmon from Barnaby's arms, caught it in his mouth and with a huge bound he disappeared into the bushes.

The children watched with open mouths, then Christie stamped her foot in anger.

'What are we going to do? What'll we tell Auntie?'

Barnaby's belligerent lower lip stuck out.

'That was mean. We'll have to say we lost the fish.'

It was lying, a sin they had promised Sergeant Coulter to forgo, but angry as they were, they knew they couldn't tattle on One-ear.

It had been a long, long time since One-ear had eaten salmon, and he finished it with gusto. When the last delicious titbit had gone down his gullet, he sat preening his satin coat.

Had he known what they wanted, and had their intended victim been Sergeant Coulter, he would gladly have obliged, could he have done so with impunity. Who knew how many cougars that murderer had wantonly destroyed?

When the children arrived at the goat-lady's, she put down the sweater she was knitting and looked at them in amazement.

'How could anybody just lose a big fish?'

The children admitted it had been plain carelessness on their part. They had put it down somewhere, forgotten to pick it up, walked on and now they couldn't remember where they left it.

The goat-lady was annoyed.

'Well, it's no good going back to look for it if you don't know where you left it. In this heat it will spoil in the sun before you find it. I could have got a dozen jars of salmon from that.'

The waste was unpardonable. Barnaby must return to the store and confess to Mr Brooks, while Christie would have to stay in for the rest of the day.

They felt badly.

'You need your hair washed and a bath anyway,' said the goat-lady to Christie. She pushed Barnaby out the door, then relenting slightly, gave him a cookie and told him to come back the next day.

Christie stood with downcast eyes.

'Get a lemon out of the cupboard. I'll put the juice on your hair to make it brighter.'

Forgiven, Christie felt much better.

'I'm getting my hair bleached with lemon juice,' she shouted to the retreating figure of Barnaby.

Even Mr Brooks was cross.

'For shame, Barnaby, a big boy like you. I hope you'll be more careful next time, or I won't feel I can trust you to do errands.'

Mrs Brooks dabbed her eyes and begged Mr Brooks not to be so harsh. Barnaby would be a child only once. She kissed Barnaby's cheek and said she was sure it would never happen again.

Barnaby looked so thoroughly miserable that Mr Brooks could not bear it.

Patting the boy's shoulder, he said: 'Now, now, it's not that serious. Just remember to be more careful next time.'

Barnaby gave a wan smile and went outside. He sat moodily on the porch, reading a crime-comic magazine and trying to think of a foolproof method of murdering his uncle.

So desperate was he that he even considered telling Sergeant Coulter. As the thought crossed his mind he looked up to find the big Mountie gazing down at him.

'Hello,' said Barnaby.

Sergeant Coulter smiled at the sight of the small, miserable figure.

'Hello,' he said.

He sat down next to the boy, took the comic book, looked at it, shook his head and handed it back to Barnaby.

'Where's your partner in crime?'

'Who?' said Barnaby, startled.

'Christie.'

'Oh, her. She's getting her hair bleached with lemon juice and having a bath. And then she's going to have her hair curled.'

'That's too bad,' said Sergeant Coulter. 'You look as if you've lost your last friend. But then, you wouldn't want your hair curled and bleached, would you?'

He paused and looked at Barnaby's grubby knees.

'Still, a bath wouldn't hurt you,' he admitted.

He offered the boy a package of gum, his panacea for all the problems of childhood.

'Did you have a good time last week at Benares?' he asked.

Barnaby looked at him blankly.

'When you had tea with Mrs Rice-Hope.'

What was the matter with the boy, was he retarded? What else could he possibly be referring to.

'Oh,' Barnaby gave an indifferent sigh. 'Yeah, I guess so.'

He peeled the whole package of gum and as usual put the lot in his mouth. Sergeant Coulter's interest waned visibly.

'Did you play games?'

Barnaby chewed silently, then, suddenly realising his hero was actually talking to him, he began speaking eagerly.

'Yes, we had a contest. She showed us how, Mrs Rice-Hope. Christie and me, we made miniature gardens. You take a piece of plywood about a yard square, with a little edge an inch high around it, and you fill it with earth. Then you make a garden. I had moss for lawn, and a piece of broken beer bottle for a lake and then I got little shells and made a path. I had flower beds too, beside the lake, with wild violets and nasturtiums and foxglove petals. It's hard to make a little garden because you need little flowers.'

Sergeant Coulter smiled. 'She liked it, didn't she?'

The boy shrugged. 'Christie?'

'No, Mrs Rice-Hope,' said Albert.

'Christie's was better. She made a little bridge of match-sticks and a beach of white sand and pebbles, and her ocean looked really real, she used a pocket mirror. And her flower garden, you should have seen it.'

'I wish I had,' said Albert.

'We got prizes. There were only two of us, so we both got prizes because Mrs Rice-Hope said they were too beautiful to choose between.'

Yes, of course she would. She would never leave one child disappointed while praising the other.

'What was your prize?'

'A little prayer book. Christie got one too. I gave mine to Christie.'

'What for?' asked Sergeant Coulter.

'Oh,' said Barnaby, 'she's collecting them.'

Sergeant Coulter stood up. A rare tenderness came over him, and reaching down, he ruffled the boy's hair.

Barnaby got to his feet.

'Sergeant?'

'Yes?'

Barnaby stood very straight.

'There's something I want to ask you. No - something I want to tell you- '

The sergeant's mind was wandering back to Benares and he murmured 'yes' absently.

'It's about my uncle.'

'Yes, Barnaby?'

'He- ' Barnaby faltered for words. 'He's not like other people.'

He knew from experience not to go too far or say too much.

The policeman's face altered slightly. Polite, clinical, disinterested, eyes missing nothing.

'Isn't he, Barnaby? In what way?'

Barnaby's lips trembled.

'He's not nice.'

Sergeant Coulter looked down at the little boy.

'I don't understand you, son. What do you mean?'

Barnaby mumbled and looked away.

'Look here, does he beat you?'

'No.'

The Mountie paused. The next question was a delicate one and he phrased it carefully.

'Listen, now, you know I'm a policeman, and it's my job to help people. Little boys like you. You say your uncle isn't nice. Does he hurt you? I mean, not spankings, does he ever hurt you in a way that isn't nice? Is this what you're trying to tell me?'

Barnaby was puzzled. How could you hurt people in a way that *was* nice? He looked sullen.

'All right,' said Sergeant Coulter, trying a new tack, 'tell me the worst thing he's ever done.'

Barnaby thought back on all of Uncle's subtle, terrible cruelties. Without a moment's hesitation, he said, 'He burned my Teddy bear in the fireplace.'

Sergeant Coulter rubbed his hand over his mouth to hide a smile.

'That sounds pretty awful,' he said. 'But sometimes these things are necessary as we grow up. I had an old patent leather doll called Felix the Cat, when I was a little fellow. The patent leather all cracked and his stuffing came out, but I didn't mind. I couldn't go to sleep without him.'

Barnaby looked up in amazement. At last he had found someone who understood.

Sergeant Coulter grinned and gave the boy a mock punch on the chin, then he leaned down and took the crime-comic book from Barnaby's pocket.

'My father put Felix the Cat in the garbage can,' he said.

Barnaby felt hopeless but in one last bid for understanding, he grabbed the policeman's hand and gazed at him searchingly.

'Sergeant, he's going to kill me.'

It wasn't Barnaby's day.

Sergeant Coulter was staring with disgust at the illustrations in the comic book.

No, it really wasn't Barnaby's day.

The picture showed a small boy trussed with ropes, while a barrel-chested man, who, by unfortunate coincidence, bore a remarkable resemblance to Uncle, wielded a long, sharp knife.

Sergeant Coulter handed the book back to the boy.

'He is, Sergeant, he is! I know he's going to kill me!'

'Well, I'll speak to him about it tomorrow. Now, how about trying to find something else to read, eh? This sort of trash isn't good for kids, you'll be having bad dreams. You ask Mrs Brooks if she's got any of Dickie's old books around. I'll bet she has. Things I used to read, *Chums*, *Chatterbox*, the *Boy's Own Weekly*. Okay?'

He patted the boy's head again and walked away.

IT HADN'T RAINED for weeks, and every afternoon the temperature crept a few degrees higher. By two o'clock the landscape hung quivering like stage scenery. The blackberry bushes and wild roses banking the roads were a confectioner's dream, powdered with a fine white dust. The arbutus leaves lost their glossy sheen, rattling gold and dry against their peeling bronze trunks. Little streamlets that formerly cavorted merrily to the ocean lingered in weary trickles, finally disappearing completely, leaving only round white polished pebbles to mark their course.

Since there was no electricity on the Island, there was no refrigeration and the old people pulled their curtains to sit panting in darkened rooms. They increased their already formidable amount of tea-drinking and assured each other that hot drinks were far more cooling anyway.

Mr Brooks cast his eyes anxiously to the mountain, watching for the first telltale plume of smoke that would herald the scarlet-tongued demon of the Pacific Coast, the forest fire.

CHAPTER EIGHTEEN

He shook his head and turning to Sergeant Coulter said, 'We're in for trouble if we don't get rain soon. The whole Island is like tinder and the wells are drying up.'

Sergeant Coulter nodded and sighed, dreaming of sitting in a cool, dim tavern, tie loosened, and sipping a beaded ice-cold beer.

No. He didn't want that. Not in the beer parlour on Benares, in any case. Sergeant Coulter had a large, painful-looking black eye, and if he had any choice, which he hadn't, he would never go in that beer parlour again. He sighed once more; he would probably be recruiting crews for fire fighting before the week was out, and that meant bearding them in the Benares beer parlour. He really couldn't blame them for grousing - it was forced labour, and the government paid only a pittance of their normal wages - but that was the Law. Able-bodied men could be pressed into service, and it was his job to uphold the Law.

Nevertheless, he didn't want to go in that beer parlour again. Before last Saturday night and the black eye, he thought he had touched the bottom of the well of humiliation, but apparently he had hardly dampened his boots. There had been a time when he had thought that the night on the beach with Gwynneth Rice-Hope had been the bedrock of the pit, he still blushed when he thought of it, but each fresh session made him realise he would never have a tough hide, he would always be vulnerable, and the next time would hurt as much as the last.

Mr Brooks leaned against the counter reading the latest edition of the *Victoria Colonist*.

'I see the Americans have caught their silk-stocking strangler,' he said, turning the page and looking up at Albert.

'About time,' replied Albert. 'He left just about every conceivable type of clue behind, including notes to the police explaining his methods. He still killed seven people before they nabbed him.'

Now if the Mounties had been handling that case, things would have been different.

But Mr Brooks had turned the pages and was reading another story. Suddenly he folded up the paper, gave Albert a startled, embarrassed look and said he was through with the *Colonist* if Albert would like to take it with him.

Sergeant Coulter thanked him, folded the paper under his arm and walked onto the porch, just in time to have his hat kicked off by Barnaby, who was swinging from the roof of the porch.

Sergeant Coulter picked up his hat, brushed it off, gritted his teeth and quietly told Barnaby to get down from there before he fell and broke his neck.

'I can't,' said Barnaby. 'Get down, I mean. Christie took the ladder away. I'm sorry I knocked your hat off. Ohhhhhh-hhh, Sergeant! What a lovely black eye. How did you get it?'

'What ladder?' asked Sergeant Coulter ominously.

'The one we found in the shed with the fire-fighting equipment. How did you get your black eye, Sergeant?'

Sergeant Coulter whispered 'Jesus' gently to himself.

'I walked into a door,' he said, and standing on the top stair he stretched up, grabbed the boy and swung him to the porch.

'Wheee!' shouted Barnaby.

Christie came racing around the corner, looking innocent.

'Oh, Sergeant!' she cried, 'you've got a black eye. Does it hurt?'

Sergeant Coulter let his breath out slowly, counted to ten and then addressed the children.

'Listen, you two! That ladder is government property, you understand? The forest rangers put people in jail for things like that. Have you got that straight? Now put it back and don't touch anything in there again!'

Subdued, they nodded.

He turned to go, then noticed the little girl standing with lowered head. He stopped, feeling awkward.

'I'm sorry, but you'll both just have to learn not to touch things that don't belong to you.'

Her head remained obstinately lowered.

'Now, don't cry,' he said as soothingly as he could. 'It's all right. Just don't touch anything in the shed again.'

She raised tearless eyes.

'You didn't swing me off the porch!' she whispered jealously.

So that was it. He sighed, grabbed her under the arms and swung her in a circle.

'How's that?'

'No. Over your head like you did Barnaby.'

Silently cursing, Sergeant Coulter decided Herod was a man whom history had judged too harshly. He lifted Christie again and whirled her as he had done Barnaby.

'Look, Barnaby!' she shrilled, 'I'm just like Peter Pan!'

Sergeant Coulter wheeled with her over his head and suddenly found himself face to face with Mrs Rice-Hope.

The dignified Mountie blushed and set Christie on her feet.

'Oh,' said Mrs Rice-Hope, who was exceedingly beautiful and none too bright, 'when I heard the screams I thought there had been an accident. You're playing with the children. How sweet, Sergeant. I always thought of you as a man who loved children.'

She smiled charmingly at him and the children, and the children smiled charmingly back at her. Again storms lashed poor Albert's heart.

'Why, Sergeant,' she said, laying a shapely hand on his sleeve in alarm, 'how did you get that awful black eye?'

It was time for Albert to dabble in the well of humiliation again.

'In the course of duty, Ma'am,' he said stiffly, touching the brim of his hat.

It was impossible for his face to get redder. Why, oh why, had he said that! He could have kicked himself. In his confusion he turned to the children.

'Come on. I'll buy you each a pop.'

'Us?' they cried in amazement.

Sergeant Coulter dispensed gum, usually to rid himself of their presence when they were tiresome, but he just wasn't a pop man.

Before they could say more and spoil her illusions, he rushed them into the store, grabbed two bottles, jerked the tops off and popped them into the children's mouths.

'Quick!' he ordered. 'Drink those and keep quiet.'

Mrs Rice-Hope came into the store and left a prescription of medicine on the counter for old Mr Allen.

'Dr Wheeler asked me to drop this off,' she explained. 'Good day, Sergeant. Goodbye children, I'll see you on Sunday.'

With a friendly wave of her hand, she moved on.

Sergeant Coulter leaned on the store counter. Thank God she was gone before he could do or say anything else foolish.

'You kids want another pop?' he asked amiably.

They looked at each other and then at their adored Sergeant suspiciously. Two pops?

As they gulped down the second drink, Christie took time out to belch and ask him how he got his black eye.

'Door,' said Sergeant Coulter.

His face was still scarlet, and the children stared at him with curiosity.

Looking out, he observed with horror that Miss Proudfoot was making her way to the store. She took a prurient interest in the affairs of the heart, and the children, even the children, knew from a glance that something ailed Sergeant Coulter.

Albert's honest face was the mirror of his soul, and in a trice he who had fought the murderous Hun and faced the assassin's bullet, fled in confusion.

When he had gone, Mr Brooks came running, in response to Miss Proudfoot's imperious ring. He found the newspaper on the counter.

'Shall I take it to him?' asked Barnaby.

Mr Brooks sighed. 'No. I suppose Constable Browning will give it to him. He'll find out soon enough, anyway.'

'Find out what?' asked Barnaby.

'Nothing,' mumbled Mr Brooks.

Sergeant Coulter pondered on the report of the stolen gun.

The Americans very logically concluded that, since they had seen the gun when they docked at the Island, it must have been stolen later. Sergeant Coulter had questioned them carefully, asking if they were sure they had the gun when they left the Island, if they remembered seeing it when they arrived on Benares. By the time they had thought it over and and talked it over, they were all absolutely positive they had the gun when they left the Island, they almost remembered seeing it when they got to Benares. Yes, they did remember seeing it when they docked at Benares. They were certain.

That made it difficult. There were twenty or thirty boats tied up at the dock of Benares during the weekend, with

God only knew how many people coming and going. It would be complicated to trace. But it would turn up. Sometime, somehow. Guns always did. In the meanwhile, Victoria had been notified and pawnshops and second-hand stores all over the province would be watching for it.

Sergeant Coulter told the tall, distinguished American that he was sorry it happened on Canadian soil, but that kind gentleman only remarked there were always a few rotten apples in the barrel, and personally he had found Canadians to be delightful neighbours, fine, helpful people, and even the children had such charming manners.

Sergeant Coulter folded the report and found Constable Browning staring at him with a look of embarrassed pity.

'What's Up?' he asked suspiciously.

Constable Browning fumbled with the copy of the *Victoria Colonist*. He wondered if he should try to destroy it before Sergeant Coulter had had a chance to see it, but, sighing, he realised his sergeant would be bound to find out.

As Constable Browning remembered Saturday night in the beer parlour, and the ring of forty jeering, hooting men laughing at Sergeant Coulter, he swallowed hard. He respected and almost loved his sergeant, and he hated to see him hurt again.

Constable Browning opened the paper and silently handed it to Albert. His finger tapped the story, three paragraphs long, on the back page of the paper, between the legal notices, auctions and United Nations reports.

'You had better read this,' he said, then, in deference to the feelings of Sergeant Coulter, he left the launch.

Albert read the story, then to make sure his eyes were not deceiving him, he read it again. He sat back, stunned, wishing for the first time in his life that he were a woman and could have a good cry.

CHAPTER EIGHTEEN

He rose and took down Professor Hobbs's book. Opening it, he stared at the two gigantic, beautiful Etruscan figures, which still challenged him from the pages.

Fakes.

It hardly seemed possible. Hobbs, the greatest living expert on Etruscan art had vouched for them.

Frauds.

He felt in some obscure way that he had been cheated personally. He rubbed his hands over his face wearily as he remembered how he had boasted of knowing Hobbs. He blushed at how he had bragged to everyone of his proposed trip to New York and the field party in Rome.

Was nothing in his life to be inviolate? He asked very little, and he got even less. Well, it would be a lesson to him to keep his mouth shut.

Put not your trust in professors. In the future the only things he would believe would be his own eyes and ears. His idol was as prone as the next to make hasty, inaccurate decisions.

It was, he knew, unfair to Hobbs, who had merely been duped with the rest of them, and who undoubtedly felt a great deal worse than he did.

Hobbs was human and made mistakes like anybody else, but my God, when he did make one, what a king-sized boner it was.

Well, it was no good brooding over it, although he knew from experience he always did brood over things that hurt him.

He took out his fountain pen and began writing his weekly letter to her.

My dear,
I'm sorry I was so stupid when you asked me about the shiner. Have I ever failed yet to behave in an inane manner when I see

you? God! Why did I have to say 'In the course of duty, Ma'am,' as if I expected you to pin the Victoria Cross on me. The truth, of course, like everything else in my life, is ludicrous.

There was a nasty brawl in the beer parlour at Benares last Saturday. Two men got cut up in a knife fight, and Browning was knocked over trying to separate them. Your hero, going to his assistance, caught his spur in Charlie Benedict's pants cuff, fell and stunned himself nicely, all with no assistance from the hostile crowd.

I know I didn't have to go into all the details when you asked, but I didn't have to say that, either. I get rattled enough when I see you, and those two damned kids don't help. Frankly I'd just as soon face a riot in a beer parlour any day. Oh, they're not bad, really, I know, although the boy still tells lies. The latest being that his wicked uncle wants to murder him. I suppose the way to look at it is that they're kids and they live in a world of make-believe.

Speaking of that, I've been living in one myself, but I had my eyes, or rather at the present time, my eye, opened today. I won't be going to New York. The statues in the Metropolitan Museum are fakes. Sometime I'll write and tell you all about it. I feel very lonely and discouraged, so I'll close for now.

With love,
Albert

He folded the letter, put it in his tunic pocket and walked wearily up to the wharf. He sat on the edge, his feet dangling over, the way he had sat when he was a boy, and gazed at the twinkling lights of Benares, across the dark waters.

With his head leaning against one of the creosoted pilings, he thought of the night he had declared his love for her. His cheeks flamed at the memory.

He took the letter from his pocket and tore it to tiny shreds, posting it where he posted all his letters to her, on the outgoing tide.

CHAPTER EIGHTEEN

He smiled bitterly as he remembered the night. She had been kind, of course. Somehow he wished that she had been kind enough to recoil in horror, or to strike him.

Instead, she had been kind enough to explain.

She understood his feelings, and they were quite natural. It was to be expected, a young man cut off from the society of women for years, and corresponding daily with someone from home. He must not be ashamed of his feelings, but they were temporary. He had created an image for himself, and he had confused her with the image. She was none of the things he thought; indeed, if he knew her better, he would see only too well her many frailties. He had wanted to love someone and that was the most natural thing in the world, but in his loneliness and need, he had fashioned her. His love was not real, it was the outcome of an artificial situation. She knew he would see the logic of it.

Logic. If he were logical, he would not have fallen in love with a married woman, especially one with an Anglican minister for a husband. Her frailties. As if he cared about her frailties. He loved them too. As if love were logical, as if he could merely say, yes, it is neither logical nor convenient to love you, as a matter of fact, if we're going to split hairs, it isn't even moral, so I have decided not to love you.

But, she had continued, she had the deepest affection for him, and she always would have. And she knew, when he had had time to adjust himself, that they would be friends, and share the many delights of true friendship, so much finer than love. The friendship of a man and a woman who had the deepest respect for each other, or was it the deepest affection. And of course, he must realise once and for all that he did not love her. And now they would forget about the whole ugly mess and enjoy their affection.

He would never forget that night on the beach. He had been so young, so honest and so desperately in love. Ten years later he loved her as shyly, as hopelessly and as desperately as ever.

That night on the beach below the old man's cottage, an enchanted night with the tide high and the moon full. By accident they had met face to face like haunted lovers, so different from the two who had exchanged innocent confidences in the lost years.

She had a Roman matron's body, deep bosomed and perfect, and she knew it. Ordinarily she hid it under ugly tweeds and knitted jumpers, but this strange night she had cast off her usual cocoon and was wearing a dated, shapeless wool bathing suit, from which the goddess's body fought to escape. She looked distraught and wild, unhappy and beaten. She looked magnificent.

She had turned to watch a gull rising from the water, her eyes huge and sad. When he saw her trembling in the night breeze, he put his coat about her shoulders, but she had shrugged it off, graciously, of course, and handed it back to him. She was quite warm, thank you. He offered her a cigarette, but she didn't smoke. She had, she said, felt restless and lonely and she had better be going back.

Then he told her.

Fair must have been the spell cast by the great grey gull who shook his wide wings from the phosphorescent waters and cried in anguish. The gull soared away, perhaps forever, but he left his hoarse cry ringing in their ears and a life memory of the lazy beauty of his wings floating in a haze of summer heat, and of seaweed and moonlight and salt winds and storm-tossed logs. Perhaps, like Albert, he too lost his way, his secret pilot confused. Perhaps, spiritless and safe, he stalked fruitful beaches, full of offal and plenty, never daring the foam-tipped waves and denying his stilled inner voice. Perhaps, on the other hand, the gull, like her, really didn't give a damn.

At the top of the cliff she had stopped, drawn his head down and given him a sisterly kiss of affection and pity. Then she delivered another homily on her unworthiness.

Mute, Albert gazed down at her. Suddenly he took her by one upper arm, as if she were a fractious drunk. Steering with a silent brutality that gave her no choice of direction, he propelled her inexorably to the safety of the wharf and Dudley.

For two weeks her arm had been girdled by a purple bracelet which finally faded to pale yellow, the only tangible outcome of his consuming passion and her deep affection.

Since that day they had never exchanged more than the most mundane and polite pleasantries.

The few women in between had never counted; far from remembering their names, he could barely recall their faces.

In all fairness, and Albert was fair, there was very little else she could have done. She was righteous and right, qualities not always particularly endearing.

He sighed, stood up and stretched. With a glance over the murmuring waters, he decided to walk to his father's cottage and spend the night there.

When he reached the cottage he lit the coal oil lamp and looked around the two little rooms. A bedroom with two iron army cots, and a kitchen-living room. It was clean, cold, inhospitable and unbearably lonely.

He couldn't stand it and walked down to the beach, feeling as though the main stream of humanity had passed him by and that he would stand on beaches, forsaken and forgotten, for the rest of eternity.

TRUE TO HIS PROMISE, Uncle still had Barnaby over one night a week for his 'treatment'. Since Barnaby was such an early riser, he was usually half asleep by the time Uncle started, and the little sessions did not appear to have much effect.

Nevertheless, Uncle was pleased with the progress he was making. There was a great deal to be said for the dropping of ideas into the subconscious mind, and the repetitious 'You cannot move, Barnaby,' was, he was sure, slowly seeping into the slumbering child's mind.

Uncle had put aside his friend, the Marquis; the book sat neglected on an end table, next to the *Petit Larousse*, for hating to miss any nuances, Uncle read it in the original French.

Uncle had a new book which he was studying assiduously as he sipped his Scotch and soda. He was not a man who did things by halves, nor was he in any hurry.

Sitting in his comfortable winged chair before the cobblestone fireplace, he paused to light a cigar, glanced at the dozing Barnaby and went back to reading his book of child psychology.

Children, said the book, were naturally curious. Like monkeys, they had to touch, see and dismantle things in order to develop normally.

Uncle looked at Barnaby again, and then at his watch.

'Time to wake up, Barnaby,' he said softly.

Barnaby stirred, yawned and opened drowsy eyes. Then he sat bolt upright, ready for any of Uncle's capers.

But there were no rogue-elephant games tonight, for Uncle had a great deal of thinking to do.

'Into bed, my boy,' he said, picking up his book again. 'Be over here the same time next week.'

Barnaby got as far as the door and paused, looking down at his worn running shoes which had the toes slit for comfort.

'Uncle,' he said timidly, 'can you get my new running shoes soon?'

Uncle looked up.

'Bless my soul, I keep forgetting. I have a memory like a sieve. I have so much on my mind these days! I'll remember for sure when I fly in tomorrow. Goodnight, my dear.'

'Goodnight, Uncle.'

The door closed and Uncle smiled.

Uncle never forgot anything and Uncle always had a reason, and the reason he did not buy Barnaby shoes was certainly not that he begrudged the child a pair; far from it. It was merely that he was quite certain that soon Barnaby would not need new shoes, and what was more important, he wanted Barnaby to continue wearing the shoes he had on. The running shoes, with the toes cut, were most distinctive, easily remembered, and of course, easily identified. Even that idiot of a policeman must have noticed them.

The next time Uncle returned from the city, he did not moor his plane by the wharf; instead, he taxied up to the pilings on Death Beach. It was so much handier and saved that long walk from the dock to his cottage.

Laden with groceries and sin, he leaped nimbly onto the rotten pilings, unafraid of the swirling, treacherous waters only two feet below. He was as sure-footed as One-ear and quite unconcerned. Uncle was a hard man to scuttle and he knew it.

The sharp-eyed children, sitting on the step of the war memorial, noted the change in Uncle's habits and pondered on its meaning. They looked at the distant plane, and then at each other. Then they shrugged.

'Come on,' said Christie, 'Let's do some work in the graveyard.

Followed by poor Desmond and Shep, they walked to the graveyard, casting puzzled glances over their shoulders.

'Come on, Desmond, you can help if you want.'

'Uh uh,' said Desmond, hastily climbing onto the fence.

'Come on,' said Barnaby. 'They're only garter snakes, they won't hurt you. They're a lot more scareder of you than you are of them.'

'Oh no they're not,' said Christie, taking a look at poor Desmond's face. 'Leave him alone, if that's where he wants to be.'

After half an hour's toil, they settled on the grave of Sir Adrian, their favourite because the long marble slab was useful for sitting on and the headstone made a convenient back rest.

'I've got an idea, and it just might work,' said Barnaby. 'I wonder why he left the plane at Death Beach?'

'Because it's closer to the cottage,' said Christie.

'Listen to this,' said Barnaby, leaning over and whispering.

'I - I don't know,' said Christie.

It was all very well to sabotage the plane so that the next time Uncle soared into the wild blue yonder he would plummet to a watery grave, but she didn't like the idea of going to Death Beach.

'I can't swim, and you know what Sergeant Coulter said about Death Beach.'

'What Sergeant Coulter doesn't know won't hurt him,' said Barnaby, 'and you don't have to swim, silly. All you have to do is get out to the plane on those logs the way Uncle went on them to the beach. You'd sure make some Mountie, wouldn't you? It's a good thing you are a girl.'

'Oh, all right, all right, I'll go,' said Christie. 'I guess I might as well drown as get killed by him.'

They were practical and they laid their plans with care.

First they would steal a monkey wrench from Per Nielsen's tool chest in the woodshed at the goat-lady's. Then they would hide midway between the cottage and the wharf, waiting until Uncle had passed them on his way to the store. After he passed they would race down to Death Beach.

A few bolts loosened around the propellers and a handful of sand in the fuel tanks, and they wouldn't have a care in the world.

They sent poor Desmond home once they had the wrench. It would be difficult enough getting out to the plane on those rotten pilings without him tagging along. They could not shake old Shep, however, and he obstinately followed them.

Hiding in the bushes, they watched Uncle pass by, and seizing the opportunity of his brief absence, they rushed down to the beach. The tide was high and the waves, as they always did there, whirled angrily.

They inspected the old, overturned rowboat which was so temptingly near the water, but even they could see it was decaying, water-logged and too dangerous to use.

There was nothing for it but to jump onto the pilings, which they did. When they had gone ten feet, Shep began whining insistently from the beach.

Christie turned and teetered precariously.

'Nevermind about him,' commanded Barnaby, steadying her.

Shep began to howl in anguish, racing back and forth on the beach, then, with one last despairing yelp, he dashed into the waves.

'Oh, hell!' roared Barnaby.

They were now halfway to the plane. Turning, he shouted.

'Go home!'

He glanced at the eddying waters and paled.

'Don't look down, whatever you do,' he gasped.

Finally they reached the plane, where Christie, with chattering teeth, put her hand on the wing to steady herself. She felt faint at the thought of playing that awful game of hopscotch in order to get back on dry land.

They watched old Shep, still only a yard from the shore, with his eyes bulging and his neck straining out of the water as he tried to breast the current.

'Oh, go back!' shouted Christie, and put her hands over her eyes.

'It's all right, you can look now,' said Barnaby, pointing.

A large wave had caught Shep and flung him back to the beach. He slipped and struggled over the glistening rocks, shook himself violently when he reached the sand, and ran off with his tail between his legs.

'Okay,' said Barnaby. 'Come on, up where the engines are. I'll start there. You come along to hold the wrench while I'm working.'

Christie gritted her teeth and nodded.

They were just in the act of climbing aboard the plane when the high-powered hum of the police launch startled them. Barnaby took one look and prudently dropped the wrench into three fathoms of water.

The prow of the launch cut through the waves like a shark, a V-shaped white wave in its wake.

Constable Browning was at the helm and Sergeant Coulter, veins of anger standing out on his temples, was on deck.

Constable Browning cut the motor and the launch glided up to the plane.

'Get the- ' Sergeant Coulter stopped. 'Get down from there,' he shouted. 'Onto the deck of the launch! Come on, both of you!'

Constable Browning cast them a look of sympathy.

Christie really wasn't too sorry to be rescued. She had a feeling it was just plain luck she'd made it out to the plane, and she wasn't at all sure she could have returned. It was merely a matter, at that minute, of whether she was more afraid of the water or Sergeant Coulter.

'On the double!' shouted Sergeant Coulter.

Silently they dropped to the deck.

Sergeant Coulter was in a most unpleasant mood.

'You've been warned about this beach. Everybody around here has warned you, and you went right ahead, didn't you? Well, you're in for it this time!'

The memory of his own near-drowning was still too fresh for comfort.

'Don't tell Uncle,' whispered Barnaby.

Sergeant Coulter wheeled on him.

'Who do you think told me?' he snapped. 'And a good thing for you two he just happened to be on the wharf with his field glasses and saw you.'

The launch, at a slower pace now, cruised back to the wharf and the shaking culprits were led up the dock.

Sergeant Coulter piloted them by the scruffs of their necks, and gave Barnaby a nasty little shove when they reached Uncle.

'Here they are! And I know what I'd do to this boy if he were mine!'

Uncle was not angry. Heavens, no. Uncle was distre-ssed.

'My dear children,' he said hoarsely, 'don't you know the danger you were in? You were told, time and again. Oh, Barnaby, how could you!'

He wiped his brow with his silken handkerchief.

'Upon my word,' he cried, 'it's a mercy you weren't drowned.'

He turned to Sergeant Coulter. 'Really, I don't know what to do with him. Barnaby, I am shocked!'

'I know what I'd do with him!' said Sergeant Coulter.

'It's my fault,' cried Uncle, overcome with remorse. 'To save myself a few steps! Children are naturally curious. I should never have left the plane in such a dangerous spot.'

He placed a pontifical hand on Barnaby's head.

'Now, Barnaby, I am not going to punish you. But you must promise me, solemnly, Barnaby, never to go on that dreadful beach again!'

Barnaby, with lowered head, nodded.

'Very well,' said Uncle. 'I trust you, Barnaby.' He turned to Christie. 'And you too, my dear. Now off you go and play somewhere else, and remember, never, never go to that beach again, children.'

Sergeant Coulter braced his shoulders and stared hard at the children.

'You two got off easily this time,' he said. 'Don't expect to next time, if I'm around.'

The miserable children slunk off.

Uncle turned to Sergeant Coulter.

'Thank you, Sergeant. Thank you a million times. I am sorry he's such a nuisance to you. I suppose I must face the fact that he is a problem.'

'A good thrashing would straighten out a lot of that boy's problems,' said Sergeant Coulter.

Uncle looked shocked again.

'Barnaby is a sensitive child,' he said. 'As you can see, a harsh word is more than enough for him. Furthermore, Sergeant, I do not approve of beating children. It solves nothing.'

He began to walk away, but turned and added icily, 'Good day, sir.'

Humming 'The Teddy Bear's Picnic' he strolled back toward the cottage. Mission accomplished.

Twice Sergeant Coulter had rescued them. He wouldn't be around the third time. It was difficult to outfox Uncle when he applied himself to a project.

Planning, thought Uncle serenely, was the basis of all successful operations. Take his escape from the POW castle at Colditz. Germans said it couldn't be done. Stupid race. No imagination. Why, it had been a romp. Absolute romp. Of course, it couldn't have been done alone, known that from the start. Had to enlist the help of the Senior British Officer, and the Escape Committee. And of course, it had been necessary to take along those two Royal Navy idiots. Committee insisted. That teamwork nonsense. But, he travels fastest who travels alone, and fortunately the pair had been captured by the Gestapo and executed while trying to re-escape. Or so the British thought. Ah well, *c'est la guerre*. Survival of the fittest and all that.

Uncle laughed. Chaps at Colditz called him Silly Billy, or, sometimes jokingly, The Murdering Major, because of his mild disposition.

' "If you go down in the woods today- " '

He bowed gallantly as he passed Agnes Duncan stagger-
ing bent-kneed under a hundred-pound sack of flour, then,
sounding his native wood-notes wild, he padded home with
his tireless lope.

The children were not punished by Mr and Mrs Brooks or
the goat-lady. Instead, their latest transgression was greeted
by wounded looks and lamentations.

The goat-lady, for once truly agitated, wrung her hands.

What would Christie's poor, overworked mother do without her little girl? Entrusting her child to Auntie, only to
have her carelessly drowned.

'If you ever go near that beach again, I'm sending you
home on the next boat!'

Mr Brooks vowed he would not have believed Barnaby would
deceive him so, after promising. And they had been warned
time and time again. If Barnaby would not think of himself,
he should at least have some consideration for his uncle. That
good and patient man, already cruelly burdened by the loss of
Barnaby's Aunt Maude. And Barnaby his only link with her!

Mrs Brooks's lips trembled alarmingly as she called for
her digitalis. She could not bear a repetition of the Dickie
saga. She could not go on living if that child were borne
dripping on a shutter to his uncle.

Their beloved Sergeant, the children had to admit, was
fair about the whole thing. After hinting that he would be
pleased to kick them into the middle of next week if he ever
found them near that beach again, he dismissed the subject,
apparently holding no grudge.

Uncle was still distressed when the children saw him at
the store later in the day. He patted their heads mournfully,

lingering especially on Christie's. He was sincerely fond of little girls.

And the children, looking on the attempt in retrospect, realised it had been a foolhardy gesture. But Christie was puzzled.

'Why,' she said, 'if Uncle wants to kill us, did he send Sergeant Coulter to save us?'

Barnaby cast her a look of disdain. She was smart enough in some ways, but she was still dumb like most girls.

'Don't you see,' he said patiently, 'it was a trap. Now, no matter what he does, no one would believe us. Even Sergeant Coulter. It's the way it always is, everybody believes him and nobody believes me.'

'Well, I don't know,' said Christie. 'It seemed like a good time to get rid of us, if that's what he wants.'

'But he didn't, did he?' asked Barnaby. He was almost amused. She still didn't understand Uncle.

'I can't think of any reason,' she continued, 'unless- ' here she paused and gave Barnaby a startled and horrified look; 'unless - oh, no, Barnaby - you don't think? Unless- '

Unless, said Barnaby, finishing her sentence, unless he was looking forward to doing it himself. People drowning accidentally wasn't Uncle's idea of fun.

THE HEAT WAVE CONTINUED and even the children were listless now. They spent more and more time playing in the store, which was cool. It was also a delightful spot for make-believe.

In one corner stood the post office, strictly off limits to them, but fascinating to peek at.

Opposite the post office were the gardening implements and clothing. From the rafters hung hoes, rakes and shovels, the metal parts of the tools blue-black and shiny, and the handles a virginal white, emblazoned with red paper crests.

Behind the counters were long piles of rubber boots, thick gray wool socks banded in white, denim work pants studded with brass nails, and fleecy heaps of winter underwear.

By the door were buckets and axes, coils of lemon-coloured ropes, candles, kerosene lamps, kettles and saucepans, brooms and fishing gear. In front of the serving counter stood barrels of flour and sugar, and a big, dry, orange-hued cheddar cheese, almost the size of a cartwheel.

There was a coffee grinding machine which smelled aromatically, and a large zinc box of tea, and shelves and shelves of canned goods with faded labels. In the center of the room was a potbellied stove, cold and unlit now.

Although dim and crowded, the high ceiling of the store gave it an air of roominess, and on soft summer evenings when the coal-oil lamp was lit, it was a comforting place.

This particularly hot day the children amused themselves weighing out sugar into small brown paper bags and sealing them for Mr Brooks. Tiring of that, they equipped themselves with brooms, hoes, axes and rubber boots, for safaris into strange lands.

They made pyramids of canned goods and gave the shelves the most thorough dusting they had had in thirty years.

They sold each other quarter pounds of orange pekoe tea and boxes of soda crackers, gravely inquiring after each other's health, and quaintly asking each other if they had heard from the old country recently.

Then, weary from commerce, they sat on a pile of blankets under the counter and chewed their daily ration of licorice.

The bell on the door rang, but they lay hidden, too indolent even to arise.

Mr Brooks came scurrying out from the back room.

'Ah, Sergeant Coulter, there's a letter here from London for you.' Mr Brooks paused and added delicately, 'I - uh - I suppose your trip to New York is off? Mrs Brooks and I were sorry to hear about that Metropolitan Museum business. Those Americans are inexcusably careless. It would never have happened in the British Museum.'

The subject was still too painful for Albert to discuss. He merely nodded and asked where the children were.

'Oh, out playing, I expect,' said Mr Brooks. 'I don't know how they can bear this heat.'

'You'd better tell them to stick pretty close to home for a while. One of Mr Allen's collies found a half-eaten deer on the mountain. It may be One-ear's work. Mr Allen found a right front paw mark, and he thought the pad was damaged. Damned dogs tramped all over it before I got a chance to see it.'

'Oh, my goodness!' cried Mr Brooks. 'One-ear here? But he was last heard of on Vancouver Island. Surely he couldn't swim all the way here? How could he do it? It's much too far for him to reach our Island.'

Sergeant Coulter took off his hat and wiped the inside band with his handkerchief.

'I'd give my eyeteeth to know,' he replied. 'It is too far, but nevertheless, he does it. He was on Benares last year. It's the same cougar all right. It's too much of a coincidence to have two with an ear missing and that right front paw.'

One-ear could have told them. It was really very simple. Under cover of darkness, he swam to a passing log-boom, climbed aboard, and sat, like a first-class passenger, till he was towed to a likely-looking island. Then he jumped off and paddled ashore.

'If he's on this Island, I'll get him,' said Sergeant Coulter grimly.

Ever since One-ear had killed the Indian child, Sergeant Coulter had been hoping his path would cross that of the unapprehended murderer.

'You know,' he continued, 'Browning saw him over on Vancouver Island. Just got a glimpse of him. He's as big as a lion, Browning says, must weigh three hundred pounds. Of course, you can't believe eyewitness accounts, even a policeman's. That one they shot in the middle of Victoria was described as being huge. Turned out to be a hundred-pounder, not much bigger than a bobcat.'

He started for the door, but Mr Brooks called him back.

'Your letter, Albert.'

As Sergeant Coulter walked toward the launch, he opened the letter and began to read it.

The children, sneaking out of the store, saw him suddenly stop in his tracks.

He walked over to the war monument, sat on the step, took his hat off, scratched his head, and read the letter again.

With a gesture of irritation, he shoved the letter into his pocket.

His broad back looked formidable and unbowed as he stomped down the ramp to the police launch.

After leaving the store, the children felt their first duty lay in warning One-ear that his presence was suspected on the Island. Perhaps, if they shouted loud enough, he would understand.

Though they hunted in all his accustomed napping and lounging spots, they could not find him.

He saw them, for he was flopped in the fork of a tree, ten feet above their heads, surveying them lazily with half-opened, slit-pupilled, jewel-green eyes.

They finally gave up their search and went over to poor Desmond's shack.

Barnaby took the precious gun from its hiding place and dismantled it on the bed. From the gun case he took an oiled rag which the former owner had thoughtfully left, and cleaned the gun with care.

Christie sat on the edge of the table, swinging her legs and gazing with renewed interest at poor Desmond.

Barnaby stared longingly at the gun.

'What time does Sergeant Coulter leave today?' he asked.

Christie thought.

'He just dropped in for his mail, so I guess he'll be going back now. He wouldn't be going hunting for One-ear all by himself.'

Barnaby smiled.

'Good, because I'm going to try shooting this gun as soon as he's gone.'

He too looked at poor Desmond with renewed interest.

Since scuttling Uncle was obviously out of the question, their attention was again driven back to Desmond. They fought against their rebellious thought, but the gun was temptingly present and so was Desmond. It was too good to pass up; they were like a couple of savages with a nice, plump missionary.

'You'd better start thinking again,' said Barnaby.

Christie nodded. She walked over to the wavy mirror above Desmond's washbasin and made faces at herself for a few minutes. She smiled becomingly, inspected her teeth and pulled her hair up to a bun on the top of her head.

'Do you think I'll look nice when I'm grown up and I wear my hair like this? I'll have a permanent then, of course.'

'Never mind your hair,' said Barnaby, 'think!'

'What do you think I'm doing?' She sat next to him on the bed and put her chin in her hands, her pretty grey eyes dreaming and secret. Finally she turned to Barnaby.

They had intended originally to instruct Desmond to say that he had found the gun.

'Why not,' said Christie, 'if Desmond's going to be blamed for having the gun anyhow, why not blame him for killing Uncle, but leave him some way out?'

'Such as?'

'Well,' said Christie, 'Mr Allen found the dead deer on the mountain, and now everybody will be afraid because there's a cougar on the Island. Won't people be out with guns looking for One-ear?'

'Yes,' said Barnaby.

'How about if poor Desmond found this gun, and he went out looking for One-ear too, only he shot Uncle by mistake?'

Barnaby nodded. She had something there.

'Yes,' he said, 'we'd have to do it, but we could teach poor Desmond to say he did it.'

'That's right,' said Christie. 'Just a mistake, and poor Desmond's so dumb he'll say anything we tell him to. And Sergeant Coulter can't hang him for making a mistake, can he?'

Barnaby sat back, pondering.

'Are you sure Sergeant Coulter won't hang Desmond?'

'Of course not, not if it's a mistake. It would be mean to hang someone for making a mistake. Sergeant Coulter is never mean, he's always fair.'

Barnaby agreed, and they both sighed with relief. Then, picking up the gun, Barnaby announced he was going out to try firing it.

Christie, rummaging through Desmond's food cupboard, nodded. She took out a box of soda crackers and a lump of stale cheese.

She and Desmond sat eating the cheese and crackers while they waited for Barnaby to return.

When Barnaby did return, his face was very white. He went directly to the bed, put the rifle down and sat rubbing his shoulder.

'We hardly heard the shot at all,' said Christie. 'You want some crackers and cheese? What's the matter with you, you look as if you're going to cry.'

Barnaby stared at the rifle the way a man looks at his dog when it has just bitten him.

'It knocked me down,' he said. 'It scared me.'

He took a deep breath and came over to the table, helping himself to the cheese and crackers.

'Well,' he said finally, 'I know what to do now, anyway. You've got to hold it very tight to your shoulder, and then it won't spring back that way.'

He paused and pointed to the gun.

'Look, you've got to learn how to shoot it too, in case anything happens to me. You won't have to fire it unless I'm dead and you've got to shoot Uncle, but you've got to learn how to load it and aim it and fire it.'

'All right,' said Christie. She hated the gun. 'Let's go to Auntie's now. What are you having for dinner?'

'Boiled beef and boiled carrots and boiled potatoes.'

Christie made a face.

'Ugh! We're having roasted stuffed salmon with chopped egg sauce and baked tomatoes with rice and mushrooms in them and lettuce and cucumber salad with oil and vinegar on it the way you like it. And we're going to have apple upside-down cake and whipped cream for dessert. Auntie told me so this morning.'

Barnaby looked hungry.

'Ask her if I can stay for dinner,' he coaxed.

'Oh, she'll let you. She always does because you always like what she cooks. We'd better come here early tomorrow to start teaching Desmond what to say about killing Uncle.'

Like Uncle, they didn't leave much to chance.

It never occurred to them that poor Desmond, who had spent most of his adult life trying to master the can opener, would be unable to load and fire a high-powered rifle without instruction.

Constable Browning turned from the police radio to Sergeant Coulter.

'It looks as if it's going to be some party for One-ear. Sven Anderson has the best pair of cougar hounds on the coast, and he's coming. Charlie Wilkinson from Courtenay is coming all the way over with his dogs, and Colonel Allardyce, who has those two big African Ridgebacks, wants to be included. They're so big they're liable to be mistaken for cougars themselves.'

Sergeant Coulter raised his head absently and nodded. He was reading *that* letter again.

'Listen,' he said, 'this letter, it's a personal matter and I'd like your advice. I wrote and told Professor Hobbs that Major Murchison-Gaunt had been at Colditz. I got this letter in reply this morning. Read it and give me your opinion.'

Constable Browning took the letter and sat down. After the first page, an expression of distaste came over his face. He finished it and handed it back to Sergeant Coulter.

'Well, what do you think of it?'

'Burn it,' said Constable Browning. 'It's the most libellous, vicious thing I've read for a long time. Your professor sounds as if he's going around the bend.'

Sergeant Coulter nodded.

'That's what I thought,' he said. 'That business of the Etruscan statues hit him a lot harder than I expected. You see where he says he'd heard rumours that he'd be on this year's honours list, but any chance of a knighthood has gone by the boards now. Then he says he's the laughingstock of the scientific world, even though he had nothing to do with the purchase or sale of those figures.'

'Yes, but he still doesn't have to make these statements about Murchison-Gaunt. There's not a phrase in the whole letter that's substantiated by common sense, let alone evidence. You can't go around saying things like that about other people. If he writes letters like this very often, I'm surprised he hasn't ended up in a libel court. You asked for my advice, well, I'd burn that letter. After all, they are on opposite sides of the world now.'

Sergeant Coulter nodded.

'You're right. I'm glad I asked your opinion.'

He sat rereading the letter, the vicious remarks leaping at him from the pages:

I had the dubious pleasure of being in the same block as that animal, and he is an animal, you know. He's the sort of person who invariably eats well during a famine. God knows, he's probably a cannibal. Silly Billy was never quite silly when it came to hoarding food.

I sincerely want you to believe I am not impugning his war record, no doubt he was a fine soldier; after escaping from Colditz he made his way back to England and was decorated by the King. There must have been a paucity of heroes at the time.

He was one of a commando party dropped into Yugoslavia by parachute, to contact wartime leaders. The Jerries transferred him from his original POW camp for security reasons, or so he said. I believe they must have tabbed him for a psychopath.

I was closely, if reluctantly, associated with him for two years and I had ample time to observe him. I cannot impress upon you strongly enough the feeling I had that the man was, at that time, anyway, unstable and actually dangerous.

Oh, I know he has a deceptively mild appearance and manner, and very few people ever saw beneath his mask. But allow me to assure you he is one of the cleverest, toughest soldiers I ever encountered, and there were plenty at Colditz.

The holograph went on and on, repetitious, and at times surprisingly foul.

I don't claim to know much about psychiatry, but-

Albert smiled grimly. Hell, he didn't even know much about archaeology.

I was never able to overcome a feeling of repugnance to the man. Frankly I detested him. If there are such things as werewolves, you've got one on your Island now.

Albert was startled at the crudity of some of the phrases. But, crude or not, the facts still emerged. Major Murchison-Gaunt had been decorated by the King, and Percival Hobbs had not. Murchison-Gaunt had been a brave, tough soldier who had guts enough to escape from the most impregnable prison in Europe, and Percival Hobbs had not.

Albert's own POW days were still sufficiently vivid for him to remember the almost homicidal dislikes that could develop between quite ordinary men who got on each other's nerves when they had no way of avoiding each other.

There was no doubt about it, and Browning was right, Hobbs's mind was affected. The letter was an addled, uncorroborated, meaningless hodgepodge of spiteful hints.

Albert felt saddened to think that Hobbs, his hero, had fallen so low.

O N CAPE MERCER fire struck the Indian village of Klomtook and half burned it to the ground. The moss-covered totem poles of the ancestors, bug-eaten and tortured by the creeping flames, toppled on the shacks that sheltered the descendants, with many an infant caught in the holocaust of a cedar attic.

The Indians drank home brew and brooded. Then they took out their old drums to bring rain and destruction on the enemy who had destroyed their past and their future.

Wearing fantastic headdresses, they shook stone-filled gourds and pranced through a vague imitation of the ancient cannibal dance. They retrieved half-forgotten relics that had once belonged to famous shamans, and they prayed.

Sergeant Coulter, investigating, without result, a rumour that gin and Scotch had been smuggled onto the reserve, felt it was a little late to deal with the fire god, but he hoped at least they would be successful in their endeavors to bring on the rain god.

Tum-tum, tum-tum went their drums. Old klootches, shod in cheap Japanese running shoes, shuffled a dance whose meaning had been lost even before the coming of the white man. The old men, with antiquated ceremonial robes draped over gaudy sports shirts, sat in a circle shaking tambourines and monotonously chanting, 'Hey-Haaaaaaw! Hey-Haaaaaaw!'

The young warriors, for mysterious symbolic reasons, kidnaped a woman of a neighbouring tribe. At least, Sergeant Coulter fervently hoped it was symbolic. He was concerned in case she had come to harm. When he asked where she was, the other maidens merely stood around chewing gum, looking at him with flat, expressionless eyes, although one turned to an ancient grandmother and said, 'Yuh seen Mabel? This guy's looking for her.'

If Grandmother knew, she was not telling any Mountie. Mabel was dead all right, dead drunk, and if the policeman wanted her, he could go and find her himself.

An old brave, being questioned about the liquor, hiccuped and said of course he hadn't been drinking. It was against the law, on the reserve, didn't Sergeant Coulter know? Then, pointing a crooked, contemptuous finger at the sky, he announced that the policeman could tell the white men that the thunder god had heard his people, and it would begin to rain in exactly seven hours.

Exactly seven hours later, despite the weather forecasts, it began to rain. And how it rained!

The children, having given up their shouting to warn One-ear of the impending cougar hunt, were making daisy chains for his thick neck. They sat quietly on his back under a huckleberry bush, alternately stringing flowers and filling their insatiable little maws.

When they heard an insistent pitter-patter over their heads they refused to believe it was rain. But the patter soon took the sound of a thump, and then it became a drumming noise with drops of water half the size of teacups emptying down on them.

Amazed, they stood, held up their hands and stuck out their tongues.

Yes, it was certainly rain. A pounding, beating, heavy and very wet rain that made their cotton shirts stick to their shoulderblades like glue and clotted their hair against their skulls.

But the thunder god began to play too roughly on his drum; he struck with wicked abandon, and they were alarmed. The god's golden finger, jagged and hot, split a tree and they clung to each other, too surprised to move.

When the god struck closer and melted a rock near them, Barnaby and Christie were unhurt but terrified. They joined hands and fled.

One-ear, as frightened as they, had his coat singed. Spitting with rage and still wearing his gay garland, he pounced into the bushes, stopping only once to turn a snarling, defiant face to the heavens.

Sobbing for breath, the children reached the edge of the forest and paused. But only for a second, for, peering through the bushes, and cunningly clad in a green suède jacket which made him almost invisible, was Uncle.

Clasping hands again, and like leaves driven before a gale, they raced on until they reached the road. They saw Mr Allen and his dogs driving sheep along and they knew they were safe while in his sight.

It was any port in a storm, and each headed for home, but not before Barnaby had turned a stricken face to Christie and said he must find a new hiding place for the gun. If Uncle followed them to the forest, he might well have followed them to Desmond's. They felt time closing in on them, and they could take no more chances.

Actually, although they had no way of knowing it, Uncle, like themselves, had been caught unawares by the storm. He had been busy watering his giant ferns in the heart of the forest when the downpour hit him.

How cosy and warm and safe seemed the drab little parlour behind the store now. The old Franklin stove was like a beacon of comfort during the storm, with the damp, fragrant driftwood glowing and spitting cheerfully. The red milk-glass lamp on the table was lit, making even the shadows look like rosy old friends, while Mr and Mrs Brooks fussed lovingly over Barnaby and his wet clothes.

His worn running shoes and dripping shirt and trousers were put on a chair before the fire to dry, and clad in a blanket he sat before the stove, gazing into the flames, wishing he never had to leave that little room again.

Mrs Brooks spread a white cloth over the fringed green velvet cover as she laid the table for tea, setting out bread, butter, boiled eggs, jam, sardines and fruit cake. Barnaby toasted cheese sandwiches for them all on the open grate, looking over his shoulder to the two old people, who sat nodding on either side of the table. It was right to have them there, waiting for him, loving him, answering his smallest needs with anxious pleasure, and he knew now that he too loved them.

When tea was finished, Mr Brooks brought out some of Dickie's old books, and just as Sergeant Coulter had prophesied, there were *Chums* and *Chatterboxes*, some of them going back thirty years before even Dickie's time.

Barnaby thumbed through them, fascinated by the illustrations. Proud little girls swimming beneath big tam-o'-shanter hats and carrying muffs, their tiny ankles encased in fragile buttoned boots, and handsome boys wearing Eton jackets or sailor suits, leading ponies and dogcarts. How good it must have been to have lived then, when everything was so comfortable and solid and so safe. Not one of those boys looked as if he had a wicked uncle, and if he had, Barnaby knew that the stalwart little Berties and Toms and Georges would have made short shrift of such villainy.

He began to read a story of a group of boys on holidays in Egypt. They were his age, and how brave! They went into the pyramids at night and found the treasure of an ancient king. Barnaby wondered if they would have been afraid if they had had to leave their warm beds, as he must, after Mr and Mrs Brooks were asleep, and go out alone into the dark and the storm, halfway across the Island to Desmond's shack, to get the gun.

He had already decided where he would hide it. Under a pew in the church.

But how he hated to leave Mr and Mrs Brooks and the sanctuary of the little parlour. Only the thought of all those intrepid, splendid boys from *Chums* and *Chatterbox* helped him through the ordeal.

It was all very well trying to be brave with Christie, but it was terrifying. It could have been such fun if he had had Steems Major and Minor along, and Tubby Toffee and the peerless Baines who was in the sixth form and captain of the cricket team.

Arranging a murder wasn't any fun on a dark night alone, with your only accomplice, a girl, probably sitting worrying if her hair would be curly tomorrow. He could almost see Christie, cosy in her flannel nighty, with Trixie and Tom, and the big black stove with the kettle bubbling as Auntie made hot cocoa for his partner in murder.

Trembling and miserable, he accomplished his mission so quietly that he did not even awaken Desmond.

The next morning poor Desmond began his third lesson. He was not an apt pupil, and the children were very discouraged. Fear, they discovered, put a slight edge to his wits, and it was reluctantly, but with a stern sense of duty, that Barnaby took the little grass snake from his pocket.

Desmond began to whimper and dived under the table, but the children dragged him out.

'Gee, Desmond, I sure hate to do this,' said Barnaby as he dangled the snake before Desmond's glazed eyes.

Christie closed the door and turned with a sorrowing face.

'Try and be brave, darling. It will only take a few minutes. Remember, it's for your own good, so you won't get hung. Now, you don't want Sergeant Coulter to hang you, so please, dear, listen carefully.'

Desmond's lesson began.

Five minutes later Christie sighed.

'I see what my mother meant when she said children could try the patience of a saint.'

'I think he's got it straight now. Okay, Desmond, let's hear it once more, that's a good boy. I'll put the snake away.'

Poor Desmond sighed with relief as the snake disappeared into Barnaby's pocket.

'I shot the uncle,' he said. 'I mistaked him for the cougar.'

'Mistook, darling.'

'All right, once more, Desmond.'

'I shot the cougar, I mistook him for the uncle.'

'No! No!' Christie stamped her foot.

'Don't shout at him, that doesn't help,' said Barnaby, taking the snake out of his pocket again.

Desmond moaned and wrung his hands.

'Only once more, Desmond.'

'I shot the uncle, I mistook him for the cougar.'

'Good boy, good boy. Now where did you get the gun, Desmond?'

'I found it on the wharf.'

The snake went back to Barnaby's pocket as the children hugged Desmond.

Barnaby went to the door, opened it, took the snake from his pocket again, patted its little head and gently set it free. It flipped its tail and slithered off the porch into the grass.

Christie shuddered with relief. She hated the snake treatment, as did Barnaby, but it was necessary for poor Desmond's salvation and there was nothing they wouldn't do for poor Desmond.

Christie's conscience bothered her, and she tried to assuage it by stuffing Desmond with sweets and cookies. She kissed his empty brow as she offered him her day's ration of licorice, plus an orange she had been saving for a week and some crumbly date squares. Barnaby gave him toffee, an apple and a wad of gum he had chewed for only half an hour.

Sated, poor Desmond put his head wearily on the table and fell asleep. The children looked at him tenderly.

'Well, we've done our best,' said Barnaby, as they tiptoed away so they would not disturb him.

THE ALMOST TROPICAL DOWNPOUR of rain replenished the water supply of the Island. The wells were filling, the gardens began to revive and dozens of little rills and streamlets again flowed bubbling and happy to the ocean.

The heavy rains subsided and were replaced by a grey drizzle. Eerie mists crept through the Island, a fog hung over the water, and the inhabitants of the Island, their blood thinned by almost three months of unremitting heat, were chilled to the bone. Dove-coloured plumes of smoke floated like gauze streamers from every chimney and overnight the atmosphere became autumn.

The children, who had no rain clothes, were outfitted haphazardly by their guardians. Barnaby wore a ragged Mackinaw which had once belonged to Per Nielsen. Auntie turned the sleeves back to the elbows, but they still reached his knuckles, and the tail of the coat dragged at his heels.

Christie was garbed in a rusty-looking Burberry cape which Mrs Brooks had bought before the First World War. They were far too concerned about Uncle to care much about their appearance, but when Sergeant Coulter saw them he burst out laughing.

They looked for all the world like two pathetic little characters from *Oliver Twist*, bent on a handkerchief-snitching mission.

Sergeant Coulter, making arrangements for the cougar hunt, was almost gay. Clad in oilskins, he looked bigger and handsomer than ever to the two children when they met him on the porch of the store.

He chucked Christie under the chin and winked at her, then, ruffling Barnaby's damp yellow hair, he said cheerfully, 'Well, Dodger, what did you steal today?'

'Today? Nothing, honest, Sergeant,' he stammered.

Christie paled.

'You're a desperate-looking pair,' said Sergeant Coulter, laughing. 'Been plotting any dreadful crimes? Watch your *p*s and *q*s or Constable Browning and I will be after you.'

He reached into his pocket and brought them out a package of gum each. Turning to go into the store, he paused, then walked back to them.

'Say, listen, when the hunters and dogs start arriving, you two will have to stay indoors. Understand?'

They nodded, but when he again turned to leave them, Christie stepped forward and grabbed him by his sleeve.

'Well?' he said, puzzled.

She remained silent and looked to Barnaby.

'Sergeant,' said Barnaby hesitantly, 'when is it going to be a full moon?'

The questions children ask.

'I don't know,' said Sergeant Coulter, 'soon, I think. Why?'

Christie still clung to his sleeve.

'With the rain,' she said in a quavering voice, 'with the rain and the clouds now, you can't see the moon at night.'

'Well, don't worry, it's still there.'

They nodded non-committally, thanked him for the gum and shuffled off toward the war monument.

He stood for a second watching them. What a pitiful-looking little pair of mugs they were in those clothes. Some-how and suddenly he felt terribly sorry for them. They looked so tiny and helpless and lost.

'Hey!' he called. 'I'll check about the moon in my tide book. You ask me later, okay?'

They gave him a wan smile, waved, and like two old pen-sioners, sat wearily on the step of the monument.

Christie examined her gum and tossed it to Barnaby in disgust.

'Peppermint,' she said.

Barnaby, as always, crammed the ten sticks in his mouth, and with a titanic effort, managed to chew them.

They sat watching Mr Duncan, laden with a pack of feed, walking up from the dock. He glanced grumpily at them as he passed, and once his back was to them Barnaby shoved the gum into one cheek in a hideous manner, while Christie crossed her eyes like an idiot and let her tongue hang on her chin.

Barnaby sighed and took the gum from his mouth.

'Listen,' he said finally, 'you're sure you remember all I told you about how to shoot the gun?'

Christie nodded.

'Don't forget to hold it tight to your shoulder. If anything happens to me, don't get scared and forget. Just keep calm and shoot him.'

'Why are you so worried about me?' asked Christie.

'Oh, I'm not,' he said, tossing the lump of gum up and down. 'I just want to make sure if I get killed, he goes too.'

Christie nodded understandingly.

'We haven't much time,' he continued. 'I'm sure it's either tonight or tomorrow night. I guess tonight would be the best time.'

Christie trembled. They were both terrified now that the actual commission of the crime was at hand, and if they had had any way of escaping from the Island to avoid the murder, they would have.

To make matters worse, during the last couple of days Uncle's schedule had been most erratic. He was always buzzing off and on the Island, and he had also taken to rambling happily along the beaches and sprinting up and down the steep cliffs with the air of a large, friendly mountain goat.

'We'll hide in the bushes on the way to the cottage,' said Barnaby. 'With any luck he's bound to pass by, and with all the hunters on the Island, nobody will notice the shot.'

How little they knew. Uncle had exactly the same plan in mind, except he was far too cunning to use a gun.

'Do you think they'll get One-ear?' asked Christie.

Barnaby shook his head.

'I don't think so. He's been hunted before and they never caught him. He's too smart to sit around and wait to get killed. Once he hears those dogs, he'll beat it.'

But One-ear had no intention of leaving. In common with Uncle and other wild animals, he also was affected by the moon, and he too planned a murder, a murder he had long wished to execute.

Barnaby stood up.

'Come on,' he said. 'Let's go over to Mr Duncan's field and get some apples. Those hard yellow ones are ripe now.'

Christie shook her head. She was afraid of the Iron Duke who was tethered in that very field.

The rain drizzled quietly down on them.

'Well, we can't sit here all day. Let's go and play with One-ear.'

'All right,' said Christie in a flat voice. All the verve and bounce of childhood seemed to have gone out of them.

Clad in their soggy, flowing vestments, they walked to the forest. The rain had stopped temporarily, but their legs were chilled by the water-laden grasses, and when they jarred against bushes, cool showers sprinkled down the backs of their necks.

It was a discouraged-looking pair that found One-ear.

Barnaby and Christie stopped and stared at him strangely. Something was the matter with One-ear. They looked at each other, then back to him.

What was it?

One-ear, for the first time since they had met him, was happy. He was extremely pleased with himself.

He purred when he saw them and rubbed his big head against Christie's shoulder, knocking her down. He leaped into the air, swatting a drifting leaf, and chased his tail like a kitten. His creamy breast was stained with blood, and there were shreds of flesh between his claws.

A grouse, looking like a damp, cross dowager, skittered along the path, its tail outspread and its head held high.

One-ear purred louder than ever and sprang after it.

His eyes were no longer green; a hidden black demon expanded the pupils. His tail, usually so supple, was stiff, and his body was one line of deadly grace.

The children drew back. This was not the One-ear who crankily allowed them to maul him. This was a cruel One-ear whose sustained mirth frightened them.

One-ear leaped six feet in the air, and the startled grouse disintegrated into a puff of gory, blowing feathers. Rippling with feline humour and lazy ease, the cougar turned to the children.

They drew back even farther. They had seen murder, and the forest was full of apples and serpents. It was the end of innocence, for they knew now that One-ear would never, never like cinnamon buns.

With dragging feet and downcast eyes they arrived at the goat-lady's for lunch. Because of the chilly rain, she had prepared a hot meal for them, with one of their favourite dishes, baked macaroni. She took it from the oven, bubbling with golden cheese, and set it before them, accompanied by the salad they liked best, chopped fried bacon, lettuce and onion, tossed with a tart dressing.

Instead of the usual ohs and ahs, they merely picked at the meal listlessly, and when she brought out the dessert, a creamy rice pudding, they shook their heads and pushed their plates away.

The change in the weather was affecting even them, reflected the goat-lady, and she did not urge them to eat more. After she had cleared the table, they sat staring at each other.

'What'll we do now?' sighed Christie.

Would they, asked the goat-lady, like to play checkers, or cards, or perhaps draw pictures?

They settled for cards, but they bickered so fretfully and accused each other of cheating so often that they gave up.

Barnaby sat swinging violently and noisily in the rocking chair, while Christie, perched on the black leather sofa, teased Tom with a dangling piece of string until he reached out and scratched her. She whined peevishly and said she hated cats when the goat-lady put iodine on the wound.

Finally, at her wits' end trying to amuse them, the goat-lady decided Mrs Brooks could have the pleasure of their company for a while. She gave them a bag of cookies and told them to take it to Mrs Brooks for tea. They could, she added, have some on the way, if they wished.

It was raining heavily again, and they had nearly finished the cookies by the time they reached the store. Although the store itself was deserted, the potbellied stove in the center was roaring cheerfully, and they could hear Mr Brooks bustling about in the parlour.

They took off their squelchy, wet running shoes and put them on a chair before the stove to dry, then, like a pair of tired mice, they crept onto a pile of clothing under the counter and munched the remainder of the cookies.

The bell on the door rang and Mr Brooks came dashing from the back.

'Ah, Sergeant Coulter. Everything ready?'

'Just about,' replied the Mountie. 'Do you mind if we use the store as a meeting place?'

'Not at all. Have you time for a cup of tea?'

'No, thank you.' Sergeant Coulter spread a map of the Island on the counter. 'There'll be six hunting parties, so I've split the Island into six sections, we're sure to get him that way. They should be arriving in about half an hour. By the way, keep the children in, either here or at Mrs Nielsen's. We don't want any accidents. Oh, yes, I nearly forgot. Tell them I checked in my tide book and it's a full moon tonight.'

The bell on the door rang again, and Agnes Duncan, dishevelled, flushed and strangely elated, came running in.

'Come quickly,' she gasped, grabbing Sergeant Coulter's arm. 'Something terrible has happened.'

As they ran from the store, leaving Mr Brooks with his mouth open, in came Uncle.

'Dear me,' said Uncle, 'what *is* all the commotion about? A pound of sugar and some matches, please.'

'It's One-ear,' said Mr Brooks. 'There's a cougar on the Island and they think it's One-ear. He may have been here for weeks, Major, and we didn't even know it. The hunting parties will be arriving soon.'

'Tsk, tsk,' said Uncle.

'I suppose you've done a lot of hunting yourself, Major. Will you be joining the guns this afternoon?'

'Good gracious, no!' cried Uncle in a shocked voice. 'I'm terrified of guns, they make me very nervous. War, you know. Can't bear killing of any sort. No stomach for it.'

Mr Brooks looked relieved.

'I'm exactly the same way,' he confided.

Behind their dark glasses, Uncle's mad eyes settled on the two pairs of shoes before the fire.

What an extraordinary piece of luck! He had planned to take them off the bodies later, but this was much better. Timing was always of prime importance, and this gave him a little edge.

Uncle was warming his hands before the fire in a leisurely manner when Mr Brooks handed him his parcel.

'If you'll excuse me, Major, I think I hear Mrs Brooks calling.'

'Of course, of course,' said Uncle. 'Such chilly weather.'

He watched Mr Brooks disappear behind the swinging beaded curtains. He left carrying his package, and, carefully concealed under his coat, two pairs of other small items.

Emerging from their hiding place, the children went to get their shoes.

'They're gone,' said Christie turning to Barnaby.

'Uncle,' said Barnaby.

'But what would anyone want with a couple of pairs of old running shoes? Mine had a hole right through the sole.'

Barnaby shrugged. He was so accustomed to Uncle's full-moon eccentricities that they hardly bore mentioning.

'Probably so we can't run so fast when he tries to kill us,' he said.

'Oh,' said Christie in a faint little voice, and put a trembling hand to her lips. 'I'm scared, Barnaby. Let's tell Sergeant Coulter again.'

'What's the use? He wouldn't believe us now, any more than he did the last time. Besides, he's too busy trying to catch One-ear. He'd just tell us not to bother him.'

Christie's common sense took over.

'You're right,' she said in a brusque manner. 'Besides, Uncle isn't going to kill us, we're going to kill him. And it doesn't make any difference about the shoes, it's practically like going barefoot wearing them anyway. Say, what are we going to do about being kept in for the rest of the day?'

'Easy,' said Barnaby. 'We tell Mr and Mrs Brooks we're going to Auntie's, and we tell Auntie we'll be at the store.'

THE PRIDE OF THE ISLAND was dead, murdered in a savage battle with One-ear.

Mr Duncan wept, Agnes rejoiced and the Islanders mourned.

Sergeant Coulter, surveying the scene of slaughter, looked grimmer than usual. He leaned down and inspected the telltale front paw pug and then gazed sadly at the remains of the bull.

Chained as he was, the mighty Duke had not had a chance, and Albert, who detested foul play, nodded to himself. By tomorrow afternoon, he silently vowed, One-ear would be on his way to a taxidermist in Victoria.

Squaring his shoulders, he went back to the wharf to greet the men and hounds.

By two o'clock a dozen vessels were moored to the float beside the wharf. From gas boats, speedboats and launches poured baying hounds and lean, gun-bearing men. Sergeant Coulter and the provincial game warden directed them up to the store, and half an hour later the various parties split up to begin covering the Island.

All afternoon, from every point on the Island, the two frightened children could hear the signal shots and the echoes of barking, snarling dogs. At six o'clock a member of each party came to the store to take back sandwiches and hot coffee for the hunters.

There was an almost festive air in the store, with Mrs Brooks and Agnes busy cutting bread and opening tins of corned beef. The old Islanders, clad in ancient deerstalkers and gaiters, were caught up in the spirit of the hunt and, briskly swinging their walking sticks, they dropped by for news.

The dogs were still fresh, said the men, and had picked up the scent. The rain made it difficult, but the hunters felt confident they would track him down in the next couple of hours. Once treed, he was finished, for the dogs would tear him apart alive if he came down.

The children sat quietly, listening. They tried to keep their minds on One-ear's fate, but they found it almost impossible. It would begin to get dark between eight and nine, and in just a little over two hours they had a man-sized job on their hands and they knew it.

The aura of excitement that hung over the usually quiet Island did nothing to calm their already taut nerves and they sat with their fists clenched, unable to eat or relax, and wondering how they could possibly bear another two hours of tension.

Like everyone else on the Island, they were shocked that One-ear had killed the Iron Duke. It struck them as a brutal, senseless act, and try as they would, they found it difficult to justify One-ear's behaviour.

'It serves him right, and I don't care. It serves him right. He's as bad as Uncle,' whispered Barnaby.

He turned to Christie.

'I don't care,' he repeated.

'You do too,' said Christie. 'And he's not like Uncle. That's the way cougars are supposed to act. Uncle's bad because he pretends to be a real person.'

'Maybe they won't catch him,' said Barnaby hopefully.

As the minutes ticked on, they wished desperately that they knew where either Sergeant Coulter or Uncle was. Barnaby whispered that Uncle was probably out looking for them, and the smartest thing they could do would be to get the gun and hide in the bushes now, even though it was still daylight.

Christie was all for going home to the safety and comfort of her bed and murdering Uncle some other night.

'You're not backing out now,' her companion informed her. 'Because I'm not, and as long as I'm not, you're not, whether you like it or not. It was your idea and you're going to stick with it.'

'I'm not trying to back out!' said Christie indignantly. 'It's just that I'm so scared!'

'You think I'm not? And if you think you'll be safe at Auntie's if he's made up his mind to do it tonight, you're crazy. I told you, you don't know what he's like. I've seen him do things - '

He stopped, his firm little mouth clamped together.

'All right, all right,' said Christie. 'We'd better tell Mr and Mrs Brooks we're going to Auntie's.'

Mrs Brooks did not like the idea at all. They were supposed to stay indoors until One-ear was shot, that was what Sergeant Coulter had said.

But they would be indoors, once they got to Auntie's, they insisted, and they would walk only on the roads and it would take them only fifteen minutes. Please, please, it was so hot and stuffy in the store, and they'd been in all afternoon.

Mrs Brooks consulted Mr Brooks. Well, said Mr Brooks, there was no place for Christie to sleep at the store, so she would have to go home sometime anyway. Barnaby could go with her, if they went straight to the goat-lady's, and stayed inside, and Barnaby would have to spend the night there.

Mr Brooks paused. Still, he said, he didn't like to bother Mrs Nielsen, and it didn't seem right to send Barnaby there without first asking her.

'Oh, she won't mind,' cried Christie. 'Barnaby can sleep on the black leather sofa, and Auntie would never let him go out to walk home by himself in the dark.'

So they received permission to leave the store, and they left, with no intention of going to Auntie's.

They decided to hunt for a suitable spot in the bushes from which they could waylay Uncle, and once having found it they would sneak back to the church for the gun.

They found a place not too heavily overgrown, and with a good view of the path, at the same time still affording them a certain amount of seclusion.

'This is as good as anything we'll find,' whispered Christie.

Barnaby raised and turned his head in a curious fashion.

'What's the matter?'

'Do you smell cigar smoke?' he whispered.

Christie sniffed and shook her head.

'I guess maybe I'm imagining it.' He sounded relieved. 'Come on, let's get the gun.'

Christie was worried in case someone saw them. There were people all over the Island now.

It was a chance they would have to take, said Barnaby. Everything would be okay once they were hidden with the gun.

Yes, answered Christie gloomily, as long as Uncle didn't act first.

'Well, let's hurry and get the gun then.'

It was eerie in the dim, silent little church, and the children were anxious to get out of it as quickly as possible. Barnaby checked the gun to make sure it was loaded.

It wasn't.

'I thought you said everything was ready,' said Christie.

'I thought it was.' Barnaby was confused and rubbed his forehead with his fist. 'I came in yesterday and cleaned the gun, it wasn't loaded then, but I thought I loaded it before I left.'

'Well, load it now, anyhow,' said Christie.

He did, and they left hurriedly, running bent over to make themselves inconspicuous.

They saw no one on the way back, and it was with a sigh of relief that they crouched in the little bush-enclosed clearing.

'Whew!' Christie wiped beads of sweat from her brow. It was raining and cold, but clad in the heavy Burberry cape she felt hot and weak.

Barnaby crouched with the gun across his knee, gazing at the path.

'I wonder how long we'll have to wait,' he whispered. 'If he doesn't come by dark, we may have to go to the cottage and shoot him through a window or something.'

There was no answer from Christie, and he sat, waiting to hear her say no, they would try again tomorrow night and she was afraid to go to the cottage.

But Christie was still silent.

Barnaby turned to her.

'Well,' he said, 'we *will* have to, tonight, you know.'

She didn't answer him.

He put the gun down and crawled over to her.

'What's the matter with you?' he whispered.

Christie's face had the expressionless calm of a death mask.

'What is it?' Barnaby repeated.

She turned her head slowly, let her breath out, and pointed.

Crudely and freshly drawn on the damp earth beside her were two little Teddy bears, with nooses around their necks.

'Oh, no,' said Barnaby and closed his eyes.

They were not hunting Uncle, Uncle was hunting them, and enjoying the chase to the full.

'He came here while we were at the church getting the gun. What are we going to do?' whispered Christie.

Barnaby looked very weary. With a great effort of will he pulled himself together.

'We can't stay here. I know him. He's scaring us now. He likes that. We're safe as long as he's doing that. It's when he stops teasing us we've got to worry. Oh, Christie, what'll we do? Where'll we go? Do you think we could make it back to the store or Auntie's?'

Christie's expression had changed. Her eyes were narrow and hard. In a rage, she took a stick and scratched out the two Teddy bears.

'That's the meanest thing I ever came across,' she said. 'No, of course he won't let us get back to the store. Or Auntie's. And we're too far away to call anyone for help.'

Barnaby sat with the rifle cradled in his arms and his head bowed. It was beginning to get dark and rain fell on the forlorn little pair.

The echoes of guns sounded in their ears, some booming, some sharp and staccato, depending on which direction the wind wafted them.

Christie raised her head.

'Listen,' she said. 'What was the signal shots the man said they would fire? Was it two with a ten-second stop if they wounded him or was that if they killed him?'

But they had been too frightened when they were in the store to pay much attention and they couldn't remember.

Barnaby suddenly straightened up.

'We can't stay here,' he said. 'If we could get into the forest, maybe we could meet some of the hunters. We'd be safe then. Come on, Christie, let's get out of here.'

Yes, it was too awful to sit there patiently waiting for Uncle's next move. Joining hands and looking fearfully in all directions, they began to run toward the gloomy forest.

The rifle was heavy and they were both barefooted. Blackberry vines dragged at their soaking clothes, hidden roots tripped them, and the mists and dusk produced a million leering, phantasmagoric wicked uncles, all waiting to clutch them.

Christie stumbled and bruised her foot cruelly on a sharp stone. She stopped, leaned her head against a stump and closed her eyes.

Barnaby, clutching the rifle and trembling violently, stood looking at her. Finally he put out his hand and touched her shoulder.

'I'm sorry, Christie.'

Christie wiped her nose on her cape and faced him.

'It's all right. It isn't your fault. Let's go.'

They joined hands and began to run again, Christie limping painfully.

A sudden crash in the bushes made their hearts almost stand still. A grouse flew noisily past them. They ran on until sheer exhaustion forced them to pause again.

'Oh, I wish Sergeant Coulter was here,' gasped Christie, sitting down and rubbing her foot.

Barnaby sat beside her, the rifle still clutched at his breast.

'It's no good,' he said quietly. 'No one can help us now. Don't you understand, Christie? He's got it all planned.'

A low chuckle from the bushes made them spring to their feet and continue their awful race.

When they reached a bend in the path, Christie stopped suddenly in her tracks.

'I'm not going in any forest!' she panted. 'That's where we saw him the day of the storm.'

'But where'll we go, Christie?'

'We're going back to the church,' she said. 'And he's not going to kill us. We're going to kill him.'

Stumbling wildly, the children turned and changed the direction of their flight to the church. In their panic it had not occurred to them how close they were to it.

Gasping and shaking, they reached the church and entered it.

They walked slowly down the aisle, then stopped and looked about them with fear.

It was almost dark. They saw a box of matches in the front pew, and past the pew the candles of the altar stood pristine and white.

'Light them,' whispered Christie.

Barnaby shook his head. He was not going to put down the rifle.

'You,' he said. 'I'll stay next to you.'

The lighted candles gave them a feeling of security, of being outside the province of Uncle's dark domain, of belonging to a concrete world, instead of a land of shadows.

Taking deep breaths, and walking back to the pews, they sat down.

And waited.

'Christie,' said Barnaby finally, 'when he gets here, talk to me. Say anything, but talk to me and don't stop.'

'Why?'

'I don't know, but do it.'

The minutes dragged slowly on, with only the distant sounds of the baying dogs and rifles to mark them.

'Oh, why doesn't he come, if he's going to,' moaned Christie.

Barnaby sat stroking the stock of the rifle.

'Because he's going to make it as tough as he can for us. I wonder if he unloaded the gun. I'm sure I loaded it.'

'But if he did, why did he leave the bullets?' whispered Christie.

Barnaby shook his head.

'I don't know. I don't know why he ever does anything. But if he did, it's because he's got a reason. He always has. I know him.'

There was a crash at the door.

Barnaby jumped to his feet, swinging the rifle to his shoulder as he did.

The handle of the door had been knocked off and hurled halfway across the church.

In the doorway One-ear stood swaying, his tail lashing and his head lowered.

Then he flopped on his belly and crawled toward them. He had been shot through the lungs, and halfway down the aisle he collapsed and coughed up blood.

The two white-faced children stood staring stupidly at him. He raised his head and gazed at them with the big, cool green eyes they loved so, then he crawled painfully forward and lay at their feet.

All his sins were forgiven as the children knelt beside him and kissed his battle-scarred head. No matter what he did or what happened, they loved him.

'Oh, I hope it doesn't hurt him too much,' said Barnaby, gently stroking his head.

The baying of the dogs sounded closer, and the cougar shook off the boy's hand. He tried to sit up, but he could not. He closed his eyes then opened them wearily, gazing at the rifle which Barnaby had propped against the pew.

'The dogs! The dogs! The men in the store said they'd tear him apart alive!' said Barnaby.

'Oh, no!' cried Christie.

One-ear turned his head from the rifle to them.

Shoot me, the eyes begged.

Barnaby and Christie looked at each other in horror.

'You'll have to shoot him,' she whispered. 'You can't let the dogs get him.'

It was then Barnaby realised he had laid the rifle aside. He picked it up and sat down on the bench, with Christie beside him.

'No,' he said. 'No. The bullets are for Uncle.'

One-ear sighed and closed his eyes and the children sat quietly looking at him. Waiting.

The tall white tapers on the altar had burned halfway down when suddenly they flickered as a cold draft passed through the church.

'Oh, Barnabee ... I'

Puzzled, the children raised their heads. They heard the whisper, but they didn't know from where it came.

'Oh, Barnabeee ... Uncle's here.'

They turned their heads but they saw no one.

'Oh, Bar-na-bee,' the sweet, insidious voice drifted through the little church.

'Bar - na - beeeee——I've come for you.'

They swept their heads in an arc, but still they saw nothing.

'Talk to me,' said Barnaby. 'Christie, talk to me!'

'What'll I say?'

'Tell me about MacNab.'

'Oh Bar - na - bee——I see you, but you don't see me, do you? I'm hiding behind a pew, but there are so many pews and you don't know which one, do you? You're so tired, Barnaby, so tired. You're going to go to sleep, Barnaby.'

'Talk!' whispered Barnaby.

'At Christmas,' said Christie, 'at Christmas, when he comes with my presents, we dance together. He's usually drunk but I don't mind, just my mother. At Christmas he always wears a funny Scotch hat he got when he was in the war.'

'Your eyes are getting heavy, very heavy, Barnaby. How thoughtful of you to bring your little friend. You are an accommodating child, Barnaby, and I shall miss you, upon my word I will. Close your eyes now, my dear.'

'That's how they met, him and my mother, during the war, when he was in London. My mother worked there. Her brother is a doctor. MacNab, he always says that's the Scotch for you, send the sons to university and the daughters into service, but my mother says I'm going to go to university.'

'You are almost asleep now. Your eyes are so heavy, so heavy, and you are so drowsy. Your eyes are as heavy as lead, and you purloined a gun to shoot poor Uncle. Really, Barnaby, that was very naughty of you.'

'He loves his Scotch hat. He always puts it on my head when we dance. He's from Cape Breton. I don't know just where Cape Breton is, but it's on the other side of Canada.'

'You are asleep now, Barnaby. Sound asleep because you are so tired, so tired, so tired. You are asleep and you can't move. It was I who took the bullets out of the gun, you know. And then I *let* you put them back in. Do you know why? Poor Barnaby, so tired, so tired. I let you put the bullets in because the gun is useless to you. You can't move, Barnaby, you can't move, Barnaby, you can't use the gun.'

'I remember now, it's a Seaforth hat, the Seaforth Highlanders they're called, but they're not Scotch, they're from Canada too. Maybe they're from Cape Breton, like MacNab.'

'Sleep, sleep, sleep. Did you really think you would have any chance against me, you silly little boy?'

'It has a silver badge on it, with a deer's head on the badge and under it says, 'Save the King,' only not in English. It's in Scotch but that's not what they call it. I forget what they call it, but MacNab speaks it and my mother doesn't, and she's Scotch. That's funny, isn't it Barnaby?'

'My voice is so soothing, so soft, so sleep-making, and you want to sleep, sleep, sleep. Do you know why you went to the church instead of the forest? Because I wanted you to. Because I waited until you were on the edge of the forest and then I frightened you. I knew you would panic and the only other place you could go was to the church.'

'It's funny because she's the one who's Scotch, not Mac-Nab. He's from Cape Breton, but I told you that, didn't I?'

'I didn't want you to go to the forest. It's much too crowded there today. I wanted you in the church. You see, they're all out after the cougar, and they'll never think of looking for you here. Of course, you won't be here long. Once they've shot the cougar and they leave the forest ... why, then we'll go there, all three of us. We'll have a little picnic and you won't even have to walk. I'll carry you both, one over each shoulder. Won't that be jolly and won't we have fun?'

Christie looked at Barnaby. He was staring straight ahead, like a bird hypnotised by a snake, and the useless rifle was firmly clamped against his chest.

'At Christmas ... at Christmas, when we dance ... when we dance ... we dance reels. Our favourite is called 'The Dashing White Sergeant' ... '
She stopped and placed her hands on her temples.
'Oh, Sergeant,' she whispered, 'where are you now?'

'Do you hear the dogs? They're a long way off. They haven't got the cougar yet and poor Barnaby can't move a muscle, he can't move a muscle, he's asleep, asleep, asleep and the pretty gun is no use and isn't that a shame? We're going to play games. Oh, I know all sorts of games. Games you've never even heard of.'

Christie looked around again.

Uncle was standing three pews behind them.

'Shoot him!' she gasped as Uncle began to move slowly down the aisle, his lips drawn back over his teeth, and in his hands a piece of long, supple wire, weighted on each end with a bar of wood.

'Shoot him!' she said again. 'Please, Barnaby, shoot him!'

Barnaby's dazed eyes were riveted. He couldn't move.

'Shoot him!' cried Christie. When she realised that he couldn't, she leaned down and tried to pry the gun from his arms, but his hands were frozen on it.

'It's no use. She can't get the gun out of your hands. Nobody can. They would have to break your arms first.'

Christie closed her eyes, then opened them and looked up at Uncle, who was slowly approaching her with a coy smile on his face.

'Oh, no,' she whispered.

'Oh, yes,' he whispered.

Things were going beautifully. With the confusion of the cougar hunt, they wouldn't be missed for hours. Already the leaky rowboat was bobbing in the waves beneath the cliff and their little shoes were placed at the water's edge of Death Beach, one pair still cunningly laced. The bodies, of course, would never be found.

Christie stepped back and stumbled over One-ear.

He gave one hiss of agony.

As Uncle took another step forward, three hundred pounds of pain-ridden, steel-muscled, hate-filled beige murder sprang from the floor, the claws leaving inch-deep scars in the wood.

Uncle, wicked, wicked Uncle, instinctively raised both hands to protect his throat. But alas, he got them tangled in the deadly, twining wire.

Like himself, One-ear was an accomplished murderer.

It was soon done, but it was a scene from hell while it lasted, with over-turned pews, blood-stained prayer books, broken candles and low snarls from two throats.

Christie stood silently with her eyes closed. At last she opened them and gave Uncle a cursory glance.

She sat next to Barnaby.

'You've got to wake up now. It's time for you to wake up. He said you couldn't but you can. He's dead, so it's all right to wake up.'

Barnaby did not move.

Christie frowned.

'It's me, Christie. Wake up now. He made you go to sleep, I don't know how he did it, but he did. He's dead, One-ear killed him, so wake up. Hurry up, Barnaby, wake up. I want you to. I don't like being here alone. I want you to wake up now, so open your eyes. You can let go of the gun too, he's dead so we don't need it any more. I don't like being here alone, so wake up and let go of the gun.'

Barnaby stirred drowsily. Suddenly he blinked his eyes, shook his head and sprang to his feet.

'What happened?'

'You mean you don't remember? But that's not fair. I had to see it all!' She sighed. 'One-ear killed Uncle. You can look at him if you want. He's over there. I did. He looks awful, but I don't care. I'm glad he's dead.'

Barnaby arose and walked over to the wicked Uncle's body. He nodded to himself, and kneeling down he untangled the wire. He gazed at it curiously for a minute, then rolled it up and put it in his pocket.

He looked from the dead Uncle to Christie, and then to One-ear, who lay on his side panting.

Barnaby sat next to Christie again, their eyes on poor One-ear, whose life blood was slowly draining away from him.

They did not speak.

As the candles burned lower and lower, the sounds of baying, snarling dogs came closer and closer. The old warrior raised his head weakly.

Shoot me, the beautiful emerald eyes were beseeching.

Christie turned to Barnaby.

'You can't let the dogs get him. Shoot him.'

Barnaby bowed his head on his hands.

'I can't. I just can't, Christie.'

Christie's eyes filled with rage.

'You!' she screamed. 'You! You're just like MacNab! You talk! But it's my mother and me who always have to do the dirty work!'

She grabbed the rifle, held it firmly to her shoulder, took careful aim at One-ear and fired.

She returned the rifle to Barnaby, then struck him as hard as she could.

Barnaby rose, tossed the rifle aside and hit her back. They fell to the floor, fighting savagely.

Sergeant Coulter stood in the doorway. Never had he been so frightened.

It was a warlock's Sabbath that met the horrified gaze of the Mountie, blood and death and flickering shadows, with the cougar hounds, leaping over everything, baying and snarling like creatures from unspeakable regions, and the two hysterical children twisting on the floor, screaming.

He kicked the dogs aside, spurring the famous hound, Mynheer, who, blood-crazed, perversely insisted on worrying the throat of Uncle rather than One-ear.

He reached the children, dragged them apart, picked them up and carried them, one under each arm, outside.

They still screamed. Overcome by relief and a senseless rage, he slapped them until they both hiccuped to silence.

He handed them to Constable Browning.

'Take them home,' he said, and re-entered the church.

D R WHEELER CAME OVER from Benares to sign the death certificate. Cause of death? Death was due to misadventure, and the case was closed.

Apart from One-ear and Uncle, the only other casualty was Constable Browning, who had injured his foot when he fell in some sort of pit in the forest, during the darkness.

It was a darned crime, he said, for people to go around leaving things like that open, and it should be filled in. But Sergeant Coulter, who was an Island boy and knew all about these things, said it had probably been there for fifty years, and it was only one chance in a million that anyone had fallen in it, so remote was its position. It was probably a trap, made by the Indians.

Barnaby, that sturdy little fellow, was a hero. Yes, Christie said, once she got her breath back, Barnaby had shot the cougar after it had killed Uncle. Barnaby modestly admitted this was so.

Reporters came from the city to take pictures and write stories of the plucky boy who, single-handed, had shot the largest cougar on record. The dread cougar who for so long had ravaged the peaceful countryside.

The Islanders were stunned by the death of poor Uncle Sylvester, but the man would no doubt be justly canonised in heaven, dying as he had to protect those helpless innocents. Mr Rice-Hope wondered if he should ask the Bishop for the rites of exorcism, for surely his little church had been invaded by a demon incarnate.

'My dear children, my dear children,' he cried, clasping them to his bosom, 'you have no idea how close you came to the fiend himself. That animal was almost human.'

He paused.

'Dear me,' he added in alarm, 'what am I saying?'

One-ear lay wrapped in a bloody tarpaulin on the deck of Sven Anderson's boat. The photographers wanted to take Barnaby's picture holding the rifle and standing beside the huge cougar, but the child went so pitifully white at the suggestion that Mr Brooks intervened.

Leading the press away, he chided them on their lack of delicacy.

'Gentlemen, gentlemen,' he said, 'the poor child saw that animal kill his uncle. Why, Major Murchison-Gaunt was like a father to the boy. Surely you must realise how shocking the sight of the beast, dead or alive, must be to him.'

He shook his head and fumbled for his pipe, at a loss for words, and shamefaced, even those hardened men left the child to his natural grief.

The one little fly in the ointment was the rifle. The children insisted they had found it in Desmond's shack. Desmond, they said, had found it on the wharf.

Sergeant Coulter knew how hopeless questioning poor Desmond would be, and since he couldn't shake the story of the children, he was forced to accept it for the time being.

But the gun had been stolen, and he knew it, and poor Desmond, in his whole thirty-five years, had never before taken anything that did not belong to him.

Albert was a patient man, and he knew that the truth, like murder, would out. The children had been subject to quite enough excitement in the last twenty-four hours. He would give them a couple of days' grace before interrogating them further about the rifle.

He and Constable Browning were in the launch, on their way to the little hospital at Benares where Constable Browning would have his ankle X-rayed.

Constable Browning sat resting his injured foot, staring reflectively at Sergeant Coulter.

'They're going to hang Gitskass Charlie.'

'Yes,' said Sergeant Coulter, 'I thought they would.'

He hated the idea that he was secretly relieved.

'I saw Skookum Charlie, Sonny's uncle, in Nanaimo last week. The way he spoke, it sounds as if they'll hold a family celebration when they hang Sonny. It doesn't seem right. After all, he is a member of their family.'

'So was his father,' observed Sergeant Coulter drily.

Constable Browning scratched his head.

'Well,' he said, 'Gitskass Charlie is crazy. It doesn't seem right in this day and age to hang people for being mentally incompetent. Don't you think so?'

'The courts found him sane. That's why they're hanging him.'

'I know, but it stands to reason, people don't commit murders like that if they are sane.'

Sergeant Coulter sighed. Constable Browning was twenty-one years of age and he could, Sergeant Coulter knew, argue interminably on a moral point.

'Listen,' said Albert, 'just try to remember that we've got a lot of intelligent people who decide what laws are legislated. We have our little say when we vote, and after that all we do is enforce them.'

'Well, do you think it's right to hang Gitskass?'

'If that's the law.'

Constable Browning was not giving in so easily.

'But what if the wrong people got in power in the government. It could happen, you know. Look at Hitler. The people put him in power. What if that happened in Canada, and laws were passed saying that all mental patients had to be destroyed. Would you still obey the law?'

'It won't happen in Canada.'

'That's it! It can't happen here!' said Constable Browning with youthful triumph. 'Well, it did in Germany. You were a prisoner of war, you know what they did well enough. What would you do then? Would you still enforce the law and help round up all the crackpots of the country and gas them?'

'What are you trying to do, make me into a Storm Trooper?'

'It's a hypothetical question. What's your answer?'

'Another hypothetical question. Why didn't you join the Brownies instead of the Mounties?'

Constable Browning gave him a wounded look, and, picking up the field glasses, he limped out to the deck.

'Don't go away mad,' Albert called after him, laughing.

Constable Browning had had two years, university, and Sergeant Coulter was undecided if they were too much or too little.

As the launch passed Death Beach, Sergeant Coulter was startled to hear.

'*Oh my God!*'

'What's the matter?' he called. 'Are you all right?'

When he received no answer, he cut the motor and dashed onto the deck, where he found Constable Browning standing with his head bowed and the glasses dangling from his hand.

Looking past him, Sergeant Coulter saw the leaky old rowboat, half filled with water, bobbing on the waves.

He grabbed the field glasses and swept them over the beach.

Then he, too, bowed his head and the glasses dangled from his hand.

The two little pairs of shoes, as sad as empty Christmas stockings, stood by the water's edge, one pair still laced the way a naughty, careless boy would step out of them. Sergeant Coulter raised the glasses again.

Yes, they were Barnaby's. The toes were slit, just as Sergeant Coulter remembered seeing them. How terrible! Spared from death by One-ear, only to be drowned the following day!

Two white-faced Mounties returned to the dock.

'Start making arrangements for dragging operations,' Sergeant Coulter shuddered. 'And I - I - I suppose I'll have to go up and see the Brookses and Mrs Nielsen.'

But before he had a chance to impart the dreadful news, he ran into the two departed spirits. They were sitting on the porch of the store chawing green apples.

'What - how - ?' Sergeant Coulter paused, unable to speak. His emotions were twofold: he was so glad to see them alive; at the same time he wanted to box their ears for going back to that beach.

Startled by his expression, they leaped to their feet.

'You've been back to Death Beach!' he shouted.

They protested their innocence so indignantly and vehemently that he believed them.

'Well how do you explain the rowboat out in the water? It was past the tide line on the beach, so don't tell me it floated out. And how did your shoes get there if you haven't been there?'

They knew nothing about the rowboat, and the last time they had seen their running shoes was when they had left them in front of the stove in the store to dry. The running shoes had disappeared and the children couldn't find them.

The boy was playing with an odd-looking weighted piece of wire.

'What's that you've got there?'

Barnaby handed it to him.

A commando garrote. Sergeant Coulter hadn't seen one in years. The handgrips of teak were worn smooth.

'Where did you get this?'

Uncle had had it in his hands when One-ear leaped on him, said the boy.

Albert stood puzzled, looking down at it.

'I want the truth,' he began, and stopped, appalled by the expressions on their faces. Their teeth chattered with terror, and without a word, they turned and fled.

Sergeant Coulter looked around. It was only poor Desmond. Why were they so frightened of him?

Ah, but having wound poor Desmond up, they had completely forgotten to unwind him.

'Desmond,' said Sergeant Coulter gently, 'have you done something to scare the kids? You haven't been a bad boy, now, have you?'

'Uh uh,' said Desmond, putting his finger in his mouth.

Still puzzled, the Mountie shook his head and turned to go, but Desmond barred his path.

He stood squarely in the way, took his finger out of his mouth and scratched his head.

Finally he remembered.

'I did it!' he said with his lucid smile.

'You did what, Desmond?'

But Desmond had forgotten again. Sergeant Coulter decided there would be no more mysteries on his Island.

In a friendly manner, he put his hand on Desmond's shoulder. 'It's all right, whatever it is, Desmond. Now you try and remember what it was you did.'

Desmond moaned, wrung his hands and begged Sergeant Coulter not to scare him with the snake.

So that was it. The damned kids had been teasing Desmond.

'It's all right, I haven't got any snake, Desmond.'

Desmond smiled.

'Now I remember,' he said distinctly. 'I killed the uncle. Barnaby's uncle.'

Sergeant Coulter swallowed hard.

'You *what?*'

'Yup.'

'Now listen here, Desmond,' said Sergeant Coulter, and his voice was very quiet, 'One-ear, the cougar, killed Barnaby's uncle. I know. I know that for sure. Right now it's about the only thing I *am* sure of.'

'Yes,' said Desmond, delighted that Sergeant Coulter was following his reasoning, 'that's it. I mistook the uncle for the cougar. I mistook the uncle for the cougar and I shot him.'

'Indeed,' said Sergeant Coulter, his eyes cold and hard. 'Then you must have had a gun, Desmond. Tell me what you know about the gun, Desmond.'

'Gun?' Desmond was in agony again and wrung his hands once more. 'Gun?'

Then he smiled. 'Yes, the gun. They put it under my bed. I found it but they told me not to touch it.'

'They did, did they? Did they tell you to say this, about killing Major Murchison-Gaunt?'

'Who?' said Desmond.

'The uncle, the uncle, Barnaby's uncle.'

'Yup,' said Desmond proudly. He'd been a good boy and remembered everything. 'Can I have a candy now?'

'Yes, of course, Desmond.'

He took poor Desmond by the arm and led him toward the police launch.

Constable Browning limped out.

'The kids are all right,' said Sergeant Coulter. 'See if Sven will give you a lift over to Benares. I want to talk to Desmond. Have you got any candy around? I promised Desmond some.'

'There's a chocolate bar in the desk drawer.'

When he had left them, Sergeant Coulter turned to Desmond.

'Don't be frightened, Desmond. I think, Desmond, that you and I will have a little talk.'

They had a lovely little talk, particularly Desmond. He had known Albert since they were children and he adored him.

Completely relaxed and unafraid, he told everything. His mind, with the fidelity of a tape recorder, reeled off conversations word perfect.

It took Desmond a long, long time, but then, Sergeant Coulter was a patient man. It all came out, the abortive raid on the police launch, the theft of the American gun, the million-dollar murder partnership, the snake pressed into service to aid poor Desmond in his memory course, and the various plans to kill the wicked uncle.

Hours later, a weary, broken man left the police launch. It was Sergeant Coulter.

When he reached Benares he found that Constable Browning would be off his feet for a few days. Albert visited Sven Anderson and asked if he might borrow his famous hound, Mynheer, for the afternoon.

He could have had an R.C.M.P. tracking dog from Victoria, but this was something he preferred to do unofficially, on his own time.

Mynheer was a friendly beast and he bounded joyfully from Albert's speedboat and up the wharf. Albert called him back and, looping his hand in the dog's collar, he led him past the store, along the path and up to the Major's cottage.

Albert was frightened again, and only his inbred discipline forced him to continue. If the children had been wrong about the uncle, it was terrible. It was even worse if they were right.

He poked around the silent, clueless rooms. Taking a high-powered magnifying glass from his pocket, he carefully examined the whiskey bottle, the brass Turkish coffeepot and the Major's toothbrush mug.

The prints were strangely blurred and he could only conclude that Major Murchison-Gaunt *had* had hair on the palms of his hands.

He was puzzled, for he had never seen anything similar. As a matter of fact the prints bore no particular resemblance to those of even one of the higher primates.

He replaced everything he had touched, and going into the bedroom closet he took out a pair of the Major's shoes. Then, leading the dog out, he held one of the shoes before its nose. The dog sniffed, lowered his head and began scampering down the path that led to the store.

Albert called him back. He already knew Uncle had been in the habit of taking that route.

The obedient Mynheer returned and obligingly sniffed again. Once more he lowered his head and this time he began running in short circles. Then, his nose on the ground like a vacuum cleaner and his tail waving proudly, Mynheer started for the path that led to the forest. He paused, looked at Albert with his big, sagging eyes, as if to inquire 'Well, what are you waiting for?' and with nose down and ears flapping, he led Albert straight to that pit.

Only Albert knew now, it wasn't a pit. It was a grave.

He looked at the ferns, the earth-packed roots carefully wrapped in sacking, ready to be transplanted, and then he followed the dog to a shallow stream where the dog flushed out the bucket used for watering, cunningly hidden under some bushes at the water's edge.

Albert sat on a log, absently stroking Mynheer's head. He took out the garrote and stared at it, sickened by the posthumous evidence of Uncle's handiwork.

They had tried to tell him. They had all tried to tell him, even Hobbs, but he would not listen. The professor was not crazy after all, he was merely shocked, as Albert now was, by even the memory of that man.

Albert bowed his head on his hands and wondered if he should resign. It was criminal negligence on his part and it was no thanks to him that the children were alive.

Mynheer put his forepaws on Albert's knee and licked Albert's hands. The policeman jerked his head back, then he put his arm about the dog's neck and sat for a long, long time, staring into the forest.

(25)

My dear,

This is probably the last letter I will be writing to you. You didn't get any of the others, and you won't get this one, but I must write it, because I must tell someone.

I have reached the crossroads and for the first time since I took the oath of 'Without Fear, Favour or Affection' I am going to do something which can only be construed as a travesty of all three.

The real tragedy of people who are in the position I now find myself in is that, having done one dishonourable thing, they move on to the next. This won't happen to me, I promise you. I'm only too aware that it's the little rift within the lute that by and by will make the music mute. You didn't know I liked poetry, did you? There are so many things we shall never know about each other. You will never know what I am going to do tonight.

I am going to withhold evidence and destroy a report. I don't know if you realise the seriousness of that from my viewpoint. I have thought about it until I am dizzy and it's the only way out. Those two children planned and very nearly committed a murder. It wasn't the uncle's fault, it was mine. He was a homicidal maniac; I am not, I am only incredibly stupid.

If I file that report, the case will be reopened. And no matter which way I write it, the children emerge as a couple of monsters. If I could prove anything about the uncle there might be some loophole, but he was too clever. And as far as the children are concerned, the facts remain. They stole a gun for the purpose of killing - it's called malice aforethought in law - the boy promised the girl the sum of a million dollars, to be paid when he was twenty-one, to help him commit the murder. Then they tortured the village idiot and tried to pin the rap on him. Nice pair of kiddies, aren't they.

The motive, of course, was the uncle, but the evidence against him is shaky and circumstantial to say the least, and inorder to establish even that, the boy will be involved in a particularly sordid and unpleasant interrogation. You see, there's more to this than someone like yourself would imagine or understand. Looking back on some of the phrases in Hobbs's letter, and the boy's general attitude, I am pretty sure the boy was molested by the uncle. If I start this particular ball rolling, I can't stop it. It seems cruel, but he will be questioned very, very thoroughly.

I can't do that to him. He begged me for help and I didn't give it to him. I have to protect him now, even at the cost of my own integrity.

All these things will come out if I file that report, and God knows what else, once they begin to talk. Make no mistake about that, I can make them talk. It's just a matter of starting on the girl, and once she does, I can break the boy easily. This sounds merciless, but it's part of the job, and I've been trained for it.

I have thought it over, and I am trying to do the right thing. I am also trying to imagine that you and I have talked it over, and what your attitude and advice would be. I know you would want the children spared any further horrors, because that's

*what more interrogation adds up to. The uncle is dead now,
and that will have to be the end of it. It is going to be the end
of it. They are young and have their full lives ahead of them,
and they must not start living with this on record. Fortunately,
they're as tough as nails, both of them, and as things stand
now, going no further, I don't think any damage done is
irreparable.*

*May God forgive me if I am not making the right decision.
This may seem like a simple thing to you, but I never thought the
day would come when I would have to protect children from the
law. I never thought the day would come when it would be
necessary for me to be unethical in order to be moral.*

Goodbye, my dear Gwynneth. I am, as always, yours,

Albert.

He destroyed both the letter and the report, and walked
over to his father's cottage. He changed his clothes. Then,
with his hands thrust into his pockets and his shoulders
hunched moodily, he set out to find the children.

They were not at the store or the goat-lady's. He finally
found them at the graveyard. They did not hear his approach,
and continued working, clad in the ridiculous Dickensian
garments, but wearing new shoes now.

He stood on the other side of the shaky cedar fence
watching, then he vaulted over and called them.

They gave him a guilty, startled look, gazed at each
other and prepared to bolt.

'Come here,' he said firmly. 'I want to talk to you.'

Hesitant and cringing, they took a step toward him and
stopped, like a couple of obedient pups waiting for a good
beating.

'I said come here,' he repeated. 'Come on, I won't hurt
you.'

With lagging steps and downcast eyes they stood before him.

He stared at them, wondering what to say. He looked around the little graveyard and was amazed to see what a good job they had done during the summer. The whole thing was more than the two of them could manage, but what they had done, they had done well. Most of the graves were neatly tended and garnished with fresh wild flowers. They had propped up the tilting wooden crosses with stones, and lined the paths with white pebbles from the beach.

They stood silently before him, their faces twitching with fear.

He came straight to the point.

'I know everything,' he said. 'Desmond told me everything. Everything, you understand? What have you got to say for yourselves?'

They were too frightened to cry and stood trembling, staring at their feet.

'Well?'

'Don't tell,' whispered Barnaby. 'Please don't tell.'

Albert looked from him to the girl.

'Don't put us in jail, please!'

What could he say to them? Now, children, don't steal any more guns, and don't go around planning any more murders, either, it's not nice.

He sat wearily on Sir Adrian's grave.

'It's all right,' he said finally. 'I'm not going to tell anybody.'

Their faces crumpled with relief.

Albert looked at the wretched little figures, and again he felt a great pity for them.

'Come here,' he said softly.

They crept toward him.

'You have nothing to worry about any more. I want you both to forget all about the whole thing. Will you do that?'

Shaking, they nodded.

'I had made out a report,' he said, 'but I have destroyed it, so that no one will ever know. It was like cheating, or telling a lie for me, I shouldn't have done it, but I did, for you two. And because I did that for you, you must promise me that you will always try to be good and honourable. Will you?'

They flung themselves upon him.

'It's all right,' he said. When he felt their frail shoulder bones beneath his hands and he remembered Uncle, he knew he had done the right thing. He hugged them and repeated, 'We'll all forget that any of it ever happened. And you must promise me to try to be extra good to make up for your part in it.'

They clung to him and kissed his chin and shoulders.

'I'll be the best boy in the whole world.' Barnaby's voice was soft. 'I'm going to be a Mountie, just like you. Oh, Sergeant, I love you more than anybody.'

'Oh, Sergeant,' cried Christie. 'I was so frightened. I thought you'd put us in jail. Oh, thank you, thank you. I'll never forget, and I promise I'll always be good. Next to my mother, I love you more than anybody. Thank you. I'll never forget. You shouldn't have done it for us.'

'No, I suppose I shouldn't have,' he said bluntly. 'But it's done now, and we'll all forget it.'

'Thank you,' said Barnaby, rubbing his cheek on Albert's shoulder. 'You shouldn't have done it for us.'

'Okay,' he said, wiping their noses with his handkerchief. 'Everything's fine now. Run along and play.'

They gazed at him, hugged him tightly and then moved on obediently.

They paused at the fence.

Barnaby waved to him and Christie blew him a kiss.

'Poor Sergeant Coulter,' she said. 'I'm sorry we made you cheat.'

Barnaby nodded. 'I'm sorry too. You shouldn't have done it for us.'

'But we won't forget,' said Christie.

Albert smiled and rose. He felt much better now.

'So long, kids.' He waved and went back to his cottage.

He hadn't intended to tell them about the report, but he had been as profoundly moved as they. It was as well he had told them; it would impress upon them as nothing else could the gravity of their behaviour.

He was glad he had done it. Poor little things, they were good, and how quickly they had responded to his kindness and love. Maybe there was something in this child psychology business.

In a glorious weekend of relaxation, Albert wandered down Government Street in Victoria. He had bought himself a new suit, and seeing his reflection in a store window, he decided he cut an impressive figure. He had just finished a hearty meal in the Empress Hotel, and there was a movie he particularly wanted to see that was running now.

And *they* were going. He felt very happy. They were finally going, back to their respective schools. Summer was over, life was beautiful and Albert's blessed little Isle would return to its usual state of grace. No more wicked uncles, no more near drownings, no more cougars, no more stolen guns and *no more lies.*

He felt as he had the day he was released from the POW camp, hesitant, unsure, and not quite able to believe in his good fortune. His heart sang, physically he felt he was almost floating, and he had to resist a boyish impulse to turn cartwheels or chin himself on the gay flower baskets hanging from the lampposts.

He stopped again to look at his reflection and found he was in front of a toyshop. He smiled happily to himself. He would buy them each a goodbye present.

Once he had entered the store, he felt awkward as he faced the clerk and stated his needs. He suddenly realised he had never bought a present for anyone before.

'A boy and girl about ten?' repeated the clerk. 'Yes, we have a good many things for children that age. Would you be interested in one of these lovely queen dolls for the little girl?'

It was, Albert agreed, a beautiful toy, elaborately dressed in a scarlet robe and gold crown, but it wouldn't do.

Not for her. If they had one of Lady Macbeth, perhaps yes, but not the Queen. It smacked of treason somehow and it wouldn't do.

The clerk brought out toy after toy, but none of them seemed to be right. Albert's face was getting red. He hated bothering people, and he felt he was being a nuisance.

And then he spied it, high up on a shelf, at the back.

'That,' he pointed.

The clerk got a ladder and lifted it down.

'I'm afraid this is a rather expensive gift for a ten-year-old girl,' she said, turning the price tag over. 'Perhaps I can give you a reduction though, it's been in stock for years. There were only two made. The original owner of the store brought this one from Australia.'

Sergeant Coulter, who had never had toys as a boy, turned it over with delight.

'It was made as a novelty for export,' said the clerk. 'That's genuine koala fur. I think I can let you have a 20 per cent discount.'

'I'll take it,' said Sergeant Coulter.

He turned it upside down, and chuckled as the music box inside tinkled 'Waltzing Matilda' and the merry brown eyes winked at him.

'Now for the little boy's present,' said the shopgirl.

She pointed hopefully to a rack of toy rifles.

Sergeant Coulter almost burst out laughing.

A popgun for *that* kid?

No, he thought, something a little older.

'A Meccano set?'

Yes, Albert nodded, Barnaby was a mechanically minded child, maybe a Meccano set. He had always wanted one himself, but of course he'd never had one.

'They start at quite a reasonable price,' explained the clerk, 'and then you can add to them. It's a sensible way - every birthday you can give him another section.

That was hardly likely. Albert smiled smugly to himself.

'Well,' he said, 'do you mind if I look around a bit, just in case there's something else?'

He was fascinated by the toyshop. He got down on his hands and knees to examine a beautiful electric train, and moved on to a model village. He smiled again as he looked at the gleaming toys. It must be fun to be a child.

'How about this?' asked the clerk. 'We just got them in. It would be a nice hobby to start a boy in.'

'What is it?' asked Albert, looking at the shining tan leather case.

'It's one of those cameras that takes instant pictures. Here, I'll show you.'

She snapped a picture of Albert.

'It's really very simple, you just have to wait a few seconds, and presto, there's your picture. Now isn't that a good likeness?'

'It's remarkable,' said Albert. He was sold on it. 'I'll take it,' he said.

After all, if the boy did like to go around shooting, this ought to direct his energies in a healthful way.

'Would you like them gift-wrapped?'

'Yes,' said Albert.

They must be wrapped exactly the same way. The children were already jealous enough for his affections, it would never do for one to have nicer wrapping than the other.

The presents were expensive, but he didn't mind. He had nothing except himself to spend his money on anyway. He might as well do it properly. In a way, it was almost like a bribe - the payoff. He'd pay anything to get them off his Island. A goodbye present, and as long as they left, he didn't mind the cost.

26

FACED WITH THE PROSPECT of being parted from their many loved ones, the children had spent a melancholy evening, though when morning arrived and nothing remained but for them to go, they seemed resigned.

All who came to the store were startled by their beauty. Was this Christie, of the floating spun-silk hair and flushed, heart-shaped face, the same shabby and sallow child who had arrived only two months ago? It hardly seemed possible.

As a going-away present, the goat-lady had knitted her a cardigan and tam-o'-shanter in a delicate, pastel Fairisle pattern, while Mr and Mrs Brooks had given her a short white pleated flannel skirt, and she flitted into the store with all the innocent nonchalance of a visiting butterfly.

By her side was Barnaby, wearing a blue-and-white-striped seaman's sweater, gift of the goat-lady, and short grey trousers donated by Mr and Mrs Brooks.

Surely this handsome child with the carriage of a toy soldier, his small manly face generous and frank, was not the rude, sullen-visaged little boor who had landed in their midst only a scant eight weeks before?

Even Sergeant Coulter, who was not given to being misty-eyed over children, stared at them in wonder when he came bearing his ornately wrapped gifts.

Some alchemy of the Island had transformed them into a pair of royal children. Magic children.

All their friends had sent presents. Lady Syddyns gave a huge armful of her most precious roses. From Mr and Mrs Rice-Hope were a tiny coral necklace for Christie and a pocketknife for Barnaby. Agnes Duncan, confined to the parental acres, sent by way of poor Desmond two one-dollar bills in an envelope, and on behalf of poor Desmond, Mr and Mrs Brooks gave them each a cheap fountain pen.

The children accepted Sergeant Coulter's gifts gravely and unwrapped them without haste.

When Christie saw the beautiful camera, she let her breath out slowly. She had always wanted a camera, and speechless, she could only gaze up at Sergeant Coulter and clasp his hand.

Before Sergeant Coulter could explain that the presents were mixed, he heard Barnaby shout: '*Rodney! Rodney!*'

Sergeant Coulter's fate was sealed.

'Oh, Sergeant! I knew I'd find him again, someday, somehow! How did you know where to find him! Oh, I'll be the best boy in the whole world, for ever and ever now!'

Sergeant Coulter didn't know who Rodney was, but if they were both satisfied with their presents, he was certainly not going to start any new inquiries.

The children shimmied up him as if he were a Maypole. They wound their arms about his neck and their legs about his waist, and they smothered him with kisses.

He hugged them, then smilingly set them on their feet.

'Well,' he said, 'it wasn't such a bad summer, was it? Things turned out pretty well, but I suppose you'll be glad to get back to town.'

'Oh,' said that star-bright child, Barnaby, 'I'm coming back.'

'What do you mean?' asked Sergeant Coulter suspiciously.

Barnaby turned to Mr Brooks. 'Tell him, Mr Brooks, tell him!'

Mr Brooks smiled at the boy and said.

'Oh, it's your good news, Barnaby. You tell him.'

And so Barnaby explained that Mr Brooks and Mr Robinson, his uncle's lawyer, had had a long conversation, and it was decided that Barnaby would attend boarding school in the city but spend his holidays on the Island with the Brookses. All that remained to be settled was for the courts to appoint a legal guardian for Barnaby. Because of Mr and Mrs Brooks's ages, both they and Mr Robinson thought a younger person should be appointed, and Mr Brooks had suggested none other than Sergeant Coulter.

Sergeant Coulter was appalled.

'Oh, no,' he said, and then, 'I really don't think I could do that.'

'Yes you can,' said Christie.

'Yes you will,' Barnaby spoke significantly.

No I won't, thought Sergeant Coulter stubbornly.

Their direct, unflinching gazes suddenly chilled him.

The report.

Oh, no, he was dreaming. They wouldn't do that. Why, why, that was blackmail!

As if reading his thoughts, they nodded.

'You shouldn't of done it for us, and we promise never to forget.' Their eyes were adoring.

No, no, they wouldn't do that. He'd done it for them, hadn't he? They wouldn't do that, they loved him. He was certain of it.

Jesus! They loved poor Desmond too, and look what they had done to him, to say nothing of the uncle, whom they had not loved. Yes, they would do it, precisely because they did love him.

'Oh, Sergeant, you *are* going to be my guardian!'

Not on your bloody life, thought Sergeant Coulter.

Then a nasty little thought which had never before occurred to him hit him like a blow between the eyes.

If the case were ever reopened, it was not at all unlikely that his superiors would imply he had done it to protect his own reputation. After all, he had had a homicidal maniac right under his nose for two months, and the children had begged for the protection of the law.

He tried desperately to justify his position, but there were certain inescapable facts.

Under questioning he would be forced to admit that Hobbs had written him a letter, warning him. And he had withheld evidence. He had also acted with fear, favour and affection.

God! The world was populated by either Gwynneth Rice-Hopes, so brimming over with morals that you almost hated them, or by people who apparently had none. As he thought of the Etruscan figures he realised that the perfidy of man was beyond belief.

Even decent, honest Constable Browning thought Albert should still go to New York to see the statues, his reasoning being that if they fooled the world's greatest antiquarians and art experts, they must be worth seeing. Even Browning would pay money to see frauds. Piltdown Man or the Cardiff

Giant would be his idea of a joke. Was there nobody honourable left in the world? Not like her, but like himself?

The whistle of the S.S. *Haida Prince* blasted its approach to the Island.

It was time to go, but the children wanted to see the graveyard on their way. The sad little procession wound its way down the dusty road.

Sergeant Coulter stood holding Rodney, the camera and Lady Syddyns's roses as the children climbed the fence. Staring down at his boots, Albert listened to the first faraway little rift within the lute.

He had a pension coming to him that he fully intended to enjoy, and he was not ruining his life and career for them. Why, even a dog was legally entitled to one bite. Surely a man could make one mistake? It was just a matter of keeping his mouth shut. He'd only see the boy on holidays, anyway. If worst came to worst, Desmond could not testify and it was their word against his. And children forgot so quickly.

If that was the way the game was played, he could be a damned sight tougher than the lot of them.

The children wandered sadly among the graves.

Mr Brooks blew his nose and said they had better hurry, the boat was in.

'You just can't keep up with those weeds,' said Christie. 'The blackberry vines are right back to Sir Adrian again.'

'I'll just clean up John Townsend's little angel,' said Barnaby, 'it won't take a minute.'

Christie helped him, and when they were through they patted the angel's head.

They climbed onto the fence, turned, paused, taking one last look at their handiwork. The *Haida Prince* blasted again.

'Hurry up!' said Sergeant Coulter. He was beginning to sweat in case they missed the boat.

They climbed down, their lovely faces secret and serene.

'Well, let's go.'

As he watched them climb up the gangplank, Sergeant Coulter no longer looked as if he were guarding the Khyber Pass. Indeed, one might almost have accused him of slouching.

When they reached the deck they turned, the girl blew him a kiss and the boy waved.

Christie clutched the holy camera to her breast and walked on, and Sergeant Coulter thought with something akin to amazement that at least he wouldn't see her again. Thank God.

It was nearly dusk as the boat pulled away, and the children stood at the rail, waving, waving, waving.

The figures on the wharf dwindled.

'It feels as if they're moving and we're standing still,' said Barnaby. 'Doesn't it?'

Christie didn't answer him.

'What's the matter?'

'Nothing.'

Barnaby turned, his eye caught by a sign at the foot of the bridge which stated in large letters that passengers were forbidden.

He nudged Christie with his elbow.

'Come on,' he said, 'let's go up. Nobody's around.'

'No,' said Christie. 'You're not supposed to.'

'Gee, what's the matter with you, Christie?'

'I told you, nothing!'

Barnaby smiled and patted her shoulder.

CHAPTER TWENTY SIX

'Well, whatever it is, nevermind. I'll still give you the million dollars, even if we didn't murder Uncle. We'll get married if you want.'

'I'm going to marry Sergeant Coulter, and I don't want your old million dollars,' said Christie crossly.

Far above, the seagulls drifted aimlessly like paper aeroplanes, and on the shining water a merry salmon leaped and flashed.

'Well, what *do* you want then, Christie?'

'I want Sergeant Coulter!'

She turned a determined face to Barnaby.

'He's half mine,' she cried jealously, 'and you got him all. And I'm coming back when I'm eighteen and I've got a permanent, and I'm going to get him!'

She raised the instant camera to frame the tiny group on the faraway wharf and snapped the shutter.

'Sergeant Coulter!' she hallooed over the glistening waves, 'look, Sergeant Coulter, I got you!'

And she did, too.

ALSO AVAILABLE IN THE SERIES

JOYCE DENNYS

HENRIETTA'S WAR

Spirited Henrietta wishes she was the kind of doctor's wife who knew exactly
how to deal with the daily upheavals of war. But then, everyone in her close-knit
Devonshire village seems to find different ways to cope: there's the indomitable
Lady B, who writes to Hitler every night to tell him precisely what she thinks of
him; flighty Faith who is utterly preoccupied with flashing her shapely legs; and
then there's Charles, Henrietta's hard-working husband who manages to sleep
through a bomb landing in the neighbour's garden. With life turned upside down
under the shadow of war, Henrietta chronicles the dramas, squabbles and loyal
friendships of a sparkling community of determined troupers.

'Wonderfully evocative of English middle-class life at the time …
never fails to cheer me up'
SUSAN HILL, GOOD HOUSEKEEPING

ISBN: 978 1 4088 0281 6 · PAPERBACK · £7.99

*

HENRIETTA SEES IT THROUGH

The war is now in its third year and although nothing can dent the unwavering
patriotism of Henrietta and her friends, everyone in the Devonshire village has
their anxious moments. Henrietta takes up weeding and plays the triangle in
the local orchestra to take her mind off things; the indomitable Lady B partakes
in endless fund-raising events to distract herself from thoughts of life without
elastic; and Faith, the village flirt, finds herself amongst the charming company
of the American GIs. With the war nearing its end, hope seems to lie just around
the corner and as this spirited community muddle through, Lady B vows to
make their friendships outlast the hardship that brought them together.

'Anyone who wants to get the feel of the period must read [this]'
DAILY TELEGRAPH

ISBN: 978 1 4088 0855 9 · PAPERBACK · £7.99

BLOOMSBURY

E.F. BE[NSON]

MRS AN[...]

...over a social merry-go-round of di[...]
...sputed queen bee of Riseborough. That [...]
...vans catches the eye of both her son and h[...]
...ving the men in her life, 'that wonderful c[...]
...t just rival to Mrs Ames's marriage, but rival to h[...]
...who of Riseborough is invited to Mrs Evans' mas[...]
...m[...] be taken. As the date looms, the irrepressible M[...]
the chance to win back her position – an[...]

'An extraordinary study in comedy' NEW YOR[...]

ISBN: 978 1 4088 0858 0 · PAPERBACK [...]

*

PAUL GALLICO

MRS HARRIS GOES TO PARIS [...]
MRS HARRIS GOES TO NEW YOR[...]

Mrs Harris is a salt-of-the-earth London charla[...] who cheerfully cl[...]
houses of the rich. One day, when tidying La[...] [war]drobe, sh[...]
across the most beautiful thing she has ever seen – [...]ior dress. She's ne[...]
anything as magical and she's never wanted anyth[...] much. Determ[...]
make her dream come true, Mrs Harris scrimps, sa[...] [s]laves away u[...]
day, she finally has enough money to go to Paris. L[...] the know ho[...]
life is about to be transformed forever...Part char[...] ry g[...]
Mrs Harris's adventures take her from her humble Ba[...]
of glamour in Paris and New York as she learns som[...]
along the way.

'Mrs Harris is one of the great creations of fictio[...]
know her, yet truly magical as well. I can ne[...]
JUSTINE PICARDIE [...]

ISBN: 978 1 4088 0856 6 · PAPE[...]

ORDER YOUR COPY: BY PHONE +44 (0) 1256 302 699; BY [...]
ONLINE: WWW.BLOOMSBURY.CO[...]
WWW.BLOOMSBURY.COM/THEBLOO[...]

BLOOMS[...]

'Well, whatever it is, nevermind. I'll still give you the million dollars, even if we didn't murder Uncle. We'll get married if you want.'

'I'm going to marry Sergeant Coulter, and I don't want your old million dollars,' said Christie crossly.

Far above, the seagulls drifted aimlessly like paper aeroplanes, and on the shining water a merry salmon leaped and flashed.

'Well, what *do* you want then, Christie?'

'I want Sergeant Coulter!'

She turned a determined face to Barnaby.

'He's half mine,' she cried jealously, 'and you got him all. And I'm coming back when I'm eighteen and I've got a permanent, and I'm going to get him!'

She raised the instant camera to frame the tiny group on the faraway wharf and snapped the shutter.

'Sergeant Coulter!' she hallooed over the glistening waves, 'look, Sergeant Coulter, I got you!'

And she did, too.

ALSO AVAILABLE IN THE SERIES

JOYCE DENNYS

HENRIETTA'S WAR

Spirited Henrietta wishes she was the kind of doctor's wife who knew exactly how to deal with the daily upheavals of war. But then, everyone in her close-knit Devonshire village seems to find different ways to cope: there's the indomitable Lady B, who writes to Hitler every night to tell him precisely what she thinks of him; flighty Faith who is utterly preoccupied with flashing her shapely legs; and then there's Charles, Henrietta's hard-working husband who manages to sleep through a bomb landing in the neighbour's garden. With life turned upside down under the shadow of war, Henrietta chronicles the dramas, squabbles and loyal friendships of a sparkling community of determined troupers.

'Wonderfully evocative of English middle-class life at the time …
never fails to cheer me up'
SUSAN HILL, GOOD HOUSEKEEPING

ISBN: 978 1 4088 0281 6 · PAPERBACK · £7.99

*

HENRIETTA SEES IT THROUGH

The war is now in its third year and although nothing can dent the unwavering patriotism of Henrietta and her friends, everyone in the Devonshire village has their anxious moments. Henrietta takes up weeding and plays the triangle in the local orchestra to take her mind off things; the indomitable Lady B partakes in endless fund-raising events to distract herself from thoughts of life without elastic; and Faith, the village flirt, finds herself amongst the charming company of the American GIs. With the war nearing its end, hope seems to lie just around the corner and as this spirited community muddle through, Lady B vows to make their friendships outlast the hardship that brought them together.

'Anyone who wants to get the feel of the period must read [this]'
DAILY TELEGRAPH

ISBN: 978 1 4088 0855 9 · PAPERBACK · £7.99

BLOOMSBURY

E. F. BENSON

MRS AMES

Reigning over a social merry-go-round of dinners and parties, Mrs Ames is the undisputed queen bee of Riseborough. That is, until vivacious new villager Mrs Evans catches the eye of both her son and her husband. Not content with captivating the men in her life, 'that wonderful creature' Mrs Evans becomes not just rival to Mrs Ames's marriage, but rival to her village throne. When the whole of Riseborough is invited to Mrs Evans' masked costume party, action must be taken. As the date looms, the irrepressible Mrs Ames resolves to seize the chance to win back her position – and her man.

'An extraordinary study in comedy' NEW YORK TIMES

ISBN: 978 1 4088 0858 0 · PAPERBACK · £7.99

*

PAUL GALLICO

MRS HARRIS GOES TO PARIS &

MRS HARRIS GOES TO NEW YORK

Mrs Harris is a salt-of-the-earth London charlady who cheerfully cleans the houses of the rich. One day, when tidying Lady Dant's wardrobe, she comes across the most beautiful thing she has ever seen – a Dior dress. She's never seen anything as magical and she's never wanted anything as much. Determined to make her dream come true, Mrs Harris scrimps, saves and slaves away until one day, she finally has enough money to go to Paris. Little does she know how her life is about to be transformed forever...Part charlady, part fairy godmother, Mrs Harris's adventures take her from her humble Battersea roots to the heights of glamour in Paris and New York as she learns some of life's greatest lessons along the way.

'Mrs Harris is one of the great creations of fiction – so real that you feel you know her, yet truly magical as well. I can never have enough of her'
JUSTINE PICARDIE

ISBN: 978 1 4088 0856 6 · PAPERBACK · £7.99

ORDER YOUR COPY: BY PHONE +44 (0) 1256 302 699; BY EMAIL: DIRECT@MACMILLAN.CO.UK.
ONLINE: WWW.BLOOMSBURY.COM/BOOKSHOP
WWW.BLOOMSBURY.COM/THEBLOOMSBURYGROUP

B L O O M S B U R Y

The History of Bloomsbury Publishing

Bloomsbury Publishing was founded in 1986 to publish books of excellence and originality. Its authors include Margaret Atwood, John Berger, William Boyd, David Guterson, Khaled Hosseini, John Irving, Anne Michaels, Michael Ondaatje, J.K. Rowling, Donna Tartt and Barbara Trapido. Its logo is Diana, the Roman Goddess of Hunting.

In 1994 Bloomsbury floated on the London Stock Exchange and added both a paperback and a children's list. Bloomsbury is based in Soho Square in London and expanded to New York in 1998 and Berlin in 2003. In 2000 Bloomsbury acquired A&C Black and now publishes *Who's Who, Whitaker's Almanack, Wisden Cricketers' Almanack* and the *Writers' & Artists' Yearbook*. Many books, bestsellers and literary awards later, Bloomsbury is one of the world's leading independent publishing houses.

Launched in 2009, The Bloomsbury Group continues the company's tradition of publishing books with perennial, word-of-mouth appeal. This series celebrates lost classics written by both men and women from the early twentieth century, books recommended by readers for readers. Literary bloggers, authors, friends and colleagues have shared their suggestions of cherished books worthy of revival. To send in your recommendation, please write to:

The Bloomsbury Group
Bloomsbury Publishing Plc
36 Soho Square
London
W1D 3QY
Or e-mail: thebloomsburygroup@bloomsbury.com

For more information on all titles in
The Bloomsbury Group series
and to submit your recommendations online please visit
www.bloomsbury.com/thebloomsburygroup

For more information on all Bloomsbury authors and for
all the latest news please visit www.bloomsbury.com